## Don Camillo and Don Chichi

**Giovannino Guareschi**, known as Giovanni to his millions of readers, was born at Fontanelle in the Valley of the Po on the 1st of May, 1908. His father wanted him to become a naval engineer. He, for the very enjoyment of going the opposite way, determined to become a lawyer, but found his vocation when he sent some cartoons he had drawn to the satirical magazine, *Bartoldo*.

Later he founded his own magazine, *Candido*, and between 1946 and 1966 wrote 346 stories featuring Don Camillo, a character who has done for Italy what Cervantes' Don Quixote did for Spain. Beloved all over the world by readers from 10 to 100, Don Camillo has been feted not only in books but also in films, in series on TV, on radio and most recently on YouTube.

Now, in this new authorised edition – the eighth book in the series – stories never before translated into English are published alongside the classic tales, including the last Don Camillo stories ever written.

## Titles in the Series So Far

An extensive biography of the author is available at the end of the first book in the series.

### The Little World of Don Camillo

Book 1, in which Guareschi introduces readers to the Little World of the village priest, Don Camillo, and his adversary, Peppone, the communist mayor – conflict time and again resolved by the gentle humour and shrewd counsel of Il Cristo from his place above the altar in the village church. E-book: ASIN: B00HAMIVUC. Paperback ISBN: 9781900064071. Audiobook: ASIN: B07CZPFQDT.

### Don Camillo and His Flock

Book 2, in which the people of the Little World again show their passion for politics, culminating in the battling priest's exile to the mountains. E-book: ASIN: B013TFT1YS Paperback ISBN: 9781900064187.

### Don Camillo and Peppone

Book 3, in which politics and prejudice remain to the fore, but the wit and wisdom of Il Cristo help bring Don Camillo home. E-book: ASIN: B01CIWE1T8. Paperback ISBN 9781900064262.

### Comrade Don Camillo

In Book 4, set against the background of the Cold War, Don Camillo steals a march on Peppone over a matter of conscience and finds himself transported incognito to Khrushchev's Russia. E-book: ASIN: B0722G6GY4. Paperback ISBN 9781900064330.

### Don Camillo and Company

Book 5: a unique treasure trove of Guareschi's enchanting, bittersweet stories made available in English for the first time in 2018. E-book: ASIN: B07DKBHFJH. Paperback ISBN 9781900064408.

### Don Camillo's Dilemma

Book 6: the local elections are upon us and the village priest discovers that the final straw can break even a Camillo's back. E-book: ASIN: B08KJ6GT7W. Paperback ISBN 9781900064477.

### Don Camillo Takes the Devil by the Tail

Book 7. Taking a serpent by the tail is not a good idea, but in the Little World of Don Camillo, hilarious and unearthly things can happen to draw the poison from his bite. E-book: ASIN: B089KLX8KK. Paperback ISBN 9781900064514.

### Don Camillo and Don Chichi

Book 8, in which the ageing Don Camillo must come to terms with huge changes in the Little World. E-book: ISBN: 9781900064552. Paperback ISBN 9781900064569.

# DON CAMILLO
# AND
# DON CHICHI

## GIOVANNI GUARESCHI

PILOT PRODUCTIONS

Published by Pilot Productions in 2021
Grove Farm Sawdon, North Yorkshire YO13 9DY

Copyright © Giovanni Guareschi 2021

The right of Giovannino Guareschi to be identified
as the Author of *Don Camillo and Don Chichi*
has been asserted by him in accordance with the
Copyright, Designs and Patents Act 1988.
Earlier translations of some of these stories
appeared in the US and UK in 1969 and 1970
respectively under the titles *Don Camillo
Meets the Flower Children* and
*Don Camillo Meets Hells Angels.*

A catalogue record for this book is available
from the British Library

ISBN 978-1-900064-56-9

Cover design by BerniStevensdesign.com

Typeset in Galliard by Mark Heslington Ltd,
Scarborough, North Yorkshire YO11 3PU

Printed and bound in Great Britain by
Clays Ltd, Elcograf S.p.A.

# Contents

## Editor's Preface

Don *Camillo and Don Chichi* concerns the years 1963 to 1966, a period of change so definitive that it is as well to remember how dislocating it must have seemed to the inhabitants of la Bassa, the Little World between the Great River Po and the Apennines where 'things happen that don't happen anywhere else. And the air you breathe is special, inspiring both the living and the dead. And even the dogs have souls.'

By chance I came across a short, charming film on the internet called *Giuseppina*, which happens to be the name of one of Don Camillo's sisters. So I clicked on it.[1] The film was shot in 1959 and won the Academy Award for Best Documentary the following year. It captures beautifully the spirit, simplicity and authenticity of life in the Emilia Romagna at the time Guareschi was writing, while its very setting – a petrol station forecourt – is indicative of the huge change that is just around the corner.

The narrative is driven by a succession of characters who drop by and seem to have stepped out of Don Camillo's Little World, such as two priests attired in their cassocks and black felt *cappelo romano* hats riding a Vespa,

[1] Go to www.youtube.com/watch?v=EIbQSLI6FjE, but be sure you wind the video back to where it starts – at the fairground: it has a way of beginning half way through.

and a carter who could be the wine-soaked Giarón, the last carter in la Bassa to carry on his trade from a cart drawn by a horse, which most certainly did have a soul.[2] Memorable, too, are the American and English tourists, but it is Giuseppina, the petrol attendant's young daughter, played by Antonia Scalari, who is the star turn, embodying the naturalness, innocence and wonder threatened by the big wheel of change at the nearby funfair, which she longs for and which her father forbids her to visit.

*

In the era of *Don Camillo and Don Chichi* a heady mix of disillusionment and optimism prevails. It is a time of great expectation and a questioning of beliefs, a time ripe for rebellion, for overturning conventions, a time to be young, a moment when a generation set about freeing itself from the systems that up until then had controlled their thinking.

Neither Don Camillo nor Peppone is young any more, for 'the putrefaction begins after forty' insists Ringo, leader of the Scorpioni, a gang of Hells Angels that rips through the village. Neither Ringo's nemesis, Michele, known as Venom, nor his fellow biker, Elisabetta, known as Cat, would disagree. 'The young are now masters of the world and nothing can stop us!' Cat yells, and don't be surprised by the violent tone, for Venom is Peppone's youngest son and Cat turns out to be related to Don Camillo.

Usually the violence in the stories of Don Camillo, 'the priest with the hefty left hook', as the British comedian Paul Merton describes him, is slapstick, a comic-book satirical element, which would emerge later as a

---

[2] See 'Menelik' in *Don Camillo and Peppone* (Pilot, 2016).

characteristic ingredient of René Gascinny's tales of Asterix the Gaul. But in this collection, for the first time, it tips over into real-world violence, the disjoint giving extra bite to Guareschi's satirical art, which is never more prescient and has a pressing finality as a commentary on what he thought about the emerging modern world. 'Humour doesn't destroy', he once wrote, 'humour reveals what should be destroyed because it's bad.'

His take on Sixties youth culture rings true and must have been waiting to find its way into the stories almost since Don Camillo first found his way onto the page in December 1946. The Hells Angels Motorcycle Club, with its own customs and code of living, was founded in San Bernardino, California, in '48. By the time 'Leader of the Pack', the biker classic by the American girl group, the Shangri-Las, became a worldwide hit in 1964, violent clashes between Rockers on their motorbikes and Mods on their Italian designed scooters were commonplace in seaside resorts in southern England. Teenage delinquents tooled up for these battles in frightening fashion, as clearly they did in Italy, sewing fish hooks or razor blades into the backs of their lapels to shred the fingers of assailants, while coshes, bike chains and flick knives were other popular instruments of pain, considerably worse than the sexton's wife Anselma's dough-paddle.

These interconnected stories have a wide remit, with a deep satirical reach into the political, social and ecclesiastical upheavals of the day. The appalling crimes of Stalin – the Gulag had consumed millions of lives – and the horrors of totalitarianism in Soviet-controlled Hungary and Czechoslovakia were in recent memory, while the Soviet nuclear threat and the Cold War were current and Guareschi couldn't believe it when the Vatican turned a blind eye and revised its intolerance of communism by lifting the earlier Pope Pius XII's Decree Against

Communism, which threatened with excommunication all Catholics who professed the Communist doctrine.

In October 1962 the Second Ecumenical Council opened under Pope John XXIII and continued until 1965. Commonly known as the Second Vatican Council, or Vatican II, it addressed relations between the Catholic Church and the modern world. In his 'Open Letter to Don Camillo', which appears here for the first time in English, Guareschi plays Devil's advocate, accusing the old priest of being a few centuries out of date, chiding him for scorning the Vatican's spirit of reconciliation with the Socialist and Communist parties and working him into a frenzy by applauding the new 'Worker-Cardinal' ideal, observing with equanimity how the Council was drawing a veil over communist abuses in Europe and then noting the ecclesiastical media's denunciation of that other totalitarian nightmare, fascist Spain, while conveniently forgetting Italy's own Pact of Steel with Adolf Hitler.

Guareschi mistrusted the whole stance as hypocritical, of course, and like George Orwell, considered Communism the greatest danger for the modern world. But being anti-Communist did not mean that he was pro-Capitalist. He was at war with hegemony, 'man's dominion over man', and it was an ideologically disinterested war.

America had emerged from the Second War as the dominant power and was now exercising its dominion over Europe not by making war but by spreading billions of dollars across it through the Marshall Plan to ensure a united front in the Cold War against Soviet Russia. While the money helped to put Europe back on its feet it also introduced it to consumerism and the best trade deal of all time. For, from America came not only the latest soul and R&B records but refrigerators, washing machines, cameras, reel-to-reel tape recorders . . . and between 1958 and 1965, the percentage of Italian families owning a television set rose from 12% to 49%, washing machines from 3% to 23%, and fridges from 13% to 55%.

Showing his true colours Peppone transforms his workshop into a large emporium selling such appliances on the never-never and justifies joining the capitalist bandwagon by getting his comrades in the local Communist Section to fund the enterprise on the basis that 'if the working-class people today want a car, a washing machine, a television, a fridge and so on, then it should be their comrades who sell them to them. That way profits will remain with the working people, because the profits of the store will be divided among its shareholders.'

Prescient of where consumerism would lead, Guareschi railed at the growing freneticism of life and the unhappiness it would cause as people ran around trying to make more money, or enjoy an even higher standard of living, or go on strike for better wages. The higher the standard of living the people would achieve, the higher the level they'd reach for. Dissatisfaction with the present would lead to impatience to want more, and the cost of that to the Earth was already the writer's song: 'Man is behaving as someone who has a beautiful peach, but throws away the pulp to gnaw on the nut,' Guareschi wrote. And 'the Devil, when he passes through our streets, no longer stinks of sulphur but of petrol.'

Meanwhile, disillusion with the traditional Christian Democrat values at the ruling party's ideological core had led to a centre-left coalition with the Socialist party, leaving Peppone's Communist party, which had previously been in a block with the Socialists, out in the cold.

Being anti-capitalist did not mean that Don Camillo approved of the new Socialist liaison with the Christian

Democrats, the party he'd originally helped into government, not least because the Second Ecumenical Council
was swinging the same way and, in his opinion, making
an altogether too desperate appeal to the next generation
of church-goers in the process.

The liturgical and ecclesiastical changes advised by the
Council were so seismic that Christ himself only just
survived it, as he confides to Don Camillo from his position above the High Altar of the village church. The
Latin Mass, the standard form since 1570, appears on the
chopping board along with liturgical prayers, east-facing
altars, sacred ornamentation, including Don Camillo's
Crucified Christ, through which he conducts his famous
colloquies with God.

The principal focus now is to be on pastoral works,
with the Good Samaritan as spiritual model. But what of
the sense of transcendent mystery which first gave the
Christian Church its impetus? Are not theology, liturgy
and pastoral works merely the means and instruments of
the Church's striving, rather than what it is striving for?
Was the Church losing its heart and soul to community
politics?

Don Camillo feared that it was. He is an observant
Catholic, just as he is a fervent patriot, respectful of the
Church's rituals, ceremonies and laws, and against
progressiveness for its own sake, especially when it
threatens to take the place of God in the soul. For some
time there has been pressure from the Bishop for the old
reactionary to toe the line and now, with the appoint-
ment of Don Francesco (aka Don Chichi) as his new
curate – the third in a line of 'bullet-headed, progressive

young leftwing priests' with a mandate to steer him into the modern world – Don Camillo digs in.[3]

Meanwhile, these developments throw the traditional antagonisms of Peppone and Don Camillo into an Alice in Wonderland world of paradox. With the parish priest plagued by politically correct leftwing curates and needing Peppone to challenge the Socialists at the local ballot box, they find themselves on the same side, even though, of course, Don Camillo doesn't want Peppone's communists to win either.

'You and I continue to fight a war that has in fact been over for a long time,' Don Camillo observes. 'Before long, we will be kicked out of office – me by my people and you by yours – and we will find ourselves miserable and broken and having to sleep under a bridge.'

'So what?' Mayor Peppone replies. 'We will continue to fight under the bridge.'

Socialism shares the same stated aim as communism, namely to create an equal society, but unlike the latter's brutal autocratic totalitarian government, socialism attaches the twin principles of liberty and democracy to its masthead. Don Camillo's anti-socialist stance is surprising, but less so than at first it appears. For in these days of exaggerated revolution, he is faced with much that goes under the name of socialism that he cannot accept, such as that poverty is a virtue akin to authenticity which 'redeems you from the sin of wealth,' as Don Chichi puts it; that in the party's sacred claims for workers' rights, the employer is always wrong; that those espousing socialism who see it as an ingenious system for

---

[3] Of the first two curates, Don Cesare was introduced in 'The Little Curate' (1961), and Don Guido in 'A Work of Art' (1963), both stories included for the first time in English in *Don Camillo and Company* (Pilot, 2018) and omitted by the publisher from the original English editions, probably as too controversial.

not working and making money anyway are within their rights to do so. And when the politically correct Don Chichi destroys the proudly self-sufficient eighty-seven-year-old Giosvè, who represents those in society who don't want the State to trespass on their lives or on their minds – whichever party they represent – the crucial advantage of socialism over communism all but disappears.

Guareschi was not alone in seeing the need to escape hegemony in any form: 'I felt that I had got to escape not merely from Imperialism but from every form of man's dominion over man,' wrote George Orwell in *The Road to Wigan Pier*. 'There's too much of an attempt to control man, rather than letting him go,' echoed the playwright Arthur Miller. 'It's part of the whole ideology of this Age, which is power mad.' The very idea of wishing to dominate and control people is fundamentally wrong, concluded the psychologist F L Marcuse.

In this context, Guareschi has been described as 'one of the most prescient and perceptive voices of the twentieth century'[4] and today the so-called free western world is the very breeding ground for domination politics by individuals through social media. 'Express a nuanced opinion online and all too often you won't be engaging in good-faith discussion, you'll be abused, "called out" and "cancelled". Have we forgotten how to simply disagree?'[5]

Going against the grain at every opportunity, Guareschi presents, in his own words, as 'a Monarchist in a Republic, a right-winger in a country which is moving, decisively and inflexibly, towards the left, a supporter of private enterprise in times of Statism, an advocate of

[4] Tobias Jones in 'Giovannino Guareschi: Italian Orwell' (*Engelsberg Ideas*, 2021)

[5] Rosie Kinchen, *The Sunday Times* (May, 2021).

unity in a time of regionalism, a supporter of Italianism in a time of anti-nationalism, an intransigent Catholic in a time of Christian Democracy I haven't been – as it might appear – an independent, but an anarchist. Not a free man, but a subversive.'

Such is the work of the satirist, whose job it is to get us to question our perceptions and to recognise, and hopefully laugh at, how readily our situation or background distorts them. But is mockery enough? What does the enigmatic reactionary actually stand for? There is no character in his stories who represents the author's own political position. He is not wholly Don Camillo, and he is certainly not Peppone, although time and again it is the Communist Mayor's ingrained integrity that shines through.

Guareschi distinguishes the politics from the man and has no time for ideology. It was a great personal disappointment to him that the films of the Don Camillo stories, made between 1952 and 1965, for all their commercial success, failed to grasp his deeper, satirical purpose to persuade us to let go of the ideas that drag us around and wake up to the reality of life that is working beyond politics, a reality of such infinite interconnectedness, interdependence and latent possibility that any single ideological template or '-ism' – be it communism, capitalism or socialism – will, like an ill-fitting gasket in Peppone's workshop, inevitably prove an inadequate interface with truth.

Don Chichi is a politicised priest who doesn't question his point of view until it is too late. Someone dies because of his near-sightedness and he suffers a breakdown on account of the guilt he feels. Meanwhile, the Great River holds the lives of everyone in its power with Old Testament finality. And Don Camillo looks beyond politics to the wisdom, compassion and enlightened advice that comes to him as the voice of universal conscience from *il Cristo* above the High Altar, who never fails to undermine his prejudices, quell his anger and, with fascinating insights and gentle humour, map the only sure way forward.

It is a voice available to all, but there is no how-to plan to tuning in to it, except to stop spouting politics, bow your head, let go of the thoughts that drag you around with them, listen, and 'in your heart you will find the right response'.

Piers Dudgeon, May 2021

## *Don Camillo Is Silenced*

COVERED IN A dust-coat from head to foot and with a paper hat on his head, Don Camillo was whitewashing the dining room, but not for a moment did he lose sight of the world outside and as soon as he saw the figure all wrapped up in a cloak cross the churchyard, making a beeline for the main door of the church, he dumped the pole to which his paintbrush was attached and bolted out of the presbytery.

Having reached the sacristy by means of the small door in the bell tower, he took up a position to the side of the High Altar. The church was dark, damp, silent as a tomb and the heavily muffled visitor got on with his business without suspecting a thing. From under his cloak he dug out a large candle and placed it on a candlestick at the foot of the altar.

None of this performance was a surprise to Don Camillo, because the same thing had happened on the eve of every election for the past fifteen years. But this time, the priest did not feel like letting it go.

'Stop right there!'

Don Camillo's startling cry froze the clandestine figure in his attempt to light the candle. The man raised his head and finding the priest standing in front of him apparently disguised as a house painter, popped his eyes in astonishment.

'The carnival is over!' the cloaked one muttered.

'Precisely,' replied Don Camillo. 'Time to stop your antics.'

'Antics?'

'Yes, antics. That a godless excommunicated person should come to church to light a candle so that the God whom he denies will make the Party of the Godless win the elections is a farce. Take your candle back, take it home and light it in front of Stalin's portrait.'

The man murmured something and Don Camillo exclaimed: 'I forgot, Stalin's been purged! My apologies, Comrade Senator.'[6]

'Not even Senator of Egypt . . . I am a senator no longer.'[7]

'You will be again. They will reconfirm you for sure. Where will they find another wretch like you?'

'Obviously they have, because I'm not even an official candidate.'

Don Camillo turned his eyes towards the Crucified Christ.

'Lord,' he said out-loud, 'is this man not truly a phenomenon? His party has removed him from the list of candidates to stand for Senator and he, forgetting his personal enmities, turns up here to humble himself

---

[6] After Stalin's death in 1953, and to Peppone's chagrin, First Secretary of the Communist Party Nikita Khrushchev began the de-Stalinisation of the USSR, purging the Stalinist myth from the collective unconscious of the Soviet people.

[7] For Peppone's original election to the Senate, see *Comrade Don Camillo* (Pilot 2017). Now, after his de-selection, he compares his situation melodramatically to that of Mark Antony, lifetime member of the Roman Senate and representing Egypt after he became Governor of Rome's eastern provinces. But only until he lost his position, finally to be declared a traitor and defeated in a civil war that destroyed the Roman Republic.

before you and offer a candle so that he might win the ear of the party that has dumped him.'

'I'm done with the Party!' Peppone exclaimed angrily. 'Ever since Stalin died, they've been selecting one sucker after another. In Rome as in Moscow. I'm not offering a candle to God to ensure my Party wins. I'm offering it so that your centre-left gang doesn't.'[8]

'Strange,' Don Camillo pondered, 'the centre-left party has a programme that looks suspiciously in line with yours. The Communist party has every interest in the centre-left winning.'

'I am not the Party. I am me and I care that your lot loses. Can I light it now, or do you need permission from the Curia?'

'Seeing as you're not lighting it to benefit Marxism, I think you may.'

Peppone lit the candle and departed. Don Camillo went rummaging in a closet in the sacristy and reappeared with a candle that could have been the twin of Peppone's. He put it on a candlestick, placed it next to Peppone's and lit it.

'Lord,' Don Camillo explained to Christ above the High Altar. 'I know that you have no interest in miserable political trifles ... In any case, you have heard Peppone's purpose in offering you that candle.'

'If I understand you correctly,' the Crucified Christ responded, smiling, 'this candle of yours is meant to "neutralise" Peppone's candle.'

'Not at all, Lord,' Don Camillo averred. 'I am offering this candle for the same, identical reason as Peppone.'

Don Camillo crossed himself, bowed and made a quick about-turn to escape, but Christ stopped him:

---

[8] For the 1963 elections, the traditionally centrist Christian Democrat party has teamed up with the leftwing Socialist party, which has ended its alignment with the Communist party. See Preface for the political background.

'Don Camillo, how is it possible that you are in such a hurry these days?'

'Lord,' answered Don Camillo, 'I want everything to be perfect for Easter and I have a lot of work in the presbytery . . .'

'It must be an enormous amount,' replied Christ, 'given that you don't even find time to read an urgent letter from your Bishop.'

'A letter from the Bishop?' Don Camillo stammered.

'Yes, Don Camillo, a letter from the Bishop. The one you put in your pocket eight days ago.'

Don Camillo, becoming entangled with his dust-coat, found the pocket and the letter with difficulty.

'In my opinion it would be the right time to open it and read it,' Christ observed.

Don Camillo, with bowed head, slowly opened the envelope and read the letter.

'Any . . . news?' enquired Christ.

'No, Lord, no news. Just the usual letter that arrives on the eve of elections, to be read, and its contents explained, to the faithful.'

'Politics is a strange thing,' Christ exclaimed. 'Here is Don Camillo who, on the one hand, lights a candle for me so that I do not let a certain fellow and his associates win in the elections, while, on the other, he explains to his parishioners that their duty is to ensure that that same guy and his associates do win.'

'Lord,' said Don Camillo pitiably, 'here is poor Don Camillo who, on the one hand, cannot lie to his God and, on the other, cannot disobey his Bishop. How will this poor Don Camillo ever be able to agree with himself?'

Christ did not answer. Don Camillo went back to work and, while he was struggling with the paint brush he'd tied to the top of a pole, Perletti passed along the street and stopped in front of the wide-open dining room window.

'Don Camillo,' said Perletti, who was leader of the left-wing blacks,[9] 'the parish priests of the hamlets have already read and commented on the Bishop's letter in church. How is it that you haven't done so yet? Didn't you get the letter?'

Don Camillo felt like smacking Perletti in the nose, but he refrained.

'The Bishop sent the letter to the parish priests. And, since I am the parish priest here, I don't see why *you* have to worry about it.'

'Reverend,' Perletti warned him, 'be careful. These days we're able to fix Cardinals, imagine how little it would take to sort out a country parish priest.'

Don Camillo felt himself once again dying to smack Perletti in the nose and, this time, he could not resist the temptation.

'Now you can go, you whitewashed deadbeat!' sneered Don Camillo, returning his pole to its main job of white-washing the walls.

Don Camillo finally read the Bishop's letter the following morning, during the 6 a.m. Mass. The faithful present included old Desolina of ninety-three, old Pirón of eighty-seven (deaf), the sexton Tognoni (a fool), and the altar boy Gamella (half asleep). Nevertheless, working like a team of slaves, Don Camillo had been able to repro-duce in box characters, on a four-by-seven metre canvas panel, the most important passages of the 1949 Papal Decree of Excommunication against the Communists

---

[9] The author describes Perletti, a leading local supporter of the 'new' socialist outlook of the Catholic Church, as '*il capobanda dei "neri" di sinistra*', summoning up images of those leftwing, revolutionary black-tunicled priests in pre-unified Italy who carried rifles and daggers and were seen banqueting at all hours when revolution was rife.

and their allies. He had it nailed to the façade of the church so that it could easily be read even a couple of kilometres away.

\*

The wise old Bishop had been sleeping in the cemetery for two years already and the new one was tough. One of those Bishops who have more inclination for demagogy than theology. Perletti's report about what had befallen him outraged the Bishop to such an extent that he didn't even allow Don Camillo the opportunity to justify himself. He simply sent him the order to move, *illico et immediate*,[10] to the most remote parish in the diocese.

Don Camillo could not even say 'Bah!' He loaded his junk onto Peppone's van and left for exile. During the journey, Peppone said to him: 'Show me the letter you read at the six o'clock Mass. Where you've been shown to be mad as hell is in the fact that you dredged up this business of excommunication. Even cats know that excommunication is no longer valid. Even if some fascist Cardinal insists that the Holy Order has not lapsed. You have no common sense, Reverend.'

'You have a lot of it, I suppose, you who got yourself removed from the list of Senators and are about to lose your position as Mayor and Secretary of the local Communist Section. Don't you understand that by insisting on being a Stalinist, you are setting yourself up in opposition not only to the Party, but even to the Soviet Union itself? If you had any brains, you should have ditched Stalin like all your other gang did.'

---

[10] 'Immediately and without even the shadow of a delay.'

'And you, Reverend, why didn't you give up on Pope Pacelli?'[11]

'What does Pacelli have to do with Stalin?'

'Well, he has something to do with it. However, we shall see: I put my hope in Mao Tse Tung!'[12]

'Not me. I continue to put my hope in God.'

'God!' sneered Peppone. 'God has something else to think about. God doesn't care about you and me.'

'The important thing is that you don't give a damn about him,' Don Camillo decided. 'Or should I keep the position of sexton open for you?'

---

[11] 'Pope Pacelli' is Pope Pius XII, born Eugenio Maria Giuseppe Giovanni Pacelli. It is his Decree Against Communism (that all Catholics that vote communist should be excommunicated) that is at issue here.

[12] Mao Tse Tung, who had earlier signed the Treaty of Friendship with Stalin, denounced the new USSR under Khrushchev as revisionist and offered himself as leader of the Marxist cause worldwide.

## Open Letter to Don Camillo

A mocking, satirical challenge to Don Camillo, written as the cultural and ecclesiastical reforms of the Second Ecumenical Council of the Vatican become a reality. The reforms have already led to Don Camillo bloodying Perletti's nose and to the parish priest's exile (yet again) to the mountains. Meanwhile, Don Guido, the young curate standing in for Don Camillo during his absence, is getting on with wholesale changes to the village church in line with new Vatican policy.

REVEREND FATHER, I hope that this letter of mine finds its way to the remote mountain exile into which that impetuousness of yours (all but undimmed by the passing years) has confined you.

I know well enough how it all came about. How Comrade Mayor Peppone would greet you in public with a 'Good morning Comrade President!' and how he turned up one day at the presbytery, along with Smilzo, Bigio and Brusco, and suggested that since he intended to adorn the People's Palace with a magnificent balcony from which to deliver his speeches, he would gladly purchase the redundant marble balustrades of the High Altar to support it, as well as the two angels that reside on either side of the Tabernacle, which, he said (if my information is correct), he planned to place above the entrance arch to the People's Palace, to frame the plaque that carries the emblem of the *Partito Comunista Italiano*. And how it was then that you took the shotgun from its place on the wall and waved it around in front of Peppone, which led to his associates finding their way quickly back through the door.

Believe me, Don Camillo, this was neither justified as a response nor even particularly witty. For is it not true – and let us not forget it – that when the de-Stalinisation bombshell exploded, you went to see Peppone in his workshop and told him that you would gladly purchase the redundant portraits and bronze bust of Stalin hanging in the People's Palace, as well as the marble plaque of 'Piazza Stalin', which you planned to place as an adornment of convenience in your own bathroom?

Now, Reverend Father, that the de-Pacellisation bomb[13] has exploded, you have no choice but to adapt your own church to the precise requirements of the New Bolognese Rite[14] and Peppone has every right to get back at you.

You're in trouble up to your eyes, Reverend, but this time it's all about that young curate your superiors have sent to instruct you on the Bolognese Rite and help you to bring up to date what goes on in the ecclesiastical life of the village. But he is not just some Peppone you can treat roughly as you treat the Mayor. Don Guido came to you with a specific mandate and, since your church has no particular artistic or tourist value, the young priest, as a worthy cleric, has every right to demand the demolition of the marble balustrades and the High Altar, and do

---

[13] Guareschi coins 'de-Pacellisation' with reference to Pope Pacelli (Pius XII) in mock defence of Catholic tradition and with a sidelong glance at de-Stalinisation.

[14] 'Rito Bolognese' (the new 'Bolognese Rite') refers to the liturgical reforms of Vatican II, the main architect of them being the Archbishop of Bologna, Cardinal Lercaro.

away with the side chapels and niches with their ridiculous representation of saints in plaster and wood, as well
as the little votive pictures, candlesticks and, in short, all
the other tin, wood and gilded plaster artefacts which,
until Vatican II, transformed churches into junk shop
storerooms.

You, Don Camillo, will have seen the 'Lercaro Show'
on TV and the people-centred Mass, *con-celebrated*
according to the New Bolognese Rite. Clearly, too, you
will have witnessed the new painfully evocative poverty
of the ecclesiastical environment, the touching simplicity
of the altar reduced to a plain, proletarian table. How can
you think fit to place in the vicinity of this humble sacred
trestle, a contrivance three metres high such as your
famous (almost *in*famous) Crucified Christ – of which
you are so fond!

A few days after the show, you will also have seen on
television the layout of the Holy Table around which the
Pope and his new Cardinals concelebrated the Eucharistic
Banquet. In particular, did you notice that the Crucifix
located in the centre of the Table was so small and
discreet as to be indistinguishable from the two
microphones?

In short, did you not observe how everything in the
House of God must now be humble and plain in order to
maximise the proletarian character of the Liturgical
Assembly, of which the Priest is but a *con*celebrant –
taking the role of President of the congregation?

And did you not hear, on the second 'Lercaro Show'
(entitled 'Cordiality'), how the Petronian faithful were
entirely satisfied with – even enthusiastic for – the new
Mass of the Bolognese Rite? And did you see how especially excited young people and women were by the
pleasure of celebrating Mass *with* the priest rather than
attending it passively and disabused of the mysterious

Latin of the Celebrant. And how uplifted now by the legitimate satisfaction of no longer having to humble oneself by kneeling to receive the Host, instead standing up to swallow it, treating God as an equal, as Signor Fanfani has always done?[15]

So, Don Camillo, that young priest is surely right. He is fighting for a Holy Cause, because the root and branch update is required by the Great Pope John[16] so that the Church – 'the Bride of Christ – can show her face without spot or wrinkle'. Our Church, until yesterday simply Catholic and Apostolic, has become – (let us always defer to Lercaro) – *the Church of God*!

You see, Don Camillo, you are a few centuries behind the times, still stuck in the days of the last medieval Pope, Pius XII,[17] who today is publicly fading from the spotlight, undermined by one and all. Witness the production of *Il Vicario* in Florence, actually sponsored by Catholic university students. It is but a question of time before this production will obtain State backing and be celebrated on film and appear on our television screens.[18]

Don Camillo, when you watched the consecration of the new Cardinals on TV did you not hear the thunderous applause for the new 'Worker-Cardinal', Cardin? And did you not hear the Reverend TV Presenter point out that the new Czechoslovakian Cardinal Beran has

---

[15] Amintore Fanfani, Secretary of the Christian Democrats and at various times Prime Minister, was responsible for diminishing the party's dependence on the Catholic Church.

[16] Pope John XIII, in office 1958–1963.

[17] Pope Pius XII, in fact in office from 1939 to 1958.

[18] In 1963, in a play called *Il Vicario*, the German author Rolf Hochhuth accused Pope Pius XII of complicity with Nazism over the holocaust, ignorant of the fact that secretly he had provided discreet aid to the Jews, which saved hundreds of thousands of lives. Productions of *Il Vicario* played to audiences in Berlin, London and Rome, where it received a ban, and in Florence, where the producer got round the public order by having it sponsored by a student organisation.

simply emerged from his 'state of isolation'? Nor notice the repressed indignation that vibrated in the presenter's voice when he denounced the abuse committed by the dictator Franco, claiming to make use of fascistic medieval privilege accorded to Heads of Catholic States to personally confer the Beretta on the new Cardinals in their country?[19]

You can scarcely have failed to notice the commendable diligence with which the Reverend TV Presenter ignored the voice of the so-called 'Church of Silence' or 'Martyr Church' from beyond the Iron Curtain (as indeed, the Holy Father himself did). Perhaps you didn't realise how the upper echelons of the Catholic Church avoid speaking of that Cardinal Mindszenty of Hungary who, with reprehensible indiscipline, persists in ignoring the conciliation between the Catholic Church and the Soviet Regime, and in refusing to pay due homage to the so-called 'Atheist Communism', even considering a Papal Excommunication valid which is today the object of laughter in all the parish oratories?[20]

Don Camillo, why do you refuse to understand what all this means? I say that because, when the young priest sent by the Higher Authority explained that it was

---

[19] Guareschi chides Don Camillo for scorning Vatican II's spirit of reconciliation with the Socialist and Communist parties and works him into a frenzy by applauding the new 'Worker-Cardinal' ideal, accepting the way the Second Ecumenical Council drew a veil over communist abuses in Czechoslovakia and Hungary and noting with equanimity the Italian media's hypocritical denunciation of fascist Spain, while conveniently forgetting Italy's own fascist Pact of Steel with Adolf Hitler.

[20] For five decades Cardinal Mindszenty was in fervent opposition to communism in Hungary, a country under Soviet control since the war. Arrested, tortured and at a show trial in 1949 he was given a life sentence for black-marketeering, treason and espionage. Pius XII subsequently announced the excommunication of all persons involved and issued his Decree Against Communism only for it to be effectively lifted by Pope John XIII during this period lampooned by Guareschi.

necessary to clean up the church and sell the candelabra, statuary of angels, Saints, Christs, Madonnas and all the other junk, including your famous Crucified Christ, you grabbed him by the lapels and slammed him against the wall. Didn't you understand that the most sacred principles of economics are at stake here? Billions and billions of lire, the most sacred principles of our economy? Which 'good' family today would want to deprive itself of the pleasure of adorning their home with such sacred object? Who can give up having a San Michele in the closet for use as a coat hanger, or a pair of golden angels as a chandelier in the bedroom, or a Tabernacle as a small bar in the living room?

Don Camillo, fashion is a force that galvanises thousands of factories and makes trillions of billions: now every respectable house will want to possess some sacred object. The quest to own the exiled saints, angels, altarpieces, candelabra, crucifixes, tabernacles, Christs, Madonnas and so on will now be so furious that, if we do not meet the demand, prices will reach hyperbolic figures. And this will prejudice the sacred integrity of the Lira, honoured around the world as the Oscar of Coinage. No longer can the Church distance herself from the life of the laity and ignore its problems . . .

Don Camillo, let me get to the point. You are in trouble and the fault lies entirely with *you*. The situation is clear: the little priest sent to you by your Superiors proposed the demolition of the old High Altar and its replacement not with an ordinary table like that featured in the 'Lercaro Show', but with a carpenter's bench that Comrade Peppone has offered cravenly as a gift, drawing attention to the fact that Christ's putative father had, after all, been a carpenter and that little Jesus, as a child, will have often helped him to saw and plane the boards.

Now, Don Camillo, here is a young, innocent cleric, full of passion and enthusiasm. Why not take that into account instead of kicking the little fellow up the backside and out of the church? Well done, Don Camillo. Good result. Now we have the little curate doing whatever he wants in your church, while you find yourself festering up here in R . . . . . . , the last miserable parish up the mountain, a lifeless region because the good men, women and boys have all upped and left to work abroad, leaving only the old people and the youngest children.

And you, Reverend, had to organise things up here according to the new directives, so after having concelebrated the first Mass with the Bolognese Rite, the old people made it plain that as long as you remain in the village they will no longer come to Mass. Don Camillo, stuff like this gets out. You – recalling the words of the little curate – explained that, now, the Mass must be celebrated this way and old Antonio replied: 'I am ninety-five years old and, for however long I have left to live what little or much I still have to live, the Latin Mass that I've known these ninety years is good enough for me.'

'This is ridiculous,' old Romilda added, 'these townies would have us believe that God no longer understands Latin!'

'God understands every language,' you replied. 'Mass is celebrated in Italian so that you can understand it. Instead of offering silent support you can now participate in the sacred rite, along with the priest.'

'What a world we live in,' Antonio chuckled. 'The priests don't want to celebrate Mass on their own anymore, they want help from us! But we want to pray during Mass!'

'Exactly, but now we can all pray together . . . *with* the priest,' you tried to explain.

But old Antonio would have none of it: 'Father, everyone has his own prayers. You can't pray all together. Everyone has his personal stuff to be entrusted to God. And the reason we come to church is because Christ is present in the consecrated Host and, therefore, feels closer to us. You do your stuff, Reverend, and we do ours. If we both do the same stuff, why would we need a priest? Anyone can preside over an assembly there are plenty capable. Like the President of the Woodcutters Co-operative.

'And then, why were all the things we ourselves offered to God, paid for by our hard-earned money, taken from the Church? It took my father eight years to sculpt that Sant'Antonio out of chestnut which you've removed to the attic. It is plain that my father wasn't an artist, but the work took all his passion and all the faith that he had. So much so that, when it looked as if he and my poor mother couldn't have children, when the statue was finished and blessed, Sant'Antonio rewarded him with grace and I was born. If you want to stir up a revolution, go do it in your place not ours, Reverend.'

Don Camillo, I understand that you had to try. But it's your fault you got mixed up in this. However, I don't just write to criticise you, but to offer you a crumb of comfort. The curate who has replaced you has already dismantled the church, but he didn't install the carpenter's bench because, with good grace, your Superiors made him understand that, beautiful and noble though the idea was, favouring carpenters in this way could have upset the blacksmiths and the other artisans. Marble balustrades, angels, candelabra, votive statues of saints, Madonnas, and small pictures, tabernacles and all other sacred furnishings have been sold and the proceeds put aside for the church – for the stereo system, microphones, speakers, heating etc. Even the famous Crucified Christ

was sold because it was too bulky, too spectacularly
looming, profane even.

But put your heart at rest, none of it went far. The old
notary, Piletti, bought it and plans to have it delivered to
the private chapel of his Villa del Brusadone. All except
the balustrade of the High Altar: Peppone bought that
and says he will use it to construct the speech balcony for
the People's Palace overlooking the piazza. I understand,
however, that the balusters and every other piece of the
balustrade have been collected together one by one with
great care, packed and placed in a safe place. And you
know what? Even though he knows you to be a
goddamned reactionary enemy of the people, Peppone
confided in me, and made me understand, that he would
be willing to negotiate. In exchange for the balustrade,
he would take the machine gun that you stole from him
in 1947. He says he doesn't have the slightest intention
of using it now because he is convinced that the clericals
will put the communists in power without giving them
the satisfaction of enacting the Revolution. He wants it
back . . . for old times sake.

Don Camillo, I am sure that when soon you return to
the village (and you will be back soon because they need
you – only Peppone, Smilzo, Brusco and Bigio now go
to church and they to spite you), you will find all your
favourite odds and ends perfectly arranged in the chapel
of the notary. And you will be able to celebrate a clandestine Mass for your few trusted friends there – the Mass in
Latin, naturally, with much *Oremus* and not a few *Kirie
Eleisons*. An ancient Mass to console all our dead who,
even not knowing the Latin, nevertheless felt all the
while close to God, and were not ashamed if, hearing
that very ancient office, their eyes filled with tears.
Perhaps because, then, the feelings and the poetry were
not deemed sinful and no one thought that the sweet,

eternally young 'face of the bride of Christ' could ever register stains or wrinkles. While today that face appears to us via the profane video, beside the deeply unpleasant face of the Red Cardinal (Lercaro) of Bologna and his faithful activists, kindly granted office by the Curia from among the local Communist Federation.

Don Camillo, keep it together: when the generals lose it, we need more than ever the soldiers' loyalty . . . I greet you affectionately and send by way of consolation a picture of the Very Reverend Pietro Nenni, etc.[21]

Your parishioner,<br>Guareschi

---

[21] Nenni, born in the Emilia-Romagna was National Secretary of the Italian Socialist Party (PSI) and, from 1963 to 1968, Deputy Prime Minister of Italy. Guareschi is referring to Nenni's presence at the three-day convocation for Pope John's encyclical on universal peace, *Pacem in Terris*, in 1963.

## The Trojan Suitcase

DON CAMILLO, HAVING returned from his month-long exile in the mountains, was napping in the dining room with the window open. All was silent until, right in front of the presbytery, some execrable creature screeched to a halt in his car, got out and slammed the door shut so brutally that the sound might have been taken for a gunshot.

Waking up with a start, Don Camillo jumped to his feet and ran to the window to tell the wretch what he thought of him and all those in a position to prevent a peasant such as he from driving a car, when clearly he didn't even have the brain to drive a wagon led by oxen.

But he remained silent because it was not the urban peasant he supposed it to have been, only Peppone, who, having lifted the bonnet of the car, was now checking who-knows-what about the engine prior to lowering the lid as if he intended to annihilate it.

'No need to be so insistent,' muttered Don Camillo. 'I heard you slamming the door before . . . when I was sleeping.'

The car Peppone was brutalising was an oxblood-red Milletré, latest model, and it sparkled in the warm autumn afternoon sun with such intensity that it made one think that Fiat had used special paints and chrome specifically to spite Don Camillo.

Peppone made his way to the window: 'I didn't know you were sleeping,' he apologised. 'Why should I? To rest, one must, by definition, first have been working.'

Don Camillo did not fall for the provocation.

'Nice car,' he said. 'Did Togliatti[22] give it to you to make you forget about not being re-elected to the Senate?'

Peppone sneered: 'To be precise, let's say that I left on foot for Rome and returned in my car, while some Monsignors, who left for Rome on foot, returned on foot.'[23]

'Better on foot than immorally motorised,' Don Camillo decided, closing the window and withdrawing. But, shortly afterwards, Peppone appeared at the door.

'Don't be angry, Reverend. I was joking: I remain a foot soldier like you. I bought the car with my own money. Togliatti does not hand out cars to his officials. Moreover, not even the Pope seems very generous with his monsignors.'

'If you want to quarrel, you can go back whence you came,' Don Camillo said, cutting him short.

'Far from arguing, I come to invite you to the official inaugural unveiling of my car. For some time I've been burning with a desire to make a trip abroad.'

Don Camillo, who was also burning with a desire for a trip abroad, took the bait:

'And where would you like to go? Getting abroad eats up a lot of time.'

---

[22] Palmiro Togliatti was leader of the Italian Communist Party from 1927 until 1964.

[23] Peppone is referring to Don Camillo, who had been made a Monsignor by the old Bishop as a ruse to relieve him of office because it meant that he'd have to leave the village and 'come and create confusion here with us in the city,' as he put it. It hadn't worked.

'If we set out early in the morning, we can be in Lugano by nine,' explained Peppone.[24] 'Leaving at nine in the evening, we can be home by midnight.'

Don Camillo wrinkled his nose. At the time a famous controversy was raging over the very laudable fact that the Swiss had expelled agitators sent by the Communist Party to sow discord among the many Italians who worked in Switzerland.

'*Timeo Danaos et dona ferentes*,' he concluded.[25]

'And what would that mean?'

'It means that when villains like you make their mouths into a smile, ninety-nine times out of a hundred they're trying to get one over on you.'

'Good God!' Peppone exclaimed. 'And I, forgetting that you are a priest, wanted to show my regard for you.'

'Comrade, you're doing the opposite, trying to use my cassock to camouflage an attempt to go and sow discord among recalcitrant Italians employed in Switzerland.'

'Father! Let us not talk nonsense. How am I going to do that? Besides anything else, the Italians there are all southerners and don't even understand Italian.'

'When it comes to incitement and roguery, everyone understands any language, even the deaf.'

'Is it possible that you have so little faith?'

'Anyone who trusts a communist is crazy. If you invite me, it means that you need me for a purpose. However, if your purpose in taking me along is to blend in, I fear you have miscalculated. Switzerland is not like here. In Switzerland, people are more suspicious of a priest than they are of a communist mayor.'

'Smart people, the Swiss,' rejoined Peppone.

---

[24] A picturesque lakeside city in southern Switzerland's Italian-speaking Ticino region. In 1959 the author made a second home at Cademario, a village in the district of Lugano.

[25] 'I fear Greeks bearing gifts.'

However, for Don Camillo's part it turned out that the temptation to go was too strong and he could not resist:

'I am coming: but if, once there, you play some Bolshevik trick, I will slap your face and report you to the police.'

'No politics, Monsignor! I swear to you on my honour that I will be going as a private citizen,' Peppone reassured him.

They agreed on the details of the expedition. At dawn, after Mass had been celebrated, Don Camillo would take the road to the fields until he reached Stra' Quarta. There, Peppone would pick him up. Don Camillo would bring – as his contribution to the enterprise – a suitcase containing a roast turkey, cold cuts, cheeses and white and red wine.

*

The expedition got off to a good start because the weather that day promised to be wonderful. As soon as they passed Varese,[26] Don Camillo's suitcase was sampled and the result was a convincing breakfast washed down with dry Trebbiano wine, which so cheered them up that they arrived at the border equipped to overcome every obstacle.

But there was none because the Italian customs officers wanted simply to look at their passports and the Swiss ones only their Green Card.[27] They had chosen a secondary checkpoint, and in any case, given the weekday there was very little traffic.

In Lugano they decided to leave the car in the railway station car park and take the funicular into the city. Peppone put two coins in the parking meter, enough for an hour, explaining that if they needed more time he

---

[26] Some 175 kilometres to the northwest.

[27] International Certificate of Insurance.

would return on the funicular and put in more. They then left the suitcase with the provisions in the boot of the Milletré and left.

Lugano, although already taken by the feverish commercialism known as Milanism, was still a city worth seeing and time passed quickly before Peppone said: 'You, Father, wait for me here in that café while I go and put more money in the parking meter.'

Don Camillo, not being one of those who, as they say, sleep on their feet, smelt a rat, deeply suspicious that this was the first step in a criminal plan and that Peppone wanted to escape his surveillance to arrange some villainy.

'All right,' he replied indifferently, but followed Peppone from a distance, cautiously taking advantage of the fact that there was a large crowd of tourists, even managing to get on the funicular car unseen by him. This was greatly facilitated by the fact that Peppone seemed absorbed in thoughts so serious that they had completely taken over his brain.

Arriving at the car park, Peppone put two coins in the parking meter. Then, instead of returning to the funicular, he opened the boot of the Milletré and started rummaging around inside. Don Camillo stood behind him as silent as a priest's shadow and watched Peppone as he opened the suitcase of provisions and took out a parcel wrapped in newspaper.

Given the shape of the package, all fell into place: the wicked fellow had taken advantage of breakfast to introduce propaganda material into Don Camillo's suitcase, which he now intended to spread among the Italian workers. Under Don Camillo's unsuspecting cassock he had transformed the priest's suitcase into a kind of Trojan horse.

Peppone had just closed the boot when Don Camillo's hand fell on his shoulder. Taken by surprise, Peppone turned abruptly, pale as death, and it took no effort for Don Camillo to take the packet of leaflets out of his hand. But as soon as he ripped open the wrapping, Don Camillo showed such surprise that Peppone did not have to use any violence to snatch the package back again.

Here were no subversive leaflets, but a bundle of brand new banknotes. Eleven packets of 10,000 lire notes. Together the two men went to sit in the station café:

'Where did this come from?' panted Don Camillo after a goodly-sized glass of cognac had allowed him to catch his breath. 'Moscow gold?'

'Moscow!' Peppone answered. 'We sold Pioppetta, my wife's farm.'

'Sold Pioppetta?' Don Camillo countered incredulously. 'What nonsense. The land is worth little but it is always better to have a piece of land than pieces of paper.'

'I know, Reverend, but for us it was a question of the sharecropper. Some day I would have smashed his head in. You know what a bastard Cincotti is.'

'But he's one of your lot!'

'That doesn't mean anything: before being liberals, socialists or communists, peasants are peasants. A cursed race. If agriculture in Russia isn't going the way it should, the fault lies with the peasants.'

'And to think that Stalin cleaned them up by having ten million shot!'

'Obviously they were the few,' Peppone muttered. 'Villeins are a false breed.'

'And who is the wretch who took on Pioppetta together with a sharecropper like Cincotti?'

'Cincotti!' Peppone replied, laughing. 'Now he enjoys being a farmer.'

'Did you sell it well?'

'We got the Milletré, enough for a fur coat for my wife, a new dining room and these eleven million lire.'

Don Camillo, seized by curiosity, had lost sight of the fundamental question posed by the bundle of banknotes and took up the subject again:

'And why did you bring them here?'

'You will see why.'

They went back into the city: Peppone had an address written on a piece of paper hidden in the ribbon of his hat. They went to that address and Don Camillo waited outside. When Peppone returned, Don Camillo asked: 'So, what now?'

'Sixteen thousand.'

'Sixteen thousand what?'

'Dollars,' Peppone explained. 'They made me pay over 650 lire to the dollar when it's not even worth 620. Anyway, they're dollars!'

'Comrade, are you not ashamed?'

'Why? Is it scandalous for a communist, with the oh so beautiful government we now have to put up with, to mistrust the lira?'

'No, it is not scandalous to have mistrust in the lira: the scandal is that you, Comrade, have faith in the dollar!'

'Let's not change the cards on the table. Here we are doing tourism, not politics.'

Peppone almost burst with joy, every now and then checking the envelope containing the 16,000 dollar bills. He recognised of course that Lake Lugano and Brè and Monte Generoso were beautiful: but, for him, the best landscape was that of the 16,000 dollar bills. Around one in the afternoon they found a suitable place outside the city to demolish the supplies in peace. When they left, only the empty bottles remained in the suitcase. At midnight they returned to base and no-one saw them. Peppone stopped the car in front of the door of the presbytery and Don Camillo got out with the suitcase.

'Leave that to me, Monsignor,' Peppone said, taking it from his hand.

In the dining room, Peppone placed the suitcase on the table and opened it. There were no more empty bottles but, in their place, an impressive amount of cigarettes, cigars, lighters and chocolate. There were also two watches.

'If Monsignor would like to make a choice . . .' Peppone said, pointing to the merchandise.

Don Camillo picked up the heavy iron shovel of the fireplace:

'Skedaddle or I'll start to play!' he screamed.

Peppone closed the suitcase and took it away with all the contraband.

'I'll give it back to you in the morning,' he said.

*

Don Camillo went to let off steam with the Crucified Christ above the High Altar.

'Lord,' he exclaimed. 'He used me and my clerical attire to do his dirty business. I don't know how to find peace within myself!'

'Do not worry, Don Camillo,' Christ replied softly, smiling: 'you are not the only naive minister of God.'

'Precisely for this reason, Lord, I struggle. I don't know how to accept being one of the many.'

## The CACAUS

PEPPONE DECIDED TO lend a hand to the Soviet Union, and his general staff, having been made aware of the project, approved it unreservedly.

'Boss,' observed Smilzo, 'we are with you on this even if it proves to be a hard fight.'

'There'll be no battle,' Peppone replied. 'We hold a majority on the City Council.'

'Yes, but the opposition have that damned priest on board who'll try and knock it on the head for sure, even if he is in the minority.'

'I wish!' bellowed Peppone. 'I'm dying to give him a hard time.'

'Boss,' Bigio interjected, 'unfortunately it is no longer possible to sort out priests like we used to in the good old days of '45. Today they're deemed necessary and we must deal with them with respect.'

'Not priests like him!' Peppone replied. 'The people from Rome didn't send him back to his parish for nothing. Even here at home, he's meddling. The new Bishop sees him as smoke in his eyes and the leaders of the clerical party are just waiting for him to do some stupid thing to get him out of the way.'

In truth, Don Camillo's situation was more or less as Peppone described it. But the Mayor himself was no better placed. He, too, had been knocked back by events in the wider world and sent back to the village. It was only the great popularity that Peppone enjoyed in la Bassa, where the damnable intellectuals (the plague of every party) were somehow still kept away like mangy dogs, that he wasn't thrown on the scrap heap.

The people of la Bassa do not change their minds easily: over here, political strategy inevitably yields to sentimental attachment, and so, while Khrushchev was the man of the moment and his son-in-law and daughter were received in the Vatican, the absolute leader of the Reds at home in la Bassa remained attached to Stalin of old, who, dead and buried in other parts of the world, was more alive here than ever.

*

The old piazza, the large one, long since named Piazza del Popolo to promote and improve the lives of the working class, was connected to the smaller Piazza della Libertà by a street known as San Martino, so-called because an ancient chapel dedicated to San Martino had at some point been built there. The flood of 1882 had destroyed the chapel but the name remained and, now, Peppone had the idea of promoting the Soviet Union at the expense of San Martino by giving the street a new name, one that would ring with the glory lately associated with Russia all over the world.

In fact, two names were to be united in this glory, albeit kept clearly distinct. It was to be a first in the field of toponymy and urban planning, the project turning the former *via San Martino* into a double-faceted street: those wishing to go from Piazza del Popolo to Piazza della Libertà would pass through *via Gagarin* while, on their return, they would travel through *via Titov*.[28] Gagarin would have the odd numbers, Titov the even

[28] Yuri Gagarin and Gherman Titov were, respectively, the first and second cosmonauts to orbit the Earth.

numbers. A brilliant idea, for, with but one street available, the pride of two important customers would be satisfied.

Poor San Martino would be left standing when Peppone's proposal passed to the Council, which it did without the slightest difficulty. The clerical opposition, these days doing all it could to facilitate the swing to the left, was willing to sacrifice not one but 200 saints to the purpose:

'The scientific victories of the Soviet Union are victories for the whole of humanity: I approve *toto corde*,' was all that Perlini was prepared to say in defence of the sacrosanct rights of San Martino. But Don Camillo, who had no sense of political expediency, marched decisively on the town hall and confronted Peppone in his office as soon as he learned of the matter.

Peppone let him talk for as long as he wanted, then said:

'Reverend, the saints are fine where they are. The streets of this low world are not made for them but for us poor mortals. And while there is no good reason for a street to bear a saint's name, there are a hundred thousand excellent reasons to exalt two heroic pioneers of space flight.'

'If it is a question of flight,' Don Camillo sneered, 'San Martino, with a few centuries advantage, made it all the way to Paradise and is, therefore, much more exalted than Gagarin and Titov.'

'The trouble is, he didn't return,' Peppone observed. 'Gagarin and Titov, on the other hand, came back.'

'Just as well it was Russia they went back to . . .'

'Reverend, this is about toponymy, not politics. You disrespect two heroes of the cosmos!'

'It is you who disrespects the whole body of saints by removing the name that the street has carried for at least three centuries. Besides anything else, San Martino is the last saint you should be disrespecting. Remember, it was San Martino who divided his cloak and gave half to the poor man dying of cold.'

'If he did so, it proved to be as much to his own advantage.'

'That's some gratitude!'

'Gratitude?' Peppone yelled. 'Why should we be grateful? Charity is an indignity that doesn't help but damages the working people by patronising them. As far as the people are concerned, only what the people win by force from the rich has any value. For us, San Martino is your typical bourgeois do-gooder and the offer of half his cloak is laughable compared to the achievements of Gagarin, Titov and glorious Soviet science, which paves the way for the future peace and well-being of *all* peoples.'

Don Camillo went away defeated and Peppone, having summoned his general staff, announced:

'Clerical obscurantism has been returned, scorned, to its lair. The unveiling of the two road signs must be undertaken with solemnity and be the glorification of our supremacy in the space race, which will lead to the Soviet Union conquering the Moon.'

\*

The stage from which Peppone would glorify Soviet supremacy in space was set up in the large piazza near the entrance to the former via San Martino: and, when it was finished and they were arranging the red flag with the sickle, the hammer and the star, and the tricolor flag,[29] a squad of young men appeared in the churchyard and began to fumble around a mysterious structure of wood

---

[29] The red flag with sickle, hammer and star was the flag of the Italian communist party. The tricolor (*il Tricolore*) is the national flag of Italy.

and canvas, from which there eventually emerged a large sign atop a long bench, on which was painted in large red letters a puzzling acronym:

CACAUS

Peppone and his associates went into alarm mode and kept their eyes glued to the churchyard: but nothing happened. However, something did happen a quarter of an hour before the time set for the ceremony to unveil the new nameplates.

A group of young men and women settled behind the counter of the CACAUS while a loudspeaker placed on the top of the bell tower explained, in the voice of Don Camillo:

'Citizens! As you know, the mighty Soviet Union, committed with all its might to the daring and marvellous undertaking of the conquest of the Moon, cannot seem to deal with the non-essential sillynesses which, in less advanced countries, are considered – clearly quite wrongly – crucial. As you will have learned from the newspapers, the Soviet Union has had to buy four million tons of wheat from America. And the United States, a capitalist country that sees everything only from a business and commercial point of view, has provided the grain and demanded gold in return. As our Perlini rightly said in the City Council, Soviet space victories are victories for all humanity and we civilized people have felt it our duty to give our support to the Soviet Union, which is working for the good of all humanity. Our programme is encapsulated in the acronym that describes us: CACAUS: "Comitato Autonomo Cattolico Assistenza Unione Sovietica" [The Autonomous Catholic Committee for Soviet Union Assistance].

'While our representatives travel the countryside to solicit offers of wheat and maize from farmers, here in the village we will collect from our citizens cake, biscuits, breadsticks, pasta, rice . . . stock cubes for broth, cans of meat and tomato sauce, solid fuel, spirit to burn . . . domestic utensils, clothes and linen both for men and for women will also be appreciated . . .

'Citizens, we must help our Soviet brothers who work so hard for our well-being and for the whole of humanity. And let's give a solemn lesson of human solidarity and civilisation to the American merchants whose true God is money!'

The thing had been cleverly organised. As soon as Don Camillo's voice fell silent, *The Song of the Volga Boatmen* and *The Internationale* burst forth from the loudspeaker and a hundred characters, selected as perfect for the purpose, lined up in the churchyard loaded with crusts of bread, bags of fodder for chickens and calves, rusty beds, obsolete bicycles, old shoes, decrepit stoves and pots and pans, which looked like they'd been retrieved from the attic.[30]

In a few minutes the whole town poured into the piazza to enjoy the show and Peppone, having recovered from the shock of it all with difficulty, dispatched Brusco and the Bigio urgently to the presbytery.

'Reverend,' Bigio began, explaining their presence, 'the Mayor says that if you don't stop your antics immediately, he won't answer for what'll happen to you and your lot.'

Don Camillo was not impressed:

'Tell the Mayor that, given the great success of our initiative, I plan to roll it out from municipal to provincial and eventually to regional and national levels. Indeed,

---

[30] The traditional Russian *Song of the Volga Boatmen* was originally sung by barge-haulers on the Volga River. *The Internationale* was the Soviet national anthem until it was replaced in 1944 by *The Hymn of the Soviet Union,* formerly known as *The Song of Stalin.*

to notify the press right away . . . Of course, if Mr Mayor were to decide to leave via San Martino where it is, we might talk about it . . .'

The two ambassadors ran off and returned immediately. Negotiations began and a compromise solution was found. Don Camillo would immediately liquidate the CACAUS and Peppone would call off the unveiling ceremony. The old plaque announcing via San Martino would be returned to the road where it began at Piazza del Popolo. Titov's plaque would remain at the Freedom Square end. So, San Martino would have the odd numbers and Titov the even numbers. A double-faceted street: but with only one Soviet face. Visitors to the village of Don Camillo who wanted to go from Piazza del Popolo to Piazza della Libertà would, henceforth, walk along via San Martino, while on their return they would walk along via Titov.

And so, San Martino would continue to ride with half a cloak and half a victory.

## Don Camillo and the Lost Sheep

PEPPONE'S ACHILLES HEEL was a bad boy called Michele, who had hands as big as shovels and a mop of hair that made one think of those acacia trees reduced to tall trunks with absurd looking leafy top-knots. He travelled around on a trendy motorbike with saddlebags studded and fringed like a cowboy's and wore a black jacket on the back of which he'd painted a white skull with the inscription 'Veleno', meaning Venom, the moniker by which he was known.

Venom was the youngest of Peppone's children and the only longhair in town,[31] but that didn't bother him because, as well as possessing the strength of a buffalo, he commanded all the other longhairs scattered around la Bassa and when he and his gang got together it was like an earthquake was ripping the place apart.

Other big news from Don Camillo's village, which nestles below the embankment of the Great River: the pharmacy has been taken over by a young city doctor , Bognoni by name, who moved to the village with her husband, also a doctor. And old Piletti had passed away.

---

[31] Michele is a 'capellone', literally a long-haired hippie, but his description marks him out as what was known variously as rocker, ton-up boy and Hells Angel, the latter implying membership of the Hells Angels Motorcycle Club. All were culturally distinct from hippies, with their anthem of peace and love.

Meanwhile, Peppone has transformed his workshop into a large emporium where he sells cars, motorcycles and appliances of all sorts on the never-never. The money to fund the enterprise had been largely provided by comrades of the local Communist Section, who were convinced by Peppone's reasoning that 'if working-class people today want a car, a washing machine, a television, a fridge and so on, then it should be their comrades who supply them. That way profits will remain with the working people, because the profits of the store will be divided among its shareholders.'

The enterprise did not find favour with Dr Bognoni and his pharmacist companion Jole, however. Both had been recommended by the regional Federation as 'highly efficient activists' and welcomed enthusiastically onto the Board of the local Section. Their view was that Peppone's initiative served only to encourage bourgeois tendencies among the working people and diminished their revolutionary zeal: 'All you're doing, Comrade Bottazzi,' Bognoni had said, 'is creating an illusion of happiness among the people, forgetting that revolution can only be achieved out of suffering!'

'Owning a Fiat 600, a television, a fridge and a washing machine won't stop people suffering!' Peppone had countered, adding that he was a man of the people and knew the people inside out.

Forced to bite the bullet, the Bognoni retreated, keeping their cards close to their chests and waiting for a suitable occasion to unleash an offensive. The opportunity arose when Venom and his gang happened to turn up at the dance hall at Castelletto. They were refused entry as undesirables, but the gang arrogantly went in anyway, only leaving after they'd removed the trousers of every man present.

The episode caused a particular stir because that same night Venom climbed one of the two very tall pylons that conveyed the high voltage line across the Po and tied one end of a long rope to the top of it, on which he hung the fifty-seven pairs of trousers in descending order, creating as it were a massive bunting.

The following day people flocked to the bank of the Great River to enjoy the unusual spectacle of pants flapping in the wind, while in a public rally the two Bognoni raged against Venom, calling him a filthy example of bourgeois hooliganism, a dishonour to the country, and concluded treacherously: 'If Comrade Bottazzi raises children like this, how can he pretend to inspire the new generation of the Party?' Finally, they added that the cause of the working people was hardly served by sitting in a shop selling old wrecks and electrical appliances.

Peppone's initial reaction was to kick the Bognoni from here to kingdom come, but then he thought about it and sent a detailed report to the regional Federation demanding an immediate response. That evening, Don Camillo jumped for joy and went to let off steam with the Crucified Christ above the High Altar:

'Lord,' he said, 'I thank you for having brought confusion and discord into the camp of God's enemies.'

'Darkness and discord are not mine to bring, only light and peace,' Christ replied. 'Your enemy is your neighbour and your neighbour's pains must also be your pains.'

'Forgive me, Lord,' replied Don Camillo 'but I cannot get too distressed about Peppone having a longhair for a son!'

'Don Camillo,' said Christ smiling, 'we must not forget that I too, during my short life on earth, wore my hair long.'

'Lord!' exclaimed Don Camillo indignantly. 'This fellow, who enjoys wearing long hair and dressing oddly, is also wicked and violent!'

'Don Camillo,' Christ reproached the priest, 'you give the sheep of your flock to the wolf too easily!'

'He is not a sheep of *my* flock!'

'You baptised that boy in the name of the Lord and he is a sheep of *my* flock.'

Don Camillo could not answer because, in that instant, in came Peppone to the church with a face that promised a storm. Don Camillo ushered him into the presbytery and once in the dining room began an apparently earnest entreaty:

'Comrade Mayor, are you finally ready to repent of your sins? Speak freely: God will listen to he whom Comrade Bognoni does not.'

'You and your goddamn Latinisms!' roared Peppone. 'Would you care to tell me what "*cum grano salis*" means?'

'It depends on the context,' answered Don Camillo.

'The context is that I reported to the Federation what those two windbags said about me in public, and the Federation replied that I have to act "*cum grano salis*". It'll be the ruin of the Party! Can't they speak in Italian? Now, even as the priests throw Latin in the trash, the officials of the Communist Federation choose to start using it!'

'Comrade,' Don Camillo began, exercising great patience, 'how could they possibly advise you to act with tact, prudence, diplomacy and intelligence when they know only too well that these are traits you wouldn't even recognise if you could see them? All they can do is to appeal to that microscopic grain of salt that they hope resides inside your great pumpkin.'

'Rubbish!' Peppone shouted. 'I'll show them a grain of salt! I'm going to sort out those cankerous doctors and I'll do it with slaps "*cum grano pepis*"! What fault is it of mine if my son's gone off his head? You know what? If that no-good had the guts to come home, I'd kill him!'

'Good idea,' Don Camillo approved. 'Much easier to kill a child than to educate him.'

'Who said kill!' Peppone was indignant. 'What I mean to say is, if I happen to be within range, I'll beat him to a pulp!'

'You'd be better off killing him, Comrade. Prosperity has reduced you to a stack of lard: if your boy lets loose a fist on you, *he'll* kill *you*.'

'Are you telling me that if I beat him he'll turn on me?'

'If he really is your son, yes.'

'Well he is, unfortunately,' Peppone admitted very sadly.

At that moment, Smilzo entered upon the scene and Don Camillo exploded:

'What the hell are *you* doing in the presbytery? Is this some kind of Party cell meeting?'

'If the Pope can receive the Soviet Foreign Minister at the Vatican, an insignificant country priest like yourself can surely receive a couple of comrades from the local communist Section!' replied Smilzo. 'Or do you consider yourself more important than the Pope?'

'What's up?' asked Peppone.

'Boss,' began Smilzo: 'Michele just piled into the pharmacy and forced Comrade Jole to drink half a bottle of castor oil. Then he went to the clinic and made Dr Bognoni drink the rest!'

Peppone, his face white as a sheet, collapsed onto a chair.

'He's done for me!' he groaned. 'Castor oil! Now they'll accuse me of having a fascist for a son![32] The scoundrel! With so much stuff around that he could have made him drink, he chose to go for castor oil!'

Meanwhile, Brusco had also arrived at the presbytery with fresh news: 'Boss, it wasn't castor oil: it was a bottle of cod liver oil!'

'God be praised,' Peppone sighed. 'They'll not be able to make political capital out of that, but I swear I'll bust the head of the thug! You two follow me but only get involved if he has a go at me and you see that I can't sort him out on my own!'

The three men made a hasty exit and Don Camillo turned his eyes to heaven, spreading his arms wide in desolation:

'Lord, a sheep of your flock is lost; the wolves they look for it. I don't know where to find it: what should I do?'

'It is written, "*Pulsate et aperietur vobis*",'[33] came the distant voice of Christ.

Don Camillo began to walk up and down the room: he didn't understand what Christ meant, but when there was a knock at the door, he ran to open it.

Enter Venom, his shock of hair all but concealing his face. The young man was very agitated:

'Reverend,' he said, 'my father is looking for me, to break my bones.'

Don Camillo viewed him with disgust:

'And you, with those paws, are you afraid of a bladder of lard like your father?'

---

[32] Peppone is referring to the practice among fascists of purging political enemies by forcing them to drink castor oil. See 'The American Indian', *Don Camillo and Peppone* (Pilot, 2016).

[33] 'Knock and the door shall be opened unto you.' *Matthew* 7:7–8.

'Sure I am! If he catches me, I can only stand and take it. You don't want me to turn against my own father . . .!'

Don Camillo regarded the bad boy with a little less disgust:

'Don't you realise the trouble you've caused by purging the Bognoni?'

'I didn't purge them for what they said about me but for what they said about my father. Save me, Don Cam . . .'

'The house of God is open to all sinners who repent.'

Venom swelled his broad chest and clenched his fists:

'I do not regret a damn thing!' he cried. 'The sin was committed by those two windbags, not me!'

'If that's what you think,' replied Don Camillo calmly, 'you have two options: you can leave immediately or, if you intend to stay, you must pay!'

'I am willing to pay!' roared Venom. Don Camillo told him the price and the boy replied that, rather than accept, he would allow himself to be slaughtered.

'Then off you go!' Don Camillo concluded.

Venom set off towards the door, but halfway there he stopped and turned:

'Reverend, the price you ask of me is *total degradation*!'

'Take it or leave it: here you pay the fixed price and there are no discounts.'

Venom returned, sat down and, gritting his teeth, agreed to pay the full price. Finally, he got up and said, 'Reverend, you have ruined me!'

'It is not my sort of work and the end product is not perfect,' agreed Don Camillo. 'However, I find that with less one is more.'

While Don Camillo put away scissors and razor and swept the great pile of hair into the garbage, Venom took a mirror out of his pocket and boy and reflection studied one another: 'Like this I am a nobody,' they said in anguish.

In truth he felt drained of all his strength, like Samson when he found himself kidnapped by Delilah, because the secret of his strength lay in his long hair.

'I no longer have the courage to show myself to people,' he groaned. 'I will leave town.'

'And where will you go?'

'I have a job: I am a conscript. I am going to be a soldier.'

Don Camillo was amazed at this decision: 'But you were among those who call themselves conscientious objectors?'

'I was, because if I'd gone into the military they'd have cut off my hair, Now that I am shaved to zero, there is no longer any moral question.'

'I see,' mumbled Don Camillo. 'Now, go to the kitchen and get something to eat and then go to bed: the bedroom is on the top landing. Sleep in peace: no one will disturb you there.'

Don Camillo went into church to confide in Christ:

'Lord, thank you. The good shepherd found the lost sheep, just as you said.'

'Yes, Don Camillo: but I did not say that the good shepherd must shear the sheep that he found.'

'This is a detail of a technical nature that concerns only the shepherd, not God . . .'

*

Venom remained hidden in the presbytery for a week and spent the time chopping and sawing all the wood that Don Camillo would need for the winter. Then, on the eighth day, Peppone surfaced, very agitated:

'The district call-up orders have been delivered,' he screamed. 'I don't know where that wretch is holed up but if he doesn't appear in time he'll be prosecuted as a draft dodger. More trouble for me if I don't find him!'

Don Camillo took him to the kitchen, and stood him in front of a window that overlooked the presbytery courtyard. Peppone saw Venom chopping wood and gasped.

'*Shaved to zero*!' he exclaimed.

'Of course,' Don Camillo explained. 'I convinced him to become a monk.'

Peppone jumped: 'This . . . *No!*' he screamed. 'Rather than see it go so badly for the boy I'll take him home right away. I swear I won't say a word against him even though it's because of him that those damned Bognoni intend to take revenge on me by creating an autonomous Maoist Section in the village.'

'He's doing well,' answered Don Camillo. 'Too bad: it sounded so good – "Brother Venom, sheep of God".'

'In the Bottazzi house there is no place for sheep!' shouted Peppone.

'Ah, yes!' said Don Camillo scornfully. 'I forgot that there was a time when you, Comrade, had written on the façade of your house: "Better to live one day as a lion than a hundred years as a sheep".'

'To hell with your confounded memories,' roared Peppone as he left. 'Between you and me, the account remains open!'

'We will close it,' Don Camillo reassured him. 'Mao permitting, of course.'

Meanwhile, the Great River flowed calmly and impassively on and it was a day like any other, but different.

## The Secret of Sant'Antonio Abate

THE LITTLE RED Spyder[34] turned purposefully into the presbytery courtyard and a thin young man, dressed in grey, with high-minded spectacles on his nose and a leather bag under his arm, got out. Don Camillo, who was sitting at his desk in the dining room with one eye on the *Gazzetta* and the other peering through the window, clenched his fists.

'Enter!' he said rather irritably as soon as his visitor's knock on the door was heard. The young man came in, proffered a greeting and handed Don Camillo an envelope.

'I can't buy anything,' muttered Don Camillo without even lifting his head from the newspaper.

'I have nothing to sell,' replied the other. 'I am Don Francesco, assigned to you by the Curia as coadjutor, and this is my letter of introduction.'

Don Camillo squared up to him.

'Seeing you dressed like this, young man, I mistook you for one of those sales reps who are forever calling round here. Considering you've come to introduce

---

[34] Innocenti, famous in the 1950s for the Lambretta scooter, branched out into cars in 1961 with the 950 Spyder, a re-bodied version of the Austin-Healey MKII Sprite, its small size, sporty appearance and low price having the young in mind. Later came a name change and the 1100 Spider.

yourself to an old cleric like me, it might have been better if you'd disguised yourself as a priest.'

The little man, a nervous type, paled before him as Don Camillo read the letter.

'Well,' he said putting the paper back in the envelope, 'so you were sent here to teach me how to be a priest.'

'No, Father: just to remind you that it is not 1666 but 1966.'

Don Camillo took the yellow handkerchief from his pocket and tied a knot in it.

'Now that you've reminded me, you may leave,' he said, which raised the little priest's hackles: 'Reverend father! The Curia sent me here and here I will remain,' he exclaimed tetchily, sitting down in front of Don Camillo's desk.

'In that case,' Don Camillo said calmly, 'let us take the opportunity to play a game. Do you know the eighty-card game?'[35]

'No,' the priest replied through clenched teeth.

On the desk were some old packs of cards: Don Camillo grabbed one of them, gripped it in his big hands and, with one wrench, tore it in two. The little priest was unimpressed: 'I can play this game too,' he said, 'but with much less effort'. He picked up another pack of cards from the desk and, very calmly, one by one, shred the forty cards in two pieces: 'Now they are eighty like yours, Father,' he said at last, all smiles.

Don Camillo nodded with an air of approval:

'I, however,' he said pointing to the two piles of broken cards, 'I can make you eat all 160 of them.'

This was the Don Camillo of harder and more violent times and the little priest was taken aback:

---

[35] An Italian deck consists of forty cards, hence the eighty-card game with two decks. See 'Return to the Fold' in *The Little World of Don Camillo* (Pilot, 2013).

'I . . . ,' he stammered. 'I was sent. If my person upsets you . . .'

'It does, but someone else's would have upset me just the same. Since his Excellency has ordered me an assistant, I will fall in line. You kindly reminded me that it is 1966 and not 1666 and I hereby return the courtesy by reminding you that I am the parish priest here. There is a room ready. Take the opportunity to freshen up and to dress as a priest: here, during the hours of service, bourgeois dress codes are not appreciated.'

The little priest was taken by old Desolina to the visitors room and Don Camillo hurried away to let off steam with the Crucified Christ above the High Altar.

In point of fact in Don Camillo's church the Mass was still celebrated in Latin and the faithful continued to receive the Host kneeling in front of the chancel rail, with its columns painted to look like marble. In all the other churches of the diocese, the altar had been replaced by what Don Camillo, with little respect, called 'the diner', but in his church no changes at all had been effected and, for this reason, the Curia – before adopting serious disciplinary measures – had wanted to place a young priest alongside the stubborn old pastor of la Bassa to induce the rebel to update himself.

Don Camillo walked up and down the deserted church focusing hard on his search for the right words to begin what he wanted to say, when Christ's voice itself called softly to him:

'Don Camillo, what are you doing? Have you forgotten that the true strength of God's priests lies in their humility?'

'Lord,' exclaimed Don Camillo. 'I have never forgotten and I stand here before you the humblest of your servants.'

'Don Camillo, it is easy to humble oneself before God. Your God became man and humbled himself before men.'

'Lord,' Don Camillo wailed in anguish, spreading his arms: *'why* should I destroy everything that always has been?'

'There is no need to destroy anything. Change the frame of the painting and the painting remains the same. Or do I detect that, for you, the frame is more important than the painting? Don Camillo, if the habit does not make the monk, nor does it the priest. Or perhaps you think you are more a minister of God than that young man just because you are wearing a cassock and he a jacket and trousers? And again, Don Camillo, do you think your God is so ignorant that he can understand only Latin? Don Camillo: these stuccos, this painted wood, this purple, these ancient words . . . they are not *faith.*'

'Lord,' replied Don Camillo humbly, 'but they are tradition, memory, sentiment, poetry . . .'

'All beautiful things that have nothing to do with faith, Don Camillo. You love these things because they remind you of your past, and therefore you feel them as yours, almost as part of you. True humility is renouncing the things you love most.'

Don Camillo bowed his head and said: 'I will obey, Lord.'

But Christ smiled because he could read the truth in Don Camillo's heart.

*

The little priest was full of enthusiasm. His motto was '*Demystify!*' That is, cleanse the Church of what is merely tinsel and can only generate superstition. But he ventured to operate with caution so as not to irritate Don Camillo.

And Don Camillo gave him free rein, albeit through gritted teeth.

Then suddenly he pulled him up.

'The altar *will* be taken down,' said Don Camillo in the detached tone of voice he had used when offering to feed the priest the two packs of cards, 'but only after I have found a suitable place for it to go.'

This was no easy task because an altar surmounted by a three-metre high Crucified Christ is no mere ornament. But Don Camillo had an idea in his pumpkin and entrusted it to Christ.

'Lord,' let me explain, 'the heirs of poor Piletti have liquidated almost all the family estate. Only the old, decrepit manor house and the adjoining private chapel, where I always celebrate Mass once a year, remains. They are willing to sell everything for around seven million lire and it is negotiable. If I could have that chapel, I should take the altar there and you as well, Lord, as Piletti intended. If I let you hang around here, no one knows where you'll end up. Of course, you would always remain the son of Almighty God even if they destroyed *all* the images of you, but I will never allow them to hide you away in some attic.

'Don Camillo,' Christ admonished him, 'you do not speak of me. You are talking about a painted piece of wood.'

'Lord, my homeland is not that piece of coloured canvas they call a flag, but the flag of my country *cannot* be treated like a rag. And you are my flag, Lord. In that chapel you would find a good home but, unfortunately, even if negotiable, seven million lire are seven million lire. How can I find that kind of money?'

'Look for it where it is,' Christ replied enigmatically, smiling.

Meanwhile the little priest was champing at the bit with impatience: 'Father, we have postponed making final arrangements for the altar,' he said at a moment he felt propitious, 'we could advance the demystification process by, for example, eliminating that horrible representation of Sant'Antonio.'

The painted plaster statue was indeed unsightly. Don Camillo had discovered it in its niche and left it untouched, merely dusting it once a year. Patron of the livestock of la Bassa, Sant'Antonio had apparently behaved very well during a serious epidemic of foot-and-mouth disease between 1862 and 1914. He had therefore known very happy times and had seen hundreds of candles burning every day before him. Then, as the anti-inflammatory injections took hold, the candles had diminished and now poor Sant'Antonio had to be content with the miserable ten-candle arrangement that Don Camillo had placed in front of the niche, masked inside an old oil lamp. Don Camillo was fond of his Saint Anthony, but accepted the priest's proposal:

'That's fine,' he responded. 'Tomorrow morning you won't find him here anymore.'

*Est modus in rebus.*[36] He agreed on the plan to evict Saint Anthony but, after more than one hundred years of honourable service, not to liquidate him with four hammer blows – as the priest would have liked. (One hundred and four years to be precise, as it appeared from the parish books that the statue had been donated to the church in June 1862 by a rich landowner called Ferrazza.)

Helped by the sexton that same night, Don Camillo took Sant'Antonio down from his niche and stored him safely in the presbytery garage. Now, it happened that during the move the Saint bumped his right foot against

---

[36] 'Moderation in all things.'

the corner of a door and lost all his toes and the tip of his shoe. Before going to bed Don Camillo meant to restore the damaged foot with a little putty, but as he was about to stick it all back together he noticed a section of black boot on the truncated section of the Saint's foot, which was not of stucco but of painted wood. Moreover, the lower part of the grey cassock which covered the Saint down to his feet was cracked and a light tap was enough to reveal something truly unexpected. Under his habit Sant'Antonio was wearing trousers and boots with spurs. Another tap and the upper part of his habit fell off like a scab and a piece of red shirt came to light.

In a few minutes, the stucco crust that covered the original wooden statue was completely removed and, lo and behold, Sant'Antonio was transformed unequivocally into Garibaldi.[37] The raised right arm of the statue still held a small crucifix in its fist, but evidently, originally, it was holding a sabre, while the pilgrim's stick, which the Saint had held in his left hand, was a skilfully camouflaged flagpole.

It was not immediately clear why Garibaldi had been disguised as Saint Anthony, but Don Camillo rumbled it shortly afterwards. On Garibaldi's red shirt there was a white heart-shaped section on the left-hand side of his chest which was not wood, but a very thin layer of plaster, as Don Camillo discovered when he tested its consistency with his knuckles and it shattered immediately, leaving a hole through which poured a tinkling cascade of Marengo gold coin.[38] Together with the coin out fell a sheet of paper folded in four.

It was an old piece of village history – a little ridiculous, a little sad. In April 1862, Giuseppe Garibaldi paid a

---

[37] A founding father and central figure in the unification of Italy.

[38] Minted to celebrate Napoleon's victory against the Austrians at Piedmont at the Battle of Marengo (1800).

visit to the provincial capital where they celebrated him as a demigod. The painted wooden statue of Garibaldi, the work of a local craftsman, was part of the celebrations. Garibaldi had spoken very harshly to the Society of Workers about the priests of Rome and 'bad priests' in general and a certain Ferrazza, probably head of the local anti-clericals in what was later Don Camillo's parish, was so enthusiastic about it that he bought the statue and, having had it transformed into Sant'Antonio Abate, offered it to the parish priest. Today such a stratagem would not be appreciated, but back then there were those who enjoyed this type of subtle but ferocious mockery. In this case, the mockery did not consist in introducing Garibaldi into the church and venerating him as a saint, but rather in making a gift to a priest (a chest full of gold coin) with a message dripping with irony:

*'Priest! (Yes, for sure, "Priest", because there is gold here and above all priests can sniff out the gold they're so greedy for at a distance!)*

*'So, priest! Contrary to what you say, no devil occupies Garibaldi's heart, but a precious treasure, which you won't be able to keep your hands off!*

*'And priest! If Mass is still celebrated by the time you read this letter (which I doubt), say one for the soul of the anti-clerical Garibaldian Alberto Ferrazza and, with the Marengo gold coin, have a good meal while toasting the everlasting glory of Garibaldi!'*

Converted into lire, the gold amounted to around six million and Don Camillo was able to buy old Pilotti's house and set up his altar in the chapel with the great Crucified Christ above it just as they had been in church. He transported the statue of Abbot Garibaldi there too, after having it covered by a specialist with a stucco crust.

Finally, the first Mass he celebrated in the chapel was for the soul of the late Alberto Ferrazza. In Latin, of course, and in the presence of a few wrecks of the old guard.

'Lord,' he then explained to Christ, 'they are block-heads. They cling to life only thanks to the strength of their memories of the past and of their dead. They do not understand that even the Church must renew itself.'

'But do you understand it, Don Camillo?' Christ responded.

'Maybe not, Lord,' Don Camillo honestly admitted. 'But I am not out of order because this was a private Mass and this chapel is now my private property, thanks to God!'

'Thanks to Garibaldi,' Christ corrected him.

'Lord, you told me that I had to look for the money "where it is" and that is what I did. It was Sant'Antonio Abate who brought my faith into question by meddling in the Garibaldi affair.'

'Perhaps, Don Camillo,' said Christ smiling. 'In a country like this, where the dead are even crazier than the living, a parish priest like you may yet be the most suitable.'

Of course, the telegraph lines were alive with the coup struck by Don Camillo. And when Peppone came across him, he asked with great sarcasm:

'Reverend, is it true that you have opened up a shop of your own?'

'No, Comrade,' answered Don Camillo. 'I always work for one and the same proprietor: Mao has not yet reached the point of sowing confusion *up there*.'

And Peppone left it at that.

*The Water of the Po is Not for Mao*

AMONG THE EIGHT hamlets of the Lower Plain administered by Peppone and his companions, La Rocca was the wildest. Only a few kilometres separated it from Peppone's village, but not all kilometres are the same and this is because men are different and, sometimes, even in a city, all you have to do is turn up some lane and you find yourself in another world.

The people of La Rocca lived in a floodplain and their centuries-old struggle with the Great River had made them hard and belligerent. As far as they were concerned, whoever lived beyond the main embankment was a foreigner. Practically all of them were Reds but their brand of communism was Stalinism and the only form of dialogue that they employed with their adversaries was basically to beat them about the head. Doctor Bognoni, therefore, did not have to struggle to convince them to form an autonomous Maoist Section and to recognise him as their leader, Mao being as hard-line a Marxist as Stalin had been.

On the day an inspector of the district Federation came to La Rocca to bring his errant comrades back into the fold, he found the town plastered with graffiti and posters praising Stalin and Mao . . . and completely empty of inhabitants.

It was inevitable that someone would take advantage of this situation. And so it was that when the newspapers published the amazing story of Mao at the age of 70 kick-starting his Cultural Revolution by swimming fifteen kilometres in the Yangtze River as if powered by an outboard motor, large yellow posters appeared on the walls of Peppone's village and La Rocca:[39]

*'Mao stunned the world with his show of strength, but what do the "Chinese" comrades of La Rocca think of the fact that their leader, Comrade Bognoni, can't even swim? How can he begin to prepare for the proletarian revolution if he can't swim?'*

A GROUP OF COMRADES WHO DO NOT KNOW HOW TO SWIM

The poster was anonymous, but everyone presumed that it was a gimmick of Peppone's at Bognoni's expense. The people of La Rocca felt provoked and, with their natural impetuousness, went on the counterattack with a challenging riposte:

*'The Maoist leader of La Rocca may not know how to swim like the great Mao, but he could beat the leader of the self-styled "group of comrades who know how to swim" any day. (Always assuming that the fat accumulated by his being a shopkeeper will allow him to stay afloat.)'*

The reply was not long in coming:

*'Little Mao of La Rocca don't get beyond yourself! After the intense cod liver oil treatment, you may feel as quick as a fish, but be careful you're not left gaping like a cod in the end!'*

---

[39] In 1966, Mao Tse Tung undertook probably the most powerful political publicity stunt in China's history. Combating rumours of his ailing health and needing to connect with the youth of China to launch his devastating cultural revolution, Mao led a reported 5,000 adoring followers in Wuhan's annual swim in the Yangtze River.

The atmosphere was warming up nicely and both sides were enjoying themselves more and more, so, naturally, when Don Camillo came upon Peppone and his General Staff, he did not fail to ask cheerfully how the training was going and if a date for the historic meeting had yet been set.

'You don't think I'd fall for such antics, do you!' Peppone replied brusquely.

'Oh, I see,' Don Camillo chuckled cruelly, 'now that the matter has gone further than intended, you, Mr Mayor, decide to back down!'

'I never back down!' Peppone screamed.

'Well said, Boss!' his General Staff enthusiastically approved. 'Priests have a face for every occasion, but with us what you see is what you get!'

The challenge of the century took place one Sunday afternoon and half the world turned up by the river. The course was across the river and back; a select cross-party committee was set up on the opposite bank to check the two champions as they turned and whoever got back first was the winner.

Bognoni was young and thin, while Peppone, despite being the stronger, was weighed down by age and flab. The first lap made the La Rocca supporters scream with enthusiasm because, so the committee adjudged, 'Bognoni was the first to touch the bank!' But their screams made Peppone furious and he forgot his years and his flab and injected into the battle the strength and breath he didn't have. On the way back he caught up with Bognoni and, after a desperate struggle, managed to overtake him. Clearly ahead, he touched the bank first, but immediately collapsed on the sand as if dead.

'A doctor!' screamed Brusco, who was there first, followed by the rest of the gang. Peppone gave no sign of life and Dr Bognoni, who, as usual, had brought a First

Aid kit in his car, appeared on the spot in a flash. Kneeling next to Peppone, he felt his pulse and yelled to his wife: 'Quick, prepare a syringe with the stimulant! There's a risk of heart attack here!'

That was enough to bring Peppone back to his senses. He narrowed his eyes with difficulty, peered at the doctor in disgust and roared: Brusco! Get rid of this quack! Can't a man be left to die in peace!'

Bognoni got up and left and Don Camillo took his place, kneeling beside Peppone.

'Now you'll be happy,' panted Peppone.

'And why should I be happy?' exclaimed Don Camillo.

'Because you are the scoundrel who printed the posters attributed to me and mounted this whole dirty business!'

'True,' Don Camillo admitted humbly. 'But it's too late now to regret it. Is there anything I can do for you?'

'Yes,' roared Peppone. 'You and all the priests of the universe can go to hell!'

'There are too many of us, Comrade,' replied Don Camillo. 'And I don't like group tours.'

Bigio arrived with a bottle of cognac and Peppone attacked it as if to drain the Pontine Marshes. Then a doctor also arrived and listened to Peppone's heart and measured his blood pressure.

'All normal,' he said.

'So, why did he lie there unconscious?' Don Camillo ventured.

'Because he's dead drunk,' explained the doctor.

Peppone was indeed drunk, but not dead, so he managed to find the strength to mutter:

'Father, if there is a God he is going to punish you.'

There is indeed a God and he is usually in no hurry to chastise his flock, but on this occasion he made an exception and punished Don Camillo just twenty-four hours later.

*

It was Monday afternoon and in the presbytery dining room, Don Camillo was arguing with the young coadjutor when suddenly a deafening uproar broke out in the street.

Seven of the craziest young motorcyclists you can imagine, with enormous mops of hair and black leather jackets, had come to a halt in front of the gate to the presbytery courtyard, cackling and furiously revving their engines. Then one of the wild bunch grabbed a weird-looking guitar and all of them, as one, sang a song coarse enough to make your hair stand on end, honking their horns to the rhythm of the refrain.

The timbre of a voice among many revealed one of the seven to be female and, hearing the oaths emanating from her coral lips, they seemed even more crude, an effect compounded by the fact that this very young hooligan, taking off her jacket, disclosed that she was dressed in a kind of black and white checked shirt, low-necked and sleeveless and so short that it barely covered her shameless backside.

'I'll see to this right now!' Don Camillo yelled, walking determinedly towards the front door. But the little priest stopped him:

'No, Don Camillo, leave it to me. I know how to deal with young people. Don't be put off by their nonconformity: they're much nicer than you think.'

Don Camillo went to the window and saw the little priest walk out through the gate and, all smiles and cordiality, engage with the wild ones. They let him have his say for a few minutes, then the girl whistled and the other six jumped off their bikes and laid into him, burying him under a storm of punches and kicks.

The know-it-all Don Francesco in his tight-fitting suit (which Don Camillo had been unable to get him to remove) had done little to commend himself, but, faced with the spectacle of his being knocked about by this bunch, Don Camillo forgot everything and bearing down upon the gang like a Panzer tank, was able to pull out the little priest, who was already reduced to a sack of rags.

The lightning-fast intervention of that marauding priest, so big and so black, confused the longhairs and seriously unnerved them. But the girl's shrill voice sounded imperious:

'Give it to that fat fool of a priest!'

They got up and all six were on Don Camillo with no uncertain a strategy, for while four restrained him by his arms and legs, the other two beat him up.

Don Camillo, who had not expected such a seeing-to, never gave less than value in extremis and behaved like an elephant attacked by a herd of petulant monkeys as he tried to shake off the rabble. But the girl's voice, angry and petulant, seemed to give her the whip hand:

'Be strong!' she screamed at her boys. 'Tear off his petticoat! We want to see him in his underwear!'

This, however, was a tactical error, because Don Camillo heard it and said to Christ: 'Lord, will you allow a minister of God to be publicly reduced to his underwear?'

'No, Don Camillo: never!' came Christ's distant reply.

As, with a whispered word in its ear, a horse lying third kicks on to overtake the field at 140 kph, so Christ's still small voice was all Don Camillo needed to tear his arms free and grab the two who were beating him by the mop, banging their heads together. The wretches fell concussed to the ground. The other four, urged on by the girl, remained commendably busy, but unfortunately for them, there was a pole leaning handily against the court-yard gate – a strong and whippy acacia stick, which, in the hands of Don Camillo, yielded to its new role with exceptional deftness and style.

No one could last long under this kind of rain and, at an opportune moment, the bad boys, full of bruises and bumps as big as plums, jumped on their motorbikes and raced away screaming:

'We'll see you later!'

Not all seven, however: the girl remained, unper-turbed, leaning against the gatepost, bold as brass, smoking a cigarette. Don Camillo was now in top gear and advanced menacingly towards the deranged crea-ture, determined to sort her out too. She didn't bat an eye and when Don Camillo stood nose-to-nose in front of her, she simply said with a smile:

'Hiya, Uncle!'

Don Camillo stopped and looked at the shameless creature. Dressed decently she would have been a beau-tiful girl of between sixteen and eighteen, but with that sassy red mop, with those eyes so misty and that miniskirt so shameless, she was simply . . . hateful.

'Who are you, you tramp? What wantonness spawned you?' he roared.

'I come from your sister Giuseppina's house. I am your niece, Cat,' replied the girl.

'I have no niece named Cat!' Don Camillo shouted back.

'My Christian name is, in fact, Elisabetta,' the shame-less girl explained with a provocative sort of smile geared to invite an angry response in the priest. 'But the boys call me Cat, short for "Caterpillar", because when I go in for a bit of fisticuffs I'm worse than a bulldozer.'

Don Camillo detected familial features in her face, which only increased his wrath.

'And you,' he yelled, 'you, my niece, the daughter of my sister, you wanted your thuggish friends to beat me up and leave me in my underpants!'

'Pardon me, Uncle. Didn't you tell my mother last week that she needn't worry about me because you'd soon transform me into the meekest and humblest "Daughter of Mary"? Do you still believe you can or would you rather I jump on my motorbike and go back to town and console my mommy?'

Don Camillo was clutching the acacia stick in his hand and the girl continued to stare boldly into his eyes.

'Anselma!' he shouted.

Anselma was married to the sexton, but was possessed of a persona more usually found in a husband than a wife. Built like a tank, she was the sort of woman who, when seriously mixing it, could make you forget your home address.

'I cannot deal with her,' Don Camillo explained to Anselma, who had followed the whole scene from a window.

'Oh, I think I can,' replied the tank, making to grab the girl by the shoulder. 'She just needs a little ironing out. Then, in a few days, I'll give her back to you.'

The girl was unimpressed:

'If you dare lay your hands on me I won't answer for what'll happen!' she said, clearly meaning it.

'Don't you worry, young lady,' Anselma reassured her. 'No hands. Us peasant folk mix it with a dough paddle.'

'Now there's a good idea!' said Don Camillo, giving his approval. 'I think that's the only way to teach it the ways of the real world.' He said 'teach it' rather than 'teach her' not through linguistic sloppiness, as in the new age of TV, but because – taking into account the girl's bad temper – he was thinking of the dough paddle.

Cat tried, with a tug, to break free: but Anselma did not budge an inch.

'Her name may be Anselma,' Don Camillo explained to his struggling niece, 'but everyone calls her "El", short for elephant. I advise you to start your makeover by increasing the length of your skirt by at least half a metre.'

'*Never!*' Cat screamed angrily.

'Too bad,' chuckled Don Camillo. 'The only alternative is to shorten your legs by half a metre.'

## A 'Nocturne' Not Made for Sleeping

THERE IS NO particular day made for paying one's dues to God, but in this case, for Don Camillo, pay-day was a Monday. Cat was, in fact, an all too real punishment from God and had already made Don Camillo realise why his sister, a widow battered with the cares of the world, had begged him to help her straighten her out.

She had clearly taken a disastrous turning along life's road. On the very evening of her arrival at the presbytery she laid her cards on the table with Anselma thus:

'It is perfectly pointless,' she said, 'you treating me like a prisoner, barring doors and windows. I have no intention of running away. I want that old fossil of a priest to beg me on his knees to leave.'

'Little Girl,' Anselma rebuked her, 'you don't know what you are saying. Remember that when things got really rough around here in the old days, your uncle fearlessly faced up to wild gangs of communists.'

'Uh! The commies!' sneered Cat. 'they're no less clowns than the priests, the fascists, the socialists, the bourgeois, the military, the policemen and all the rest. They're the walking dead. The young are now masters of the world and nothing can stop us!'

'What about God?'

'God!' Cat laughed. 'God is dead.'

Anselma, being the sexton's wife, considered herself to be directly dependent on God and found this particularly difficult to swallow.

'If you were my daughter,' she said through gritted teeth, 'I would give you a slap in the face. But, since you are not, I will give you two!'

Like certain internal combustion engines, Anselma was rather ahead of herself, so by the time she said 'two', the slaps had already arrived.

'They will help you sleep,' she said by way of explanation.

'But they'll make sure you don't,' Cat replied portentously, walking up the stairs to her room.

Her words were indeed prophetic: at two in the morning, the church bells began to ring out and the whole town got to its feet. Don Camillo, too, jumped out of bed and once downstairs found himself confronted by Anselma who looked a picture of humiliation.

'What the hell is going on?' Don Camillo shouted.

Anselma opened her arms in desolation:

'Father, it so happens that the attic window overlooks the roof of the rectory and, from the roof of the rectory, a deranged person can apparently reach the roof of the church and slip through the round window of the bell tower.'

'So?'

'So, since your niece is a deranged person, she is now up there having fun, after pulling up the ladders and sealing off the hatches to the various belfry landings.'

Down below, people had begun to gather and from among them Peppone stepped forward:

'Reverend, either you put a stop to this scandalous behaviour, or we will take matters into our own hands!'

'Take them, Comrade Mayor,' answered Don Camillo. 'If you have a helicopter, take it out and get on with it.'

In the bell tower Cat had discovered how the carillon worked and was having a wail of a time ringing out a melody to a 'beat' rhythm accompanied by inhuman screams.[40]

Hearing her shrieks, Smilzo sneered:

'That must be our parish priest's new lady friend singing for her supper!'

Don Camillo did not like jokes of this kind and grabbed Smilzo by the lapels of his jacket, whereupon Peppone stepped in:

'Reverend, you would not deny that those are the screams of a woman!'

'They are the roars of a tiger!' Don Camillo shouted. 'What sin have I committed for that crazy girl to torment me so?'

Brusco intervened: 'Ah, Father! So this is all about your witty young niece who arrived yesterday afternoon with her friends and tried to reduce you to your underpants!'

Peppone and his hateful gang had a good laugh at Don Camillo's expense while, in the meantime, Cat was stepping up the bell ringing with ever greater vigour.

'Lord!' Don Camillo moaned. 'How can I make her stop?'

The good Lord took pity and the sexton approached and told him, in a low voice, that someone was waiting for him in the attic. There was indeed someone up there; a sort of Diabolik figure of a man straight out of a comic

---

[40] A carillon is a musical instrument consisting of some twenty-three cast-bronze, cup-shaped bells, which are played serially (typically in the belfry of a church) to produce a melody. Guareschi uses the colloquial English 'beat' in his otherwise Italian manuscript to indicate that Cat had managed to create a cool rhythmic accompaniment to her clearly original singing style.

book:[41] black jumpsuit, black gloves and a black balaclava, which left only his eyes uncovered:

'Father,' the man said to Don Camillo, 'I will take care
of this.'

'Venom!' Don Camillo exclaimed. 'How come you're
dressed up like this?'

'I need to be able to melt into the darkness of the
night,' replied the bad boy. 'Also, I don't want anyone to
see me shaved to zero.'

'What about the army?'

'All good,' replied Venom. 'I'm in on the next recruit-
ment round.'

'She took up all the ladders to the belfry and blocked
the hatches,' Don Camillo warned. 'How are you going
to get up there?'

'If the lightning rod gets there, I can get there too.'

'No: it's too dangerous.'

Venom only laughed: 'Dangerous for a priest, not for
me.'

He left by the window that gave onto the presbytery
roof and reached the roof of the church by clinging onto
the metal cord of the lightning rod before disappearing
into the night.

'Lord!' Don Camillo pleaded falling to his knees:
'Help him!'

'Don Camillo,' replied the distant voice of Christ. 'Am
I wrong or did you tell me that he is not a sheep of your
flock?'

'No, Lord, make no mistake: I was wrong. But, for
God's sake, don't get distracted! Keep a hand on his
head!'

---

[41] Diabolik is one of the most popular characters in the history of Italian
comics. Initially a ruthless criminal, he developed honourable principles and
respect for noble souls, directing his skills against other criminals.

'And if he slips, how do I save him by grabbing him by the hair, since you shaved it off?'

Don Camillo's brow was dripping with sweat and, meanwhile, the infernal chime continued. Then suddenly, it stopped. Don Camillo rushed down to the room at the base of the bell tower; you could hear the bustle up in the tower: the hatches of the various shelves opened and the ladders were lowered down. Finally the last trapdoor opened and down came the ladder, then Venom appeared with a bundle under his arm. And the bundle was Cat. To manoeuvre her more easily, he'd wound a bell rope around her and put a stop to her endless shrieking by stuffing one of her leather gloves in her mouth.

On touching *terra firma*, he handed Don Camillo the bundle, but the priest withdrew, roaring:

'Throw her in the corner!'

Then he shouted for Anselma, who came post-haste.

'Take the rubbish out!' Don Camillo yelled, pointing to the girl. 'Tell people the show is over and they can go back to bed.'

*

The operation had been tiring and Venom gladly sank a couple of glasses of the presbytery's wine with Don Camillo. They were alone in the dining room and Venom had taken off his balaclava to give his bald pumpkin a little air. Don Camillo would have liked to know the details of what went on between Venom and Cat, but the boy shook his head:

'Father, put it from your mind, let's talk about serious things. You brought the plague into your house. *I know that one!*'

'How do you know her?'

'In Castelletto, two months ago. She was with the Scorpioni, a gang of Hells Angels.[42] They had descended on Castelletto for a punch-up but, as Castelletto is in our manor, we beat them up and they left town with their heads busted. The six who accompanied the girl here yesterday are the leaders of that gang. You have done them and they will not forgive you. *They will be back.*'

'No problem,' muttered Don Camillo. 'I still have a few acacia sticks in the woodshed.'

Venom shook his head; 'I have an informant in town and he phoned me that the Scorpios have a big expedition in mind. They want to come here *in number*, throw everything up in the air and free the girl by force.'

'Come with me,' muttered Don Camillo. 'We'll alert the *carabinieri*.'

'Father, nothing can be done: they will arrive when least expected. There are about fifty of them and well organised. They know that the *carabinieri* cannot shoot at them and they will strike.'

Venom frothed with rage and paced like a raging lion up and down the room. 'But why?' he finally bellowed, stopping in front of Don Camillo. 'Why did you shear me?'

'And what does your hair have to do with those thugs?'

'It has to do with them because, if I still had my hair, I could mass organise my crew and give the Scorpioni a total service! You have to bear in mind that we young rebels have our own systems and can settle things between us without courting tragedy. Ah, if I still had my hair!'

'Hair!' Don Camillo laughed. 'Nonsense!'

---

[42] The Hells Angels Motorcycle Club (*sic*), with its own customs and code of living, was founded in San Bernardino, California, in 1948. Today it is reputed to have 470 chapters in 56 countries.

'I certainly can't introduce myself to my boys bald as this. It's a question of honour, of prestige.'

'A man is the same man whatever the length of his hair.'

'Then let me tell you, Father, that a priest is always the same whatever his dress. But what would happen if you celebrated Mass in your underwear?'

'Stuff and nonsense!'

'Yes, nonsense, but when yesterday those scoundrels wanted to strip you down to your underwear, you created an earthquake!'

'Okay,' Don Camillo cut him short. 'It's better this way: it will avoid a clash between two gangs.'

'Yes, but you will not be able to prevent someone from the town, defending themselves from the Scorpioni, pulling out a shotgun and shooting someone! Father, if a boxer punches a little man, if the little man is armed he will defend himself by shooting, and the boxer is a dead man. But if two boxers in the same category hit each other, you have only a boxing match and nobody dies. I mean what I say.'

Don Camillo was tired of arguing: he rummaged in a desk drawer and took out an envelope, which he handed to Venom:

'Milan,' he said, 'it's not far. And in Milan you can find everything we need. Samson was ruined by Delilah, but he couldn't go to Milan. You can.'

At twenty past three, Michele Bottazzi, known as Venom (or Veleno, in Italian), exclaimed, 'Okay!' as young people say today, put on his balaclava, went out and disappeared into the night.

*

Cat remained under house arrest until the afternoon of the following day. Around six in the evening on the

Thursday, Anselma unloaded her in the courtyard of the presbytery where Don Camillo, stretched out on his deckchair, was enjoying a bit of fresh air.

The little criminal was no longer wearing a miniskirt but she was bundled up in a high-necked black robe, long to the ground and with sleeves that hung twenty centimetres beyond the tips of her fingers. Also, she had covered her head with a black scarf and had whitened her face, not with makeup but with flour. She looked like an agricultural crisis.

'How do I look, Uncle?' she asked insolently, as she lit a cigarette.

'No,' Don Camillo replied calmly, 'the cigarette is out of place: a guy like you should smoke Tuscan cigars. But sit down.'

Cat wanted people passing by on the street to see her, so she replied that she preferred to remain standing. And the people who passed and saw her laughed. Everyone knew what the girl had done in the bell tower. Moreover, the evening before, in the City Council, Peppone, after having recalled that the nearby town of Busseto had financed the studies of its son, the great composer Giuseppe Verdi, asked if something similar might be done for the niece of the Reverend Parish Priest as, during the public performance of her nocturne, she had shown a great disposition for music.

People, therefore, passed back and forth in front of Don Camillo's garden, laughing. But, suddenly, powerful engines were heard roaring and people huddled together on the pavements. Shortly thereafter, six long-haired motorcyclists in black leather jackets paraded in a line side by side; then, on his own, and followed at a safe distance by the entire gang, came the Leader astride his powerful 1,000-CC motorcycle, with studded and fringed leather, his powerful and swollen chest fit to burst and bearing on his back the white death's head and the word, 'Veleno'. His eyes flashed and his very long, shiny, soft hair fluttered in the wind. Venom was majestic, monumental. When she saw him, Cat's eyes popped.

'That damn . . .!' she began with hatred and ferocity. 'I'll make him pay for what went down at Castelletto and the rascally antics of the other night!'

'Little girl,' Don Camillo advised with a smile: 'Try to stay away from him. That's a bad guy who wouldn't think twice about making you swallow half a bottle of cod liver oil.'

'You don't know anything about us!' replied Cat, furious. 'You can't even imagine what it means to go up against the Scorpioni! They'll pull his lousy hair out strand by strand! I want to hear him scream in anger and pain!'

'That would be difficult,' Don Camillo chuckled, but not too much, because he was thinking of how much Venom's wig had cost him.

Cat had lost her temper and, turning her back on Don Camillo, she made her way resolutely towards the gate that gave onto the forecourt to the sexton's house. But she forgot that she had on a dress with a hem that rubbed along the ground and got caught up in a hydrangea bush, bringing her headlong down into it.

'A love for flowers is a sure sign of kindness of heart,' Don Camillo observed to anyone who might hear.

## A Cellar Proves More Important than a Roof

IT WAS NOT a good time for Don Camillo. As if Cat were not enough, the little priest sent by the Curia continued to upset him with his desire for reform. It was, therefore, inevitable that Don Camillo spent most of his time in the manor house he had acquired with the help of God and, in a certain sense, with the help of Garibaldi.

The old High Altar, together with the great Crucified Christ, had been installed in the chapel along with the Abbot of St Anthony and all the other little things that Don Francesco's zeal for reform had eliminated from the parish church. Don Camillo's interest was reserved principally for the chapel, but as this was attached to the manor house, which, though massive and solid, had a very battered roof, when he was not in the chapel talking with Christ, he was on the roof repairing joists and replacing tiles.

So it happened that one afternoon he noticed from this commanding position a pickup truck come to a halt in front of the rusty gate to the wilderness of nettles that passed for a garden. When Peppone, Brusco and Smilzo emerged from the truck, it was clear that they'd not expected to find Don Camillo.

The first to notice the priest was Smilzo, who sounded the alarm, shouting at Peppone:

'Boss, what bird is that up there on the roof?'

Peppone looked up and replied, as loud as he might:

'It's a black crow. A species which, fortunately, is all but extinct!'

A tile fell from the sky, skimming past Peppone and shattering at his feet, making him jump.

'Hey, Reverend!' he screamed. 'What kind of joke is that?'

'Oh, sorry Comrade Mayor,' Don Camillo shouted down from the roof. 'I mistook you for that butcher, the Executioner. Trouble is you are all of a type, you comrades.'

This was a bit close to the bone on the part of Don Camillo, because there was no external or internal similarity between Comrade Giuseppe Bottazzi, called Peppone, and Comrade Egisto Smorgagnino, aka 'Il Executioner'.

*

At the end of the war, Smorgagnino had returned to the village a hero and became practically the spiritual leader of the 'Reds' because of his heroic past as a fighter in the Resistance. Then, in 1947, it emerged that his war record was not quite as heroic as it had at first seemed and Smorgagnino, who had indeed earned the qualification of 'the Executioner' for the great number of people he had killed, was sentenced to life imprisonment . . . for murder. He had then cut loose and taken refuge behind the Iron Curtain. Twenty years later, he'd been pardoned without having spent a minute in jail and was back as fat as a pig and as full of himself as ever.

Peppone and his comrades had not felt good about any of this and when a big shot from the Federation had told the Mayor that on such and such a day Smorgagnino would be arriving home and that Peppone should organise celebrations and, as a priority, an adequate protection service, Peppone had replied: 'Right: I'll tell the *carabinieri* to keep an eye on him to prevent him from murdering anyone else.'

Given how things stood, the big shot hadn't pressed him. Nevertheless, on the day the Executioner returned, the walls of the village were covered with posters full of words of exaltation and welcome. And the man's car was followed by a great procession of vehicles loaded with people and flying the Red Flag. There was even a truck with a marching band playing *The Red Flag* and *Bella ciao*.[43]

Peppone, however, had nothing to do with it: it was all stuff organised by the Bognoni doctors and the Maoists of La Rocca. The procession paraded through the deserted streets of the village and came to a halt in the piazza. There, the Bognoni, standing with the Executioner on the official pickup, had made resounding speeches of welcome to 'the brave comrade who brought back the spirit of the partisan and proletarian struggle to la Bassa' and didn't miss the opportunity to cock a snook at the comrades who had become 'bourgeois shopkeepers'.

At this point, Peppone, who, together with his General Staff, was listening from the concourse of the Town Hall, issued an order:

'Gigiola, proceed!'

Gigiola, head traffic warden, had been a true tough guy in the Resistance and was still a force to be reckoned with. He went down into the piazza accompanied by four local police and began to slip penalty notices under the windshield wipers of all the cars belonging to people

---

[43] An anthem of the Italian Resistance beloved of partisans in the Second War, but with its roots in a 19th-century protest song sung by the *mondina* (rice paddy) workers in protest at the harsh working conditions in Italy's rice belt, which includes the Emilia-Romagna.

in the procession and parked in prohibited parking areas. Starting, of course, with that of the Executioner. From his place on the platform of the truck, he saw what was going on and leapt down, threatening Gigiola:

'Comrade Gigiola!' he shouted. 'Do you not know me anymore?'

'I don't know anyone when I'm on duty,' replied the other. 'You can redeem the notice for 1,000 lire. It is forbidden to park here.'

The Executioner, oozing grease and hatred (equally) from every pore, paid up and said: 'I'm going to park in a spot where *true* communists are allowed to park!'

Which is what he did. Followed by the whole Maoist gang, he went to La Rocca and found his new home there, becoming the spiritual leader of the autonomous Communist Section.

*

This is the truth of the matter and it was pure wickedness to liken Peppone to the Executioner in any way at all. But Don Camillo was not at all happy seeing Peppone and his gang wandering around his property. What had they been up to? They hadn't come to see a priest on a roof and they couldn't have dropped in by chance; to get there you had to take a long private road that led only to the gate into the nettle patch. They were up to no good, and that was shown by the fact that they'd been put out when they realised that the house was occupied.

'Reverend,' shouted Peppone, 'aren't you going to invite us in?'

'I am not in a position to receive guests,' replied Don Camillo. 'As you can see, I have builders in the house.'

'I only see a priest on the roof,' Smilzo sniggered. 'And it's not a pretty sight.'

'If you wait a moment I'll try to cheer you up with a little music,' replied Don Camillo grabbing a tile and making as if to throw it at his head.

'Now that he has got himself a cheap old ruin, he thinks he's Lord of the Manor!' Smilzo said, jumping back.

Grumbling, they got back into the van and drove off. As the sun set, Don Camillo got down off the roof and went to confide in Christ.

'Lord, what wicked purposes brought them here?'

'Don Camillo, men do not always act out of evil intention.'

'Lord, the house has been empty for years, why did they come just now that I have bought it? Obviously they have some conspiracy in mind that involves me.'

'Don Camillo,' Christ admonished him, 'why do you imagine you are at the centre of their plans? If suddenly this floor collapsed under your feet, would you think that a vaulted ceiling built 300 years ago was just waiting for this moment to spite you by collapsing?'

'No, of course not, Lord. In any case, there's no danger of the floor collapsing because, beneath it lies only solid earth.'

To give greater strength to his argument, Don Camillo stamped a few times on the stone floor and heard a distant echo. There was no earth below, nothing but emptiness. It seemed ridiculous to imagine that there was a crypt under a chapel built no more than 200 years ago in a wing of the manor house. It was more logical to think that the underground cellar beneath the manor house extended under the entire building.

Don Camillo picked up his torch and went down to inspect the cellars of the house where he knew ancient junk was rotting. Against the transversal main wall that divided the chapel from the rest of the building he noticed for the first time a large pile of barrel staves, and, after moving the staves, Don Camillo found a rectangle of wall, which despite the care that had been taken to camouflage it, now seemed to be of fairly recent construction.

With a piece of timber, Don Camillo knocked out the wall and revealed a narrow door and soon found himself under the chapel. There, diligently greased and wrapped in greaseproof paper, were ninety machine guns, eighty pistols, and a great heap of watertight metal boxes crammed with ammunition.

As in many old manor houses built along the lines of a castle, there was a deep well in the cellar that had long been disused, but still full of water, now black and stagnant. It was a tremendous effort, but in a couple of hours Don Camillo had managed to throw weapons and ammunition into the well, and further to complete the work, he added a few tons of large stones and debris collected from elsewhere in the basement. The black water swallowed and covered everything. To move more quickly, Don Camillo had set to work in his long johns and T-shirt: having finished his work, he went upstairs again, washed himself, dressed again and threw himself down on an old sofa, falling into the abyss of a deep sleep.

Shortly after midnight he woke up: there were people around the house. Three individuals were speaking loudly, clearly convinced that no one else was there.

Inevitably, Don Camillo, after having cleaned up one of the machine-guns with extreme care so that he could see exactly what it was, had omitted to throw it into the well with the rest of the armaments. And it was precisely that disagreeable weapon that the three men found themselves facing when Don Camillo turned on his torch and stopped them.

'Oh,' Don Camillo exclaimed, 'it's the Mayor! To what do I owe the honour of this visit?'

Peppone didn't have time to answer because other people could be heard also arriving. Not entering through the door this time, like Peppone and his associates, but through a window on the ground floor. They weren't afraid of making a fuss in tearing the railing off. Don Camillo turned off his torch and he and the first wave of interlopers holed up in a corner. There were also three in the second wave and they spoke loudly, confidently.

'The goods are still in the cellar under the chapel,' explained one of the three. 'I checked last night. We need to get the stuff back in thirty-two minutes because in thirty-two minutes Gino will arrive with the tractor and trailer loaded with boxes of tomatoes. It's the tomato season and all time of day and night the streets are full of farm carts taking tomatoes to the factories for processing. When the boy arrives, everything must be ready on the main road to be loaded.'

They went down to the cellar but were back after a few minutes and were furious. 'Boss,' said one of the three, 'they've screwed us!'

'It could only have been that traitor, Peppone. He was the only one besides me who knew the hiding place. I'll make him sing, that sack of . . .! Anyway, you have to make haste and warn the boy not to come with the tractor and the tomato!'

'Perhaps not,' said Don Camillo, switching on his torch and stepping forward, while Peppone and his associates remained holed up in their corner. 'Listen to me, Executioner: let the tomato come. A ride in the cool will do him no end of good.'

The Executioner looked intrigued by Don Camillo's machine-gun.

'Do you notice how carefully I treat it, Executioner?' Don Camillo said. 'Ditto for the rest of the arms. Go back to La Rocca quietly. When Mao orders you to unleash the proletarian revolution, all you have to do is come to me and withdraw your weapons.'

Once more the Executioner, fat as a pig, sweated lard and hatred in equal measure and Don Camillo felt sorry for him.

'You are free to go,' he said, accompanying them to the door. Smorgagnino found the way first into the cool starry night, an atomic kick from Don Camillo helping him to navigate the twelve steps of the staircase in a single leap.

'Your graceful exit lacked only that one stamp,' explained Don Camillo. 'Now you may go in peace and wait for God to consign you to the sewer of Hell.'

His two partners received the same viaticum, all three returning to La Rocca with warm backsides. Once shipment of these three parcels had been completed, Don Camillo turned back to the first wave of intruders.

'If this story were made known, it would make half the world laugh,' Don Camillo explained quietly. 'But I am selfish, I want to be the only one laughing. The roof must be made good within a week, Comrade Bottazzi! Comrade Smilzo is right: a priest on the roof is not a pretty sight.'

'Don't expect me to go on the roof!' said Peppone indignantly.

'Never! Comrade Brusco is foreman and whomsoever he sees fit he will send to work on the roof. The important thing is that you *pay*, Comrade.'

'This is filthy blackmail!' protested Peppone, trying to sound deeply hurt, but failing because, after all, everything was fine.

*They Came Out to Play and Returned All Salty*

THE PROGRESSIVE LITTLE priest sent by the Curia to put Don Camillo back on track was called Don Francesco but, on account of the dry and nervous little person that he was, his tight-fitting salesman suit, his constant tail-wagging and fidgeting, he had been renamed by the people, Don Chichi. It was a nickname that referred not to any particular characteristic of the man, but conjures up the whole affected idea of him perfectly.

Don Chichi, having demystified the church to all appearances externally, had now launched a more deeply laid offensive from the pulpit with a series of sermons which amounted to a sustained, ardent denunciation of the wickedness and serious sins of the rich.

More and more people fell absent from Mass, and Don Camillo, meeting Pinetti by chance, asked him why he had stopped coming to church.

'Me?' replied the other, 'I have worked honestly all my life to get what I now have and I don't want to come to church to be insulted by Don Chichi.'

'One doesn't go to church out of respect for the priest, but out of respect for God,' Don Camillo replied. 'And by not going to church you spite God, not the priest.'

'Yes, Father: my brain understands that, but my liver doesn't.'

It was not great reasoning, but it had a certain logic of its own and, as the defections increased, Don Camillo talked about it with the little priest.

'It is written: a camel will pass more easily through the eye of a needle than a rich man through the door of the Kingdom of Heaven,' replied Don Chichi peremptorily. 'The church door must be no wider than the door to Paradise. God created the world so that it belongs to all men, but the rich man is rich because he has taken from others what in fairness should be theirs. If the rich man did not exist, the poor man would not exist, just as the robbed would not exist if there were no thieves. The rich man is therefore a thief and his property stolen goods. The Church of Christ is synonymous with the Church of the poor, because only the poor can enter the Kingdom of Heaven.'

'Poverty is a disaster, not a virtue,' replied Don Camillo. 'Nor is it enough to be poor to be classed as righteous. Nor is it true that the poor have only rights and the rich only duties: before God *all* men have only duties. What's more, besides the rich you are also alienating non-rich people from my church. Your campaign against the war, for example, may be right, but it is not right to treat as a criminal those who fought in the war and, perhaps, have lost their health or even their life as a result.'

'He who kills is a murderer,' shouted Don Chichi. 'There are neither just wars nor holy wars: every war is unjust and diabolical. God's law says: "Thou shalt not kill", "love thine enemy". Father: the hour of truth is upon us and we must call bread *bread* and wine *wine*!'

'Not, perhaps, when the bread and the wine are the flesh and blood of Jesus!' muttered Don Camillo, sticking stubbornly to his guns.

Don Chichi looked at him with an air of sincere compassion:

'Don Camillo, the Church is a large ship which, for centuries, has been at anchor. Now we have to weigh anchor and get back to sea! And we need to refresh the crew: mercilessly rid ourselves of the bad sailors, about turn and steer a different course. Only then can we muster the new energies that will rejuvenate our crew. This is the time for *dialogue*, Father!'

Don Camillo shrugged:

'Twenty years ago, when you uttered your first words, I was already fighting with the communists!'

'I'm not talking about bias, intransigence, violence!' Don Chichi yelled. 'I speak of dialogue, of coexistence.'

'Arguing is the only possible dialogue with the Communists,' replied Don Camillo. 'After twenty years of quarrelling, here we are all still alive: I see no better coexistence with them than that. The communists bring me their children to be baptised and they get married before the High Altar while I confirm them in their duty to obey God's laws. My Church is not the great ship you talk about, it is a humble little boat; but she has always sailed from one shore to the other. Now it is you who steers her and I allow it because I was ordered to do so: but I advise you not to overdo it. You are alienating many of the old crew and plan to take on new recruits, but be careful you don't lose the old ones and then fail to find new ones on some other shore. Do you remember the story of those little friars who relieved themselves upon the small and ugly apples because they were sure that there'd be big, beautiful apples further on and then when they didn't come upon them, had to return and eat the small ugly ones?'

'The story of the friars has had its day,' exclaimed Don Chichi laughing. 'The good sower does not throw his seed upon the earth unless he first clears the troublesome tares that will inhibit their growth.'

Don Camillo was a poor country priest and, unlike Don Chichi, had read few books and fewer newspapers. Apart from the liturgical reforms, he didn't understand what this new path was that was to be taken by the Church, first of all because, for twenty years, Don Camillo had taken great trouble to walk his own path to the benefit of his diverse congregation. It stood to reason, therefore, that he didn't feel much sympathy for this rookie sent to teach him, whose 'new path' only served to empty his church.

*Sic stantibus rebus*[44] when Pinetti turned up at the presbytery. 'My daughter is to be married,' he said. 'But I want to be sure that that she is married just as my wife and I were married, and my father and my mother before us were married: in front of the same altar and with the same marriage service.'

'Your daughter will marry in the manner dictated by the Church!' Don Chichi answered forcefully. 'Don't think for a moment, Mr Pinetti, that this is a shop where you can choose whatever item you like best. Remember also that, before God, money doesn't count for anything!'

'It counts for something for my daughter and her future husband,' replied Pinetti abruptly. 'So, as those two want me to dish out a dowry, it looks like they'll have to marry before the Mayor.'

Don Chichi jumped to his feet: 'If this is all your faith means to you,' he cried, 'it's no big deal for the Church to lose a Christian like you!'

'Just as it's a bad deal for the Church to take on priests like you!' replied Pinetti, making his way towards the door.

Don Camillo had not said a word, but when Pinetti left, he sighed:

---

[44] 'Thus did things stand . . .'

'It will be the first civil marriage ever to be undertaken in my parish.'

'Is that reason enough to suffer that blackmailing rascal?' exclaimed Don Chichi

'He is not a rascal, nor did he ask for anything contrary to God's law.'

'The Church must renew itself!' shouted the little priest. 'Clearly, you don't know anything of what was said at the Second Ecumenical Council.'

'I have read about it,' answered Don Camillo. 'But it's very hard for me. I can look no further than Christ: Christ spoke in a simple, clear way. Christ was not an intellectual, he did not use difficult words, only the humble and easy words that everyone knows. If Christ had participated in the Council, his simplicity would have made the most learned Council Fathers laugh.'

'You like a joke, Reverend!' answered the priest. 'But if Christ returned to Earth, he would speak differently now than he did then.'

'No,' Don Camillo stated firmly. 'Because if he did, the ignorant poor, like me, would not understand him.'

'Don Camillo, the truth is that you don't *want* to understand!'

'I only understand the facts. For me, the civil marriage of Pinetti's daughter is a much more important *fact* than all the very learned speeches of the progressive Council Fathers. A civil marriage is a mortification of the Church, an outrage against God. And this is precisely what happens when the Church opens up to the world and finds that the world largely does not believe. That is the real problem. Millions of people no longer have faith. This is the one thing, above all, that I have understood of what was said in the Council. And it is most important, because the Pope said it.'

Don Chichi spread his arms wide:

'Let's not exaggerate the importance of this business,' he said. 'I agree with you that it would be better if that civil marriage did not take place. Why don't you marry them in your chapel? It is a private chapel and therefore it would be perfectly in order.'

'It is something that must be meditated upon for a fitting length of time,' answered Don Camillo. In reality he didn't need to think about it for a second, as it was just what he had had in mind.

So it was that Pinetti's daughter was married in Don Camillo's chapel and there were so many people present that they filled not only the chapel but also the whole garden. Among the throng were all those whom Don Chichi had alienated from the church and this was a great consolation for Don Camillo. A consolation much to be desired, because his terrible niece was making his life more of a misery every day.

*

Cat, short for Caterpillar . . . Evidently whoever had stuck this nickname on Don Camillo's niece knew the girl only superficially, for not even the most disreputable bulldozer would be able to cause half the trouble that this hellish girl could.

Anselma had clear ideas and a pair of heavy hands, which she would deploy on Cat at the least provocation: but this did nothing to resolve the situation.

'I'll pay you back for all that you do to me – *with interest*,' Cat said on every occasion.

Anselma laughed but would not have done so had she known what the girl was planning. As Venom had predicted, the foul deed took place on a very ordinary, sunny and sleepy weekday afternoon. The town was silent: in the piazza, chairs and coffee tables stood empty, red-hot in the sun. Under the arcade, shopkeepers sprawled on wicker armchairs in front of their shops. In the bars and taverns, the old stagers sat in muted conversation, each with his glass of red wine.

It was like when the tornado of '65 suddenly swept across the country: one moment all was quiet, the next all hell broke loose. Thirty Scorpioni in heavy black jackets burst into the square, their motorcycles roaring. There'd been fifty of the longhairs when they'd left the city, but at a certain point twenty had taken the road to Castelletto, while the others hid out behind a hedge.

Once in Castelletto, they had found their way like swirling winds into every nook and cranny of the small hamlet and broken everything that could be broken. Forewarned by telephone, the Marshal and four of the six *carabinieri* entrusted with the safety of the entire Municipality rushed to Castelletto, leaving only one police officer and one constable in the barracks in Don Camillo's village. It was then that the gang of thirty Scorpioni threw themselves upon the defenceless community.

Thirty wild longhairs tore the tables and chairs in the piazza to pieces with their crazy carousels. They then jumped off their motorcycles and took to devastating the shops, ferociously beating up anyone who tried to oppose them. Meanwhile, a select nucleus of the gang found their way by way of side streets to the area of the church and presbytery. As soon as Cat, who had organised everything by telephone, heard the roar of the motorbikes, she signalled from the door of the sexton's house to come inside and instructed the wild ones:

'Before you get me out of here I need you to help fix something for me.'

Anselma slept on the first floor. She had bolted the door of her room, but it could hardly resist the angry shoulders of the four invading Scorpioni. Cat was the first to enter. Holding the dough paddle, she pointed it at Anselma, who was trying to cover her shoulders with a blouse:

'You keep her still,' Cat ordered the four, 'while I pay her what's due.'

Anselma resisted like a lioness, but the four young men soon managed to restrain her, face down on the bed. Cat lifted the dough paddle high:

'You'll not be able to sit down for the next three years,' she promised fiercely. 'Neither you nor your old fossil of a priest, because we'll fix him too!'

It all happened in an instant: a hand the size of a shovel latched like a claw on Cat's hair as another tore the dough paddle from her grasp. Venom had arrived with eight of his longhairs. The four Scorpioni occupied with Anselma were easily overcome. It turned out to be rather a laborious business jettisoning the first of them through the window, but thereafter, for the other three, it was more of a laugh. The old houses of la Bassa are small and a flight from the first floor is nothing too scary. In any case, these four were tough guys and, on reaching the ground, only a few minor bones were broken.

'Anselma,' said Venom, 'we have to go: do you feel like trussing up this brat yourself?'

'Don't worry,' Anselma reassured them. 'I'll cook her goose for her.'

In the piazza the Scorpioni were resisting the rustic longhairs rather too well, but the arrival of Venom and the other eight beasts marked their complete defeat. Venom was a pragmatist and when he realised that the Scorpioni had taken enough of a battering, he said to his men:

'If we continue with this, we'll have to take them home: better they get there on their own. Let them go.'

Struggling back onto their motorbikes, the Scorpioni set off at full speed. The timely intervention of Venom and his band of rustics had convinced the men of the village, who organised quickly to repel the invader, not to meddle in the battle. But they didn't want to let the Scorpioni go without something to remember them by. The Scorpioni travelled with their bellies glued to the petrol tank of their bikes, like racers do, and those backsides in the air prompted the idea of sprinkling them with a few small shots, like you might a bird on the wing. But the leader of the village men who, albeit superficially, knew a few words of Latin, held them back:

'No lead, comrades. We must act *cum grano salis.* They had loaded the cartridges with grains of salt. Anyone who has had their bottom shot with salt will know that it is difficult to think of returning to a country where souvenirs of this kind are distributed.

The twenty-six city butts, when they crossed the town boundary into the shooting sector, were suitably salted. Twenty-six only because the four bosses that Venom and his crew had thrown out the window were left moaning in the sexton's garden. Peppone took charge of the four battered Scorpioni and just as he, helped by Smilzo, Brusco and Bigio, was loading them on a truck to deliver them, together with their motorbikes, to the *carabinieri*, Don Camillo arrived. He had spent the afternoon lost in the green of the presbytery garden, unaware of all that had happened.

'Who are those four lice?' he asked.

'Visitors, Reverend,' explained Peppone. 'Thanks to your sweet niece, we now have a burgeoning tourist industry. She's a very smart girl, Don Camillo. You should introduce her to me!'

'She already knows enough crackpot gadabouts,' muttered Don Camillo.

## Revenge, Tremendous Revenge

THE AGGRESSIVE DRIVE of the little priest continued to depopulate the church and, as Don Camillo had readily foreseen, those who Don Chichi planned to recruit 'from some other shore', however he might coax and solicit them, did not materialise to fill the empty pews.

But, to Don Camillo's recriminations, Don Chichi would calmly reply that the good sower, before sowing the seed, must first free the earth from stubborn weeds.

'The good sower,' Don Camillo objected, 'before sowing the seed, also makes sure that the earth is fertile.'

'There is no infertile land!' shouted the little priest. 'A little water is enough for vegetation to flourish even in the arid desert sand. Here is the error of the traditional Church; the world divided into good and bad. It is precisely in this arid land that the Reformed Church intends to sow the good seed, after having made it fertile with its sweat, with its tears, with its blood, if necessary! I will bring Christ to the rejected creatures on the margins of society: to the human wreckage forced to beg, to the sinners who sell themselves for a piece of bread, to the unfortunate girls seduced and abandoned, whom hypo-critical society isolates by raising a wall of contempt around them!'

'I see,' said Don Camillo: 'you intend to move to another location.'

'Why do you say so?'

'Because the lost souls you are looking for are not to be found here,' Don Camillo explained. 'The few beggars you see are professionals who come from afar by bus or by rail on market days. As for the sinners, there are some as in all the countries of the world, but they do not make it a profession.'

'Does that mean there are none . . . not even unmarried mothers?' asked Don Chichi with much sarcasm.

'Yes, there are several unmarried mothers.'

'I will bring Christ to these poor wretches!'

Whereupon old Desolina came in with the post.

'You may begin your work immediately,' Don Camillo said to the priest. 'Desolina is one of those poor wretches whom you intend to bring to Christ.'

'He'll be lucky!' Desolina said with a nod to Don Chichi. 'As far as Christ is concerned, I know where to find him without the help of this half-baked priest.'

Don Chichi was deeply offended: 'Is this the way that a sinner speaks to a minister of God?' he cried. 'A little humility wouldn't go amiss.'

'Maybe you come from a family of sinners,' Desolina hit back at him. 'At sixteen I had a son and I raised him by honest work; then, when he started a family, I helped him raise his children. Now that the eldest of these boys has an eight-month-old baby, I'm raising that child too and I even find time to do a few hours of service at the presbytery. I seem to have humbled myself quite enough in sixty-two years of my life!'

Desolina went away with her head held high and Don Camillo explained to the little priest: 'This is an extreme case of an unmarried mother who is also an unmarried grandmother and unmarried great-grandmother. But there are also many less singular cases. Unfortunately, they are all girls who live with their parents and it is not a good idea to seek them out: they have fathers and brothers unsympathetic to those who stick their noses in their family business.'

'What kind of wild country do I find myself in?' Don Chichi shouted.

Don Camillo spread his arms wide and said:

'You will just have to pray to the good Lord to send beggars here too, lost women and unmarried mothers rejected by society . . .'

'The prospect does not enchant me, Reverend,' the little priest said. 'Rottenness, injustice will exist here, as everywhere, even if hypocrisy hides them under a shameful cloak!'

'Courage!' said Don Camillo. 'He who seeks, finds.'

*

Don Chichi sought . . . and found.

Here, in this patch of fertile earth that basks under the sun on the south bank of the Great River, the villagers have recently discovered that making bread and pasta at home and taking care of a piece of garden is a fairly useless conceit and instead they buy everything they need, even wine sometimes.

Giosvè was the only man who had a vegetable garden with a little orchard and two rows of Moscatello vines and so, with a rickety cart, dragged along by a decrepit old horse making its way on three cylinders, he'd go around the countryside selling vegetables and fruit. One hot summer afternoon Don Chichi came upon him on the side of the highway – with half a leg in the mud he was trying to put his cart back on the road after one of its wheels had slipped into the ditch.

Don Chichi emerged from his red Spyder, gave the old man a hand and then started a conversation.

'How old are you, Grandpa?'

'Eighty-seven.'

'And you still have to work for a living?'

'No: I live to work.'

Don Chichi was indignant:

'This is infamy! You have earned the right to rest!'

'There is no hurry: I will have time to rest when I am dead.'

'No, you have to rest now. Society has a duty to support you.'

'I support myself very well on my own, young man!'

'Don't call me young man; I am the assistant pastor.'

'A priest, you? Dressed like that?'

'And what does one's dress matter?'

'It matters. How much do the alpine hat and the *bersagliere* hat count for? I fought in the war, 1915 – 1918, and I know what I'm talking about.'[45]

'Nonsense, Grandpa! The fact is that the country is in debt to you and has to support you.'

'The club has always paid me out what I put in. See you don't bother me, young man!' said Giosvè giving a whip to his horse, which convinced the animal that he had to give it his all and make a grand prix getaway.

Don Chichi was now off the launch pad and nothing could stop him: the priest ran into the Mayor and explained to him that leaving a poor eighty-seven-year-old in that state was a disgrace.

'One of these days they will find that poor man dead on the side of a ditch and you will have killed him!'

'Me?' Peppone muttered.

---

[45] Bersaglieri are wide-brimmed hats decorated with black capercaillie feathers worn by the Italian Army's infantry corps; the Cappello Alpino hat is the most distinctive feature of the Italian Army's Alpini troops uniform.

'Not you personally, but the authority you represent.'

Don Chichi had an easy way with words and buried Peppone under an avalanche of heavy accusations, so much so that Peppone asked him:

'Reverend, tell me what I should do.'

'There is an old people's home in the village; have him admitted.'

'Giosvè is a stubborn old man and I can't think that I'm going to convince him.'

'Have him hospitalised before it is too late.'

Peppone undertook to look into the matter and it transpired that, a few days later, they did find old Giosvè unconscious in his cart stopped on the bank of the canal. Peppone, taking advantage of the opportunity, had the old man taken to the home, which was a building with a large garden, one kilometre from the village. Don Chichi heard about it immediately and went triumphantly to tell the whole story to Don Camillo.

'It's the worst, most stupid thing you could have done,' answered Don Camillo very brusquely.

'Father, they found him dying.'

'Dying! He'd simply had a few drinks and the heat overcame him. It always happens like this in the summer-time. I'm going to have him discharged in the morning.'

Don Chichi puffed out his small chest:

'I will stop you, Don Camillo! . . . If necessary, by force.'

'You mean with the force of law?' Don Camillo giggled. 'Because with your own force I don't think you'd really manage it.'

Don Camillo did not discharge Giosvè: the oldster freed himself. That same night, having come to and found himself in the home, he climbed over the boundary wall. Unfortunately he landed on the other side head first, but he managed to drag himself to the cemetery and there, the next morning, they found him dead – dead in front of the door of a small Chapel of Rest along the third avenue.

'And it was *his* little chapel,' Don Camillo explained to Don Chichi. 'Giosvè continued to work in order to be able to finish it. He said; "I want to be buried like a gentleman in my little chapel with my wife: and I will not die until I've finished it."'

'What nonsense,' exclaimed Don Chichi. 'We are all equal in the face of death. Of what importance is where we are buried? I would have a law passed that establishes a single type of burial for all and a single type of funeral. Giosvè was a dotty old prisoner of superstition. I put him in the home for his own sake.'

'In your opinion, then, is it better to die of frustration, a prisoner in an old people's home, than to live free and happy with your work?'

'Old people have a duty to rest!' said the little priest.

'I would say that they also have the right to live,' grumbled Don Camillo.

A few days passed and there was no more mention of Giosvè: the death of an old man of eighty-seven is not news. It was the Crucified Christ who returned to the subject.

'Don Camillo,' he began, 'can you not hear that poor little priest walking up and down, every night, in his room?'

'No, Lord: I pretend I don't hear it.'

'And can you fool your conscience?'

'No, Lord, but it does not seem right to me this wanting to find evil at all costs, even where it does not exist, this wanting to revolutionise everything!'

'Don Camillo, I too was a revolutionary.'

'Lord, there is no comparison!'

'Then why do you let that poor young man suffer on his cross?'

And so Don Camillo went to the little priest and said, 'I don't like the look of you. Go to the doctor and have him prescribe a tranquiliser.'

'No pill can stop me seeing that old man in front of me every night. What does he want from me?'

'Probably that you help him finish his little chapel.'

But Don Chichi had read too many books and replied:

'Why throw away money on a dead man who needs nothing, when so many living need so much?'

'You don't have to tell me: tell old Giosvè when he comes to upset you.'

'Giosvè is dead and the dead don't bother anyone.'

'Tell him that. Get Giosvè to behave like the dead should!'

Don Chichi began to laugh: but Don Camillo heard him walking up and down in his room again that night. Then, one morning, Don Chichi burst out:

'And how do you know that he intended to finish his damn little chapel?'

'It's simple,' Don Camillo replied. 'He shared the project with me. The chapel was a secret between me and Giosvè. He wanted to surprise everyone. He said: "When poor old Giosvè is dead, while everyone is expecting him to be thrown into a hole in the ground, they'll see him borne into a chapel like a great gentleman." And, since he likes company, he's moving his wife in there too. He was amused to think of the faces people would make. Whenever he had some money he would bring it to me and I would have the work done. It would take 250,000 lire to finish everything.'

Don Chichi reaffirmed that it would be madness to throw away so much money. Then he sold his flaming

Spyderino, settling for a second-hand Fiat Cinquecento, paid his debt to old Giosvè and, finally, was able to sleep.

You may say: 'Fairy tales!' You may say: 'Stuff and nonsense!' But then you don't appreciate how stubborn and pig-headed those who die can be, down there in the land of the Great River. It is a very special land: flat, and at one with the sky, so that it never ends. There is all the space you could want for the dead, while the living are crushed by that immense sky, which makes its people feel even smaller than they are.

Even Cat, after her violent rebellion, got things into perspective. And maybe it was that sky that made her a girl like any other. As a result she made good use of the hours of parole before her release and never took the opportunity to make trouble. It was clear that she had cut ties with the past.

Don Camillo jumped for joy and when, in the late afternoon of a hot August day, Peppone and his gang crossed the churchyard where he was enjoying a bit of shade, he cheerfully greeted his Comrade Mayor:

'My good fellow! How are your pretty little Chinese people from La Rocca?'

'I'm not complaining, Reverend,' replied Peppone. 'What about your pretty little niece? It's been a while since she's been heard ringing the church bells.'

'Signor Mayor,' said Don Camillo, 'I promised my sister to transform that girl into a good "Daughter of Mary" and I'm about to get there!'

'I am pleased,' replied Peppone. 'I am pleased for *you*, Reverend. Not for the girl; I thought her more intelligent and witty than that.'

'Boss,' Smilzo interrupted, 'you cannot blame her for having a priest for an uncle!'

'You're right,' Peppone admitted. 'Having a priest for an uncle is a serious misfortune.'

Don Camillo felt his nose itch.

'Do you think it bad luck for an unruly girl to have an uncle who rescues her from a bunch of shameless thugs and brings her back to a community of honest and civilised people?'

'I have not made myself clear, Reverend; I mean that a girl can behave honestly and civilly without getting involved with a herd of self-righteous spinsters. I fervently hope not to see the poor girl chanting in procession with a candle in her hand.'

'I feel sorry for you, Signor Mayor, but you will see her soon and she will be a magnificent sight to behold.'

Peppone spread his arms wide and at that moment there was a great commotion on the other side of the piazza as the head of a long procession appeared at the entrance to the road leading to the sports field.

'What's up?' Don Camillo said. 'Has the proletarian revolution begun?'

'Relax, Reverend,' Peppone reassured him, laughing. 'We no longer need to have a revolution to get into power; the electorate gets us there these days and these people marching are part of the *Festa de l'Unità*.[46]

The procession was advancing into the piazza and the brass band that led it was playing *The Red Flag*. Proceeding behind the band, pulled by a tractor, was a farm trailer decorated with red drapes. A high stepped podium had been erected on the floor of the wagon, adorned with festoons of red carnations. On it was set a gilded throne and, standing, leaning against the throne, was a girl draped elegantly in a red train, but with a murderous slit from the left hip to the ground, so that a fine full leg was in plain sight.

---

[46] *Festa de l'Unità*, an annual festival in Italy originally organised by the Italian Communist Party to finance and spread its official newspaper, *l'Unità*.

On her head the girl wore a golden crown surmounted by a crossed hammer and sickle and over her shoulder she had a large silk band bearing the words, 'Miss *Unità*'. It was an exciting sight for she was a really pretty girl whose left leg guaranteed consistent excellence in every department under her mantle, otherwise only to be guessed at.

The tractor came to a halt at the edge of the churchyard, while the band played *Bella ciao*. Then, after greeting the applauding crowd with a clenched fist, the Queen of the festival descended majestically from her throne by means of a wooden ladder on a red runner, which a team of youngsters had swiftly placed alongside the trailer.

Don Camillo could barely catch his breath.

'Not bad for a "Daughter of Mary",' said Peppone who, together with his staff, clustered around Don Camillo as if in thrall to the Queen.

'Of course,' added Smilzo, 'it must be a great satisfaction for the parish priest to see his niece so wildly venerated!'

Cat, a picture of impudence, moved towards the presbytery like a model down the catwalk, followed by four vestal virgins, who held her train. As she passed in front of Don Camillo, she smiled at him and, raising a clenched fist, said:

'Bye-bye, Uncle!'

Blocked by Peppone and his associates, Don Camillo could not even lift a finger. But so striking was the determination in his eyes to kick Cat up the backside that the girl anticipated and jumped a little to dodge it.

Reaching the sexton's house, Cat looked out over the piazza from the first floor balcony, greeting the screaming crowd with another clenched fist and throwing flowers and kisses down to them.

Don Camillo was by now panting and for a moment thought he was going to have a stroke. When he recovered he said to Peppone:

'Comrade, you have committed a grave crime.'

'Not as serious a crime as getting me into that swimming competition with Bognoni. I was almost a gonna. In any case, you now have the great satisfaction of reading *l'Unità* for a year. Among the prizes awarded to your niece is an annual subscription to the official organ of the Party.'

'I'll deliver it personally each morning,' promised Smilzo.

He got away with it only because, even from Don Camillo, a look cannot kill.

*Vinyl Heart, Rubber Soul*

OF ALL THE evil tricks that the pestiferous Cat had played on him, that of getting elected 'Miss *Unità*' was for sure the worst for poor Don Camillo: he was so upset that the doctor had to give him an injection to calm him down.

He saw the girl again only the following afternoon:

'You shouldn't have done that!' he shouted at her, but he didn't chastise her, because Don Chichi was present.

'And why's that?' asked Cat insolently. 'I knew it would get to you big-time and I'm glad I did it.'

Smilzo had slipped the Party rag under the front door of the presbytery, as arranged, and Don Camillo threw the newspaper down in front of the girl:

'Look what you've done, you wicked girl!' he shouted. 'Think what joy your mother and grandmother Celestina will feel when they see this filth!'

'Oldie and Zombie don't read this newspaper!' Cat chuckled as she contemplated the crisp photo they had taken of her as she greeted the crowd with a clenched fist from her throne on the float.

'People will make sure they'll see it, be sure of that!'

'So what? What's wrong with being proclaimed Queen at a festival? Also, what they've written is okay: "Cat, the beautiful and likeable niece of the parish priest, Don Camillo, has been proclaimed Miss *Unità* etcetera." Again . . . "How proud must her uncle be!" You see how discreet I have been; I only gave them my *nom de guerre* and told them no more than that I am your beloved niece.'

'They may as well have used your birth name!' Don Camillo screamed furiously. 'They elected you Queen to make the connection with me, those scoundrels!'

Don Chichi laughed:

'Don Camillo, why are you so angry? Making her Queen of *Unità* is a no bad thing. It serves to revitalise the dialogue between you and the Communist Party.'

'Young man!' roared Don Camillo. 'If I once did a stupid thing by rescuing you from this young idiot's friends, I can still do a job on you myself! Get out of my sight and take your nonsensical views with you!'

Don Chichi said no more and left forthwith, while Cat exclaimed, giggling:

'This quarrel between Big Crow and Little Crow is so funny!'

Don Camillo remembered the fifth commandment, which was just as well, but, to avoid succumbing to temptation and strangling the girl, he needed also to lose himself in the fields for a while. And that was less of a good idea. For when he got back to the presbytery, things had moved on, and in a disastrous direction.

While Don Camillo had been trying to regain his cool, a taxi had stopped in front of the presbytery and old Celestina, Cat's paternal grandmother, got out and ran into the dining room, where Cat was admiring her photo in the newspaper.

Old Celestina appeared to have gone quite mad. Snatching the newspaper from the girl's hands, she vented her fury on her:

'You scoundrel; I've always defended you, but this time, *no!* This time you've committed a heinous crime, having yourself elected Queen *by that lot!*'

'This lot or that lot, it's all the same to me,' Cat replied laughing, 'I don't understand why you're getting so hot under the collar. I just wanted to spite the old Crow and I succeeded!'

'Yes, you managed to spite your uncle, but worse still you insulted your father!'

'My father?' Cat looked at her aghast. 'What does he have to do with it, poor fellow? He died when I was two months old!'

'I'll tell you what he's got to do with it, *they* killed him! And his killer is now back here – free and full of himself – without having spent a single day in jail. What fun the Executioner's going to have now!'

It was at this point that Don Camillo returned.

'Celestina!' he shouted. 'You wretch. Be off with you!'

To be sure that she understood, he grabbed the old woman by the arm and carried her away bodily as if she was light as a feather, shoving her into the taxi that was waiting in front of the presbytery. When he returned to the dining room, the girl was sitting quietly, smoking:

'What was she going on about, the old woman?' she asked.

'I don't know. Maybe she just remembered that your father was her son. Old women have strange turns sometimes. Anyway, let's not talk about it anymore.'

'Alternatively, do let's talk about it,' replied the girl. 'Let me in on my history.'

'Your grandmother has already explained it to you and there is nothing to add.'

'Why hasn't anyone ever told me before?'

'Because it's better that children don't know everything there is to know about their fathers. Because children make their way towards the future better without being weighed down by a past that has nothing to do with them. And, finally, because you are a freak like your father

. . . but much worse than him, in that you inherited *only* his faults.'

'And what were his faults?'

'He was impulsive: he did things first and thought about them afterwards. You are worse, because you do things without thinking about them at all, either before or after. He was a man who was not afraid of anything or anyone and he always said what he thought. In the war he was a paratrooper and had been trained to despise danger.'

'Why did they kill him?'

Don Camillo opened his arms: 'Child, forget the past. Forget that Old Celestina told you anything. She is a good woman and wise, but on seeing that damn picture of you, she lost her mind. We must forgive her. Listen to me: forget it. If I got angry it was not because you were so full of spite for me, but for the pain I feared you would cause your mother and your grandmother.'

'Well, now the eggshells are broken and the omelette has to be made; you must tell me why they killed my father. Or I will make others tell me.'

'Child . . .'

'Child be *damned*!' shouted Cat. 'I was born in October 1946 and in a few months I will be twenty. And when I come of age, I will show you . . .!'

'I guess you can't do anything more stupid than you have done already . . . So, here it is. In 1946, the air burned hot as hell. The war had just ended. The *world war*, I mean, because civil unrest now took hold of minds poisoned by hatred and politics. Extremists, raised in a school of violence, were now the masters at it and life retained the relative value it has in war. The Reds were convinced they were on the verge of seizing power and did not like people who sang from a different hymn sheet. Il Krik . . .'[47]

'Who's Krik?' asked the girl.

'Your father. They called him Krik because of his strength. He was a guy a lot like Venom . . .'

'A stupid beast then?' Cat interrupted, clenching her fists.

'Venom is neither a beast nor a fool. In those days il Krik spoke forcefully as he behaved. In public he spoke clearly in cafés, in the piazza and even at the political rallies if he heard someone say something that he didn't agree with. So, one night, as he was returning home, they shot him in the back. You were only two months old, Cat; it happened in December 1946. Your grandfather and grandmother, Celestina, sold the farm and went to live in the city with your mother and helped her raise you . . . with the fine result that we see before us.'

'And this Executioner, after having murdered my father and a lot of other people and after having been sentenced to life imprisonment and escaping behind the Iron Curtain, he comes back here now, having received a pardon, with honour and in triumph . . .'

'That's more or less how it goes, yes,' grumbled Don Camillo.

'Nice piece of s . . . , the world you've given us!' Cat exclaimed in disgust. 'I felt there was a void in my life . . .'

'In your head!' replied Don Camillo.

'No, Very Reverend Uncle Priest, the void is in your head as in all old hypocrites! If we young people are rebellious and restless, there is always a reason. We feel that yours is a filthy world of cowards before Truth. And your laws serve to disguise your cowardice as a civic

---

[47] A krik is a jack, a hydraulic device for exerting a large force, more usually to be found in the boot of a car.

virtue. We young people don't have the strength to destroy this lousy world, but we have the courage to spit on it. Anyway, my father was a fool: otherwise he'd not have put himself in a position to be killed.'

'He was honest!'

'When dealing with bandits, honesty is not a good policy.'

'Honesty is always and only honesty; your father was right.'

'Dying is never right.'

'Not true!' Don Camillo shouted. 'The justice of God fixes everything.'

'I heard you say that!' giggled the girl. 'Unfortunately, in this case, since miracles have gone out of fashion, a dead man is *not* going to be resurrected.'

Don Camillo had been terribly afraid that Celestina's intervention would upset the girl. Seeing, instead, that Cat, while seething with indignation, had assimilated the revelation with detachment, almost with indifference, he thanked God and brought the discussion to a close by admitting that everyone is master of how they think.

*

The girl continued her usual rebellious routine and, after a week, Don Camillo concluded that Cat must have a Beatles record for a heart.[48] Then, one afternoon, Anselma arrived at the presbytery to tell him that Cat had forced the woodshed lock and disappeared with Don Camillo's motorbike.

---

[48] *Rubber Soul*, the Beatles' sixth album appeared in December 1965 and was followed in March '66, as Guareschi was writing, by the controversy surrounding John Lennon's remark that the band had become 'more popular than Jesus'. The seed for the album's title was sown after Paul McCartney heard a man in the US refer to the Rolling Stones' music as 'good, but plastic soul'.

'Have a nice trip!' Don Camillo responded. 'She's gone home: better for everyone.'

'I don't think so,' Anselma muttered. 'She left all her stuff here, even her record player and goddamn records.'

'Girls like her, if they had to choose between saving their son or some of their records, would throw the son overboard. We will see her again soon. We'll take care of her when she comes back.'

But Don Camillo thought again when, having gone up to his room, he found the double-barrelled shotgun and the over-and-under shotgun hanging on the wall, but the five-shot Browning was missing.[49] And the cartridge belt was empty. Then his head went blank and said: 'Jesus, think for me: I'm not in residence up there anymore!'

Peppone was at home and was checking the registers with the help of his wife when Don Camillo appeared in front of him with a face he had never seen on the man before.

'Peppone!' roared Don Camillo, 'I didn't know you were so contemptible a scoundrel. Now I do know and I swear that if anything happens to her I'll shoot you like a dog.'

'Reverend, you are crazy!' Peppone blustered, getting up.

'You rogue, you should have been content with getting her elected Queen of *Unità*: you didn't need to publish the photograph of Krik's daughter in your damned newspaper!'

'Il Krik's daughter?' stammered Peppone 'Who are you talking about?'

'Cat!' Don Camillo shouted. 'Il Krik is Cat's father. Ela Krik's mother saw her picture and came up here and told

---

[49] The over-and-under shotgun has one barrel mounted over the other, as opposed to the classic side-by-side double-barrelled version. The five-shot Browning is a single-barrel, semi-automatic shotgun.

her everything! And now the girl has disappeared with her motorbike and my five-shot Browning!'

Peppone turned white and collapsed into his chair:

'I didn't know,' he gasped. 'You have three sisters, how could I have known that she is the daughter of il Krik? She didn't use her real name. Do you think me so evil?'

'No. You didn't know. But that's neither here nor there!' Don Camillo shouted. 'She's a madman like her father and I swear she intends to kill the Executioner: you are responsible for whatever happens now.'

'Reverend, you're running too fast with this,' said Peppone's wife. 'Maybe she went out to shoot frogs.'

'God let it be!' exclaimed Don Camillo. 'What if, instead, she went to shoot executioners and kills the Executioner?'

Peppone jumped to his feet:

'That's the least of our problems,' he said. 'Fact is that the Executioner always travels with two bodyguards and may manage to kill her too! The Executioner is out and about making propaganda: we must find him, stop him. Or find the girl!'

Peppone organised the expedition: he would set out with the Millecento, Brusco with his Fiat 600, Bigio with the pickup truck and Smilzo with the motorbike.

'We don't know where the Executioner went and there are five roads leading out of La Rocca: Cat won't be lying in wait for him in the village because that bighead lives in the piazza. She'll be waiting for him along one of those five roads. So, we'll make it up to La Rocca fast, then about turn and each of us takes one of the roads out. Maria,' he said turning to Peppone's wife, 'as soon as Michele arrives, you send him to La Rocca and tell him to drive back via the highway.'

'In the meantime, I'm going ahead,' said Don Camillo. 'I have the bicycle. I'll cross the Stivone, which is dry, and take the highway as far as La Rocca. Then I'll make my way back.'

*

Cat knew perfectly well where the Executioner had gone and which of the five roads he would take on his return. At that very moment she was stationing herself along the highway behind a decrepit roadside shrine, flanked by wild shrubs. She had made a detailed study of the terrain and knew exactly what she planned to do. On the bank leading up from the ditch by the road, to one side of the shrine, there was a poplar and Cat had sawn it almost through at the base, leaving a piece of bark intact facing the road. A rope anchored to the shrine kept the plant upright. It was enough to cut the rope for the tree to crash down and block the road. The motorbike was lying in wait behind a hedge. She knew all she needed to know: she knew the Executioner's car and its registration number. She held his pig face clearly in memory.

'You will have to pass this way, *Canchero*, and you will have to stop your car and get out to clear the road. And if your two gorillas get out instead of you, I'll shoot you through the window.'

Don Camillo, meanwhile, having reached the main road, pedalled towards La Rocca:

'Jesus,' he was praying, just as he neared the shrine, 'give me plenty of energy and the sharpest of eyes.'

At that moment a car whizzed passed him and almost immediately came to a screeching halt, because the poplar, which normally stood at the side of the shrine, had crashed onto the road in front of it.

Don Camillo pressed mightily on the pedals of his bike and reached the car as the three who were on board got out to remove the obstacle. He recognised the Executioner and approached him to warn him that he had better get back in, because he could be in mortal danger. But he didn't have time.

'Get out of my way or I'll kill you too!' Cat was heard to scream.

Don Camillo stood in front of the Executioner, shielding him with his body.

'Clear off!' shouted Cat, furious. 'And you two stand where you are and put your hands up or I'll liquidate you!'

One of the two tried to get smart and Cat shot at his foot so that he jumped around like they do in the films.

'Clear off, you!' Cat yelled for the third time. 'Don't think you can make a fool of me, Executioner, like you made a fool of my father!'

Cat looked mad, her face a scary sight to behold. But Venom, who had bypassed the scene and come up fearlessly behind Cat, disarmed her and grabbed her by the scruff of her neck with a strength that took her breath away.

'Father, take the gun while I tie up this fool,' said Venom.

Don Camillo moved away from the Executioner and walked forward to retrieve the gun, while Venom, taking off Cat's studded belt used it tie her arms tight enough to break her wrists.

'Beast! Like that rascal of a father of yours who had me elected Queen to entertain my father's killer!' Cat screamed, trying to wriggle free.

'If the father of that hooligan is that traitor Peppone,' said the Executioner, whose bravado had returned, 'no way would he ever entertain me. But I'll make sure now that any jokes are on him.'

'In the meantime, perhaps, they're on you,' said Venom, throwing Cat on the ground like a bundle of rags and approaching the Executioner.

The Executioner was a true executioner, but the Russians, in addition to having taught him to call long-hairs hooligans, had fattened him up like a pig, so the first slap that Venom put on his snout made him squirt lard from every pore.

Venom was twenty years old but, longhair that he was, he had an unfortunate respect for those older than him. So he didn't use his fists, he just slapped him about with his paws. And, for the same reason, had even put on a pair of gloves.

Meanwhile, one of the two gorillas, having pulled a jack out of the car, came up behind Venom.

'Forget it, Falchetto,' Don Camillo advised, waiving the Browning in his direction, 'it's their business, not yours. You can have your turn later, if you want it.'

He did not want it and, as Venom's gloves began to disintegrate, he stopped giving the Executioner a facial.

'That was for calling me a hooligan,' Venom explained. 'You'll get the rest from my father personally: I don't deal in politics.'

The Executioner departed with his bodyguards and shortly afterwards Bigio arrived with the pickup, into which Venom threw Cat, Cat's motorbike and Don Camillo's bicycle. Don Camillo got into the truck next to Bigio. Venom with his rumbling motorbike escorted the vehicle to the presbytery.

By now it was evening and Venom joined Don Camillo and Cat for dinner, the latter saying not a word until they had finished eating:

'Perhaps you can tell me now why you butted in?' she asked Don Camillo aggressively. 'Why didn't you let me kill him?'

'For two reasons,' Don Camillo explained. 'First, because we old priests are still quite attached to the Ten Commandments. Second, because if you had killed him, you would have gone to jail for thirty years and there'd have been no pardon for you.'

Cat eyed Don Camillo defiantly: 'You say that we young people have no reason to be enemies of a lousy society that honours murderers and takes it out on boys for wearing long hair. And at the same time, you expect us to wage war to defend your filthy society!'

Cat then turned to Venom and, oozing sarcasm, said:

'You go and do your military service, you animal! It takes more courage *not* to sign up than to sign up. But military service is perfect for cowards like you, who don't dare stand up to the *carabinieri*.'

'The girl does have a point,' muttered Venom.

Cat looked at him now with contempt:

'Yes, I have a point, but you will sign up. Military service is perfect for those like you who cower before the stinking laws of this society of hypocrites. And when the army has shaved you to zero, will you still wear the jacket with Venom on the back?'

Sweating under his wig, the boy blushed and got up, managing 'Good night to you both' as he left.

'That is no way to treat a man who has saved you from committing an irreparable folly,' reproached Don Camillo.

'Only I am judge whether the things I do are stupid or not. Not that nowhere man.'

'He's no fool, as I've already told you.'

'All men are jerks!' Cat shot back ferociously.

'Watch what you're saying, you little puppy!' Don Camillo sounded deeply hurt: 'I am a man too!'

'What do you have to do with it?' the girl replied. 'A priest is not a man. He's something less! . . . Or something more. It depends.'

Don Camillo didn't expect that coming from Cat: it quite literally took his breath away.

## The Devil Doesn't Always Have Horns and a Tail

FOLLOWING THE HIGHWAY holdup, Cat changed as night to day. She abandoned all idiosyncratic pretension and dressed modestly, like an ordinary girl from a traditional middle-class family. In short, she appeared to be the beautiful girl she was and a good girl, even participating devoutly in all religious offices, so much so that Don Chichi – who, due to the treatment meted out to him by Cat's long-haired friends, did not have much sympathy with her – had to admit to Don Camillo:

'Your niece looks like a different person. I don't understand what happened to her.'

Don Camillo spread his arms wide and, although he knew very well what, replied:

'God only knows.'

Cat listened attentively to the rousing sermons of the little priest and, one day, approaching Don Chichi timidly, she confided:

'Yours are not the usual sermons one generally hears. You speak of God but with your feet firmly on Earth. I would like the guys in my group to hear what you have to say.'

Don Chichi laughed: 'The guys in your gang don't have much sympathy for me, judging by how they roughed me up on that infamous afternoon.'

'The boys made a mistake,' explained Cat. 'They mistook you for one of the old-fashioned priests like Don Camillo. From the pulpit you don't simply parrot lessons learned in the seminary. You're not afraid of the truth and in this respect, given that you condemn war, I'm amazed that you have never addressed the subject of conscientious objection.'

'It's a sensitive subject, Signorina.'

'I realise, Don Francesco. But there are some priests who nevertheless confront it at the risk of being dragged to court.'

'It is not a question of fear, but of respect,' the priest said. 'Your uncle was a military chaplain and has different ideas . . .'

'He is wrong!' exclaimed Cat. 'My uncle is a fossil! And as for respect, he has very little of it for you! As I see it, it is dishonest to celebrate Mass secretly in his private chapel, using the old rite.'

'He doesn't do it secretly,' answered Don Chichi. 'He keeps me informed. It is not really a bad thing if he gathers around his old altar those who no longer come here because they feel offended by my frankness.'

'It is wrong, nevertheless! You, Don Francesco, drive out false Christians from our church and he readmits them to his chapel. You condemn them and he absolves them. He destroys your work, misunderstanding continues and a dissident church, an opposition church, an anti-church is the result! Don Francesco, you know I'm sure that his position is not only divisive, it is nothing less than heresy!'

'That is too dramatic!' Don Chichi exclaimed. 'Many of Don Camillo's remarks are sensible. On Sunday I will deal with the subject of conscientious objection.'

'I admire you, Don Francesco!' said the girl, clearly moved.

\*

The following Sunday, when he sailed up into the pulpit for his sermon, Don Chichi was taken aback to see forty Scorpioni with their black jackets and long, dishevelled hair, looking darkly up at him with folded arms. They were sitting in a group by the door ready to defend their motorbikes, which they'd left leaning against the west wall of the church, guarded by two sentries. And there was Cat, in a modest dark dress and black lace scarf over her copper hair, sitting in the middle of the first row of longhairs, smiling up at Don Chichi. She looked almost angelic.

The little priest threw himself into the fray: he condemned all conflict, from Cain and Abel to Julius Caesar, to the Crusades, to Korea and Vietnam. His sermon established that the only attitude of the good Christian towards military service must be conscientiously to object to war. Nor did he forget to lash the patriotic war mongering of military chaplains with his derisive tongue. The forty longhairs from the city nodded their bushy heads and Cat's smile was so radiant that it would have dazzled a bishop.

At the end of the Mass, she went to congratulate the priest in the sacristy:

'I had warned them,' she explained. 'And what I said about you so interested them that they came here despite the serious risk they ran by doing so. Don Francesco, you were wonderful: those forty boys will return to their homes much better off!'

In reality they returned much worse off, because Venom and his rural longhairs were waiting for them outside the village, armed with big acacia sticks. It was real cinema once again: Venom, God knows why, had a personal thing going with Ringo, leader of the Scorpioni.

While the two biggest beasts of his gang held Ringo, Venom gathered his very long hair at the nape of his neck, tied it with string and clipped it to zero.

Meanwhile Cat looked ever more angelic, latent tears flickering in her big eyes filled Don Chichi's heart with tenderness. But only for a little while, for Don Camillo, hiding in the organ loft, had been listening to the sermon and the veins in his neck stood out like six-year-old vines.

'Don Chichi,' he began menacingly, 'better to be chaplain to soldiers, as I was, than chaplain to a bunch of thugs, like you! And as for you, you little brat, out!'

Cat retreated with her head held bowed, sobbing. At that moment, Don Chichi hated this big brutal priest who had made that meek and delicate creature suffer so. Seeing her shoulders shaking with sobs, the little priest was amazed that they did not sprout white wings. Such was his indignation that he threw himself forthwith into his Fiat Cinquecento and shot off to the city.

\*

The next day, Don Camillo received a letter from the Curia which took his breath away: while awaiting his transfer to Rughino, the very farthest parish in the mountains, and to avoid more serious censure, Don Camillo should desist from 1. any further subversive, secessionist activity, 2. celebrating Mass in his private chapel and 3. any involvement in the affairs of the parish which, on his departure, would be passed to Don Francesco.

Don Camillo developed a fever and threw himself onto his bed. The Devil is not as ugly as he is painted. The Devil, in fact, must be beautiful, otherwise how could he seduce and deceive people?

True, but good or bad, the Devil is always and only the Devil, and Cat *was* the Devil. When she learned that Don Camillo was indisposed, she went to visit him.

'Very Reverend Uncle,' she began on entering his bedroom, 'what are your last wishes?'

'Go to hell!' Don Camillo yelled at her. 'Pack your bags and go home.'

'You would throw a poor orphan out on the street?' moaned the hooligan.

'No I would not!' exclaimed Don Camillo, instead throwing her the letter that he had placed on the bedside table. 'It is you who has thrown me onto the street!'

Cat read the letter and shrugged: 'And what have I got to do with this?'

'You have climbed inside Don Chichi's head. I didn't think you were so wicked. However, you have won. Blessed is your father that he died before seeing what a daughter he had brought into the world. And now get out or I'll shoot you with my shotgun!'

Cat went downstairs humming to herself and, as she left the presbytery to go to Anselma's house, Venom appeared before her.

'So much for Ringo,' he said, throwing the leader of the Scorpioni's hair at her feet.

'Murderer!' Cat screamed in horror. 'You scalped him!'

'No, but I will if he comes around here again. Before he is able to get out of bed, his hair will have grown to his knees,' said Venom as he turned and walked away.

At the gate he turned and said: 'Fact is, little girl, whoever listens to you will always come off badly,' he muttered. 'And don't end it all by getting a snake to bite you, like Cleopatra did. In your case the snake would die – not you.'

Cat angrily kicked Ringo's scalp into a corner of the churchyard. Whereupon Don Chichi arrived. Upon learning from Cat what had happened to Don Camillo, he was not happy:

'I didn't think it would end like this,' he said. 'They've got the whole thing out of proportion!'

'No, they haven't,' replied Cat. 'They've made the right decision. I know Rughino: it's the perfect parish for him. All the young men and women have moved out to find work and the only people left are old fossils and the very youngest children: he can't do much harm up there. This parish, on the other hand, is full of life and needs a young, modern parish priest. Don Francesco, don't get sentimental on me or I'll lose the great esteem I have for you. Although . . .' She cut off there and, with a smile full of sadness, left the little priest.

It was two days before she let him see her again and the first thing Don Chichi said to her was:

'Although . . . what?'

'Forget it, Don Francesco. If I told you, you'd be upset. It's not something that can be said to a priest. Priests are born not made . . .'

'Wrong, Signorina Cat,' replied Don Chichi. 'I am a priest not out of inspiration but out of reasoned conviction, because I realised that in the Church I can do so much good for those who suffer on Earth. Nurture faith in those who have it, give it back to those who have lost it, give it to those who don't.'

'I understand perfectly,' exclaimed Cat. 'Faith is the most precious thing, but, in a world so different from that of 2,000 years ago, in a world steeped in materialism, faith can only be deemed meaningful with deeds, not with words. Too many promises have been made in the name of Christ. Humanity is tired of being promised Heaven after death.'

'Signorina Cat,' protested Don Chichi, 'faith helps us to live.'

'No, Don Francesco, it helps us to die. If a man has no shoes, even if he firmly believes that in Heaven he will have wonderful golden shoes, his feet get wet and he contracts pneumonia. "Oh poor man who walks barefoot on the frozen snow, in Paradise you will have golden shoes: but meanwhile, shelter your feet with these humble, but waterproof, cowhide shoes!" Wouldn't it be better to be able to tell him that?'

'Yes, and this is precisely why the Church has put itself on the social policy level,' exclaimed Don Chichi.

'Quite the right decision!' exclaimed Cat. 'What benefit can faith promise those dying of hunger today? Faith is the bread of the spirit, not of the body.'

'*Signorina*,' the little priest tried to protest. 'Forgive me, but this is all too materialistic a turn of phrase.'

'I realise that, Don Francesco. But the Pope did not ask for faith and prayers for hungry India, rather for money, rice, medicines, trucks – neither spiritual nor ethical values but expressions, however trivial, of *reality*.'

'Yes, but the Church cannot . . .'

'Exactly,' Cat interrupted him. 'The Church cannot solve these practical problems. And, then, don't you think how much good you could do to humanity if you used your intelligence, your culture, your enthusiasm, your sweet and persuasive words, your deep, sincere Christian faith in the practical field? You would never imitate those who try to place Christ in the service of politics, but you *would* place politics in the service of Christ!'

'But I . . .' Don Chichi stammered.

'Wouldn't you,' Cat continued, 'be able then to treat workers fairly if you became an employer? Or, if you were a deputy or a senator, would you not know how to research and propose laws in favour of the poor? Would you not be able to direct the working masses on the right path if you were a powerful union leader? Would you not be able to pursue a peace policy if you were Foreign Minister?'

'Really,' Don Chichi stammered 'I don't know if I could . . .'

'But *I* do!' Cat shouted excitedly. 'I know! I would sacrifice all my life, all my fortune, all my love for it.'

She stopped and shook her head sadly.

'Forgive me,' she whispered, 'I'm saying some crazy things . . .'

Then ran off sobbing. And, on that occasion, Don Chichi had no reason to be surprised that he was convinced he did see Cat had sprouted two angel's wings from her shoulder blades.

*

A week later Don Camillo, having calmed down, found his strength and, getting out of bed, went downstairs and sadly began to pack his trunk.

'What are you doing, Very Reverend Uncle?' asked Cat with her usual impertinence.

'I'm getting ready to give way to Don Chichi,' Don Camillo replied grimly.

'Well you can forget it: Don Chichi left last night.'

'Where did he go?'

'No idea. He must have had that famous spiritual crisis over which many priests abandon the priesthood and get married. Poor Don Chichi! He will never come back here.'

'How do you know?'

'I know because, rather than marry an ex-priest, I would go and bury myself in a convent of friars.'

Don Camillo look at her in horror.

'You!' he screamed. 'You, wretch, you had the shamelessness to . . .'

'Of course: me! You couldn't have turned his head and got rid of him.'

Don Camillo puffed out his chest:

'*Vade retro, Satana!*' A terrible scream. '*Vade Retro!*'

The girl looked at him quizzically and laughed, 'Sorry, Very Reverend Uncle. It is true that "Cat" derives from "Caterpillar", but she does not have a reverse gear.'

Don Camillo raised his eyes to heaven:

'Lord,' he said, 'will you ever be able to absolve this wretched woman when she appears before the court of God?'

'It cannot be said, Don Camillo,' replied the distant voice of Christ. 'It all depends on the quality of her lawyer for the defence.'

It was a distant voice and only Don Camillo could hear it.

*Old Parish Priests Have Strong Bones*

THE ROAD THAT crossed the village from east to west divided the large piazza into two parts, one of which, defended on three sides by squat stone bollards, was considered the exclusive property of the church.

One morning, some men from the Municipality arrived in the piazza and began to dig up one of the bollards with their picks. In a trice, Don Camillo was on the spot.

'This is the churchyard,' he said, 'and nothing on it may be touched.'

'The Mayor has ordered us . . .' the gang boss began.

'Tell the Mayor that if he wants to dig out the bollards, he must come and see me *in person.*'

In the past, Peppone would not have hesitated for a moment to swoop into the churchyard armed with a pickaxe, spade and sledgehammer. But the years pass for communist mayors like anyone else, so he took things gently and arrived in the piazza all of an hour later, behind the wheel of one of the enormous excavating machines that were engaged in work on the New Bridge.

He brought the big beast to rest a few metres from one of the bollards and lowered the arm of the great machine. He then got out, harnessed the steel rope dangling from the top of the arm to the bollard and Don Camillo let him do it. Then, as Peppone got back on the monster and began operating its arm, the priest quietly sat down upon the bollard.

Even had the Vatican Council appropriated all the power of parish priests in favour of the bishops and the laity, it would still not be permissible to uproot a church-yard bollard on which a parish priest is sitting. The piazza was filled with people in an instant.

'You cannot obstruct public utility works decreed by the Municipality!' Peppone shouted to Don Camillo.'

'You cannot remove these bollards erected on church property in 1785 by the Very Reverend Parish Priest, Don Antonio Bruschini,' replied Don Camillo, lighting up his half Tuscan.

But Peppone had done his research.

'Reverend,' he shouted, 'you forget that in 1796 this territory became part of the Cispadane Republic and therefore . . .'[50]

'So!' Don Camillo responded, drowning him out. 'If Napoleon didn't take out these columns then certainly neither can you, who, if you will allow me to say, are far less important than Napoleon.'

Peppone had to surrender because Don Camillo also threw the connections of Napoleon's consort, Marie-Louise, with the Duchy of Parma, Piacenza and Guastalla into the arena.

However, two days later, the Bishop's secretary fell into the presbytery. The young man, like all progressive priests of the Aggiornamento,[51] despised and detested the old parish priests; and his attitude was not helped by Don Chichi's lacklustre performance in the parish.

The man went on the attack immediately:

---

[50] The short-lived Cispadane Republic was founded in 1796 in northern Italy with the protection of the French army, led by Napoleon.

[51] Following a speech made by Pope John XIII in 1959, 'Aggiornamento' became a buzz word in Vatican II when referring to the wind of change the progressives wanted to see blowing through the Church.

'Father, it seems that you don't miss an opportunity to demonstrate your insensitivity to political and social matters? What does this new clowning about mean? Am I right that the Mayor, in order to bolster tourism and adapt the village to the increased number of cars, wants to create a decent parking space in the piazza and that you are setting up in opposition?'

'No: we simply do not wish to allow them to appropriate the property of the Church.'

'What, a churchyard! You cannot justify taking up half the piazza with a churchyard. Can't you see that, when all's said and done, the plans are of benefit to you too? Don't you realise that a lot people don't go to Mass because churches don't have space to park their cars?'

'Yes, I hear you, but unfortunately,' answered Don Camillo calmly, 'I don't think that the mission of a pastor of souls is to organise parking lots or dumb-down the Mass to offer the faithful a religion equipped with all modern comforts. The religion of Christ is not and cannot be comfortable or fun.'

This was less than weighty priestly reasoning on Vatican II and the Secretary exploded:

'Father, it is clear that you have not understood that the Church must modernise and must assist progress, not hinder it!'

'You, on the other hand, do not seem to understand that, for many people, progressiveness for the sake of it has taken the place of God in the soul. And the Devil, when he passes through our streets, no longer stinks of sulphur but of petrol. Perhaps, finally, the *Pater Noster* should no longer say "deliver us from evil" but "deliver us from Welfare".'

Unable to argue with a fossil of this kind, the Secretary cut to the chase:

'Don Camillo, do I understand, therefore, that you refuse to obey.'

'No. If His Excellency the Bishop orders us to turn the churchyard into a parking lot, we will obey, even if ironically the Vatican Council has established that the Church of Christ must be the Church of the poor and, consequently, should not worry about the cars of the faithful.'

The 'order', of course, did not arrive; but inevitably the Bishop's secretary would emerge above the surface again.

\*

Punctually, every morning, Smilzo continued to slip a copy of *l'Unità* under the door of the presbytery and Don Camillo, no less punctually, leafed through it with justified indifference, justified either because it was the official organ of the communist party, or because it reminded him of the sad episode which had led to Cat winning a free subscription to the newspaper.

But, one day when he was leafing through it, Don Camillo jumped with surprise: on the third page there was a photograph of an altar above which hung a large crucifix and a second photo, a close-up of the crucifix itself. They weren't very sharp photographs in the newspaper, but there could be no doubt: it was Don Camillo's High Altar and Crucified Christ.

Don Camillo read the article quickly, then jumped on his bicycle and made haste to his secret chapel.

'Lord!' he panted, showing the newspaper to Christ on the cross above the High Altar.

'There is a photo of you in *l'Unità*!'

'So I see, Don Camillo,' replied Christ, 'let's hope that I have not got you into trouble like your niece did. If so it transpires, it is *not* my fault.'

Behind the photographs lay an extraordinary story that dates back to 1944, when a German unit had been sheltering in the village. Among the group was an officer, who, even though he had to be a warrior for now, had not forgotten that he was also a famous professor of the history of art.

He had been struck by the figure of Christ and certain ornamental details on the altar and he'd photographed them as carefully as he could at the time. Then, returning home, he had studied the photographs and realised that they were unusually fine works of art, made by a famous German artist of the 1400s who specialised in sacred sculptures in painted wood. After twenty-two years, the man had returned to Italy to photograph the altar and the crucifix with greater precision and in colour, but had not been able to find them. He had then published the story of his wartime discovery in an important German magazine, illustrating it with some of the photos taken in '44, and *l'Unità* had reprinted the article and the photos, limiting the commentary – *sic et simpliciter* – to a few words:

'Where did that poor Christ end up? Like so many poor Christs, was he, too, forced to emigrate?'

Other newspapers reported the article from the German magazine, giving rise to a sort of scandal, which, one fine day, led to the Bishop's secretary making a second visit to the presbytery. He was indignant and rushed at Don Camillo:

'Reverend Father, you seem never to tire of making trouble! Where is Christ and where is the altar that the newspapers talk about?'

'You ordered us to remove everything from the church and everything has been removed,' replied Don Camillo calmly. 'Indeed, you will find that since we did not carry out your orders sufficiently promptly, you sent us a political commissar to speed up the process.'

'You should have told us that it was an important work of art!' the Secretary objected.

'How was I supposed to know? How was I, a poor country parish priest, even to suspect it, given my profound ignorance . . . In any case, we have ensured that both altar and crucifix are safe.'

'Thank God!' the Secretary rejoiced. 'Retrieve them immediately. Pack them with great care and call us as soon as everything is ready. We will come and collect them and find them worthy accommodation in the diocese.'

Don Camillo lowered his head as a sign of obedience.

*

'Signor Mayor . . .'

Peppone raised his head from his paperwork and, finding himself looking at Don Camillo, clenched his fists.

'What do you want?' he muttered aggressively.

'I wanted to communicate to the Mayor that I have thought again about the idea of a car park,' answered Don Camillo. 'You can have the bollards removed.'

Peppone looked at him with distrust. 'When a priest gives you as much as a button,' he said, 'you can bet that at the very least he'll want a full dress suit in exchange. What's the deal?'

'Comrade Mayor,' Don Camillo explained humbly, 'we see that, for some years now, your party has dealt with small and indeed large problems of the Church with great love and devotion. We would simply like you and some of your comrades to be present at the release of our precious crucifix which, after 350 years of honourable service in the area, moves to the city where a good place in the diocese awaits it.'

Peppone jumped out of his chair: 'You are mad, Father! That Christ is a work of art. It belongs to the town and will remain in the town.'

Don Camillo spread his arms wide.

'I understand you, Mr Mayor. Unfortunately, I do not yet defer to your party, but still to my Bishop. And so I will have to deliver Christ and the altar to the Bishop's secretary. I understand that the Christ is part of the most precious artistic and spiritual heritage of our parish and his place should be the one he has occupied for 350 years, above that altar in front of which you too took your first Holy Communion and were married. Before which your mother prayed for your safekeeping when you went to war. Your poor old parish priest understands all this but can only obey the Bishop. And he will obey, unless someone takes violent exception to his doing so. In the face of violence, what can a poor old parish priest ever do? Comrade Mayor, please, explain my distressing situation to your superiors! And take note of it yourself when deciding what to do.'

'Reverend,' screamed Peppone 'if you think I'm going to let myself be fooled by your lot, think again!'

Peppone clearly meant it, for the next morning the town was carpeted out with huge posters denouncing the attempted misappropriation and ended with two lines in large characters:

*The Christ is ours!*
*Hands off our Christ!*

Around noon, Don Camillo, who had not been in the least disturbed by Peppone's position, went quietly by bicycle to the secret chapel in the old house away in the fields, where a big surprise awaited him: the toughest of

Peppone's squad had camped out in the large overgrown garden and spent their time clearing it of weeds.

'Do you realise that this is private property and that I could sue you for trespassing?' Don Camillo said to Brusco and Bigio, who were in charge of the detachment.

'Yes, Reverend,' said Brusco.

'May I come in to pack the Christ and the various pieces of the altar?' Don Camillo asked.

'Yes, you can enter, but you can't pack anything. You are a priest, not a freighter.'

'I don't want to make trouble with the unions,' Don Camillo agreed as he went off home.

The controversy flared up: the newspapers dedicated a lot of space to the disputed Christ. Peppone, at his wildest, held rallies and unleashed his propaganda department upon the countryside. Never as on that occasion had such consensus been seen. Suddenly, the country shook off its indifference and rebelled. It was a campaign of revolt against the city that has always despised, exploited and tried to kill the countryside. Putting all political rivalry aside, the whole region was united around Don Camillo's Christ. Like the great square of Villafranca.[52] Even atheists spoke of *their* Christ and of the historical, artistic and spiritual heritage that the city was trying to steal from the country. Day and night the garden of the old house, lost in the fields, was full of people. And, since Don Camillo had forgotten to lock the door of the building, they could sleep indoors.

A mixed commission made up of representatives of all the parties and associations ventured to the city and was

---

[52] On June 24, 1866, near Villafranca during the third war for independence, astride the road to Verona, the Italian infantry (peasants, labourers, artisans and workers together) famously resisted the imperial cavalry (Austrian, Hungarian, Czech, Slovak and Polish knights) by arranging itself in a "battalion square".

received by the Bishop, to whom Peppone expressed the respectful but energetic protest of the population of the Municipality.

The Bishop listened attentively then opened his arms wide, smiling: 'It is only a misunderstanding,' he said. 'Given its exceptional artistic and spiritual value, there is nothing to prevent the altar in its entirety being returned to where it has always been, provided the Holy Mass is celebrated with the new rite and that the pastor does not have particular and valid reasons to oppose it. The decision is therefore up to him and to him alone.'

When the commission reported to Don Camillo what the Bishop had said, Don Camillo humbly replied: 'We are here to obey the orders of His Excellency the Bishop.'

It was a sweet Autumn morning and both the air and the fields were dusted with gold. During the night, a team of volunteers had returned the altar to where it had been for centuries and now the people of the Municipality – the old, the young, the women and men, all as one, no-one excluded – were stretched out in two endless rows on each side of the road leading to the lonely old manor house.

The band came out of the gate and filled the golden fields with the sound of brass. Behind the band came a billion children; behind the children, Don Camillo was holding the great Crucified Christ and advancing with a slow and sure step. Behind him, came the municipal banner and then Peppone, festooned with the Italian Tricolor, followed by the entire municipal administration.

As the procession advanced, the people on the side of the road joined it. The large wooden cross was heavy and the strap of the leather pocket that held the foot of the cross cut into Don Camillo's shoulders. And the road was long.

'Lord,' whispered Don Camillo at a certain point, 'before my heart breaks, I would like to get to the church and see you installed there once more above the altar.'

'We'll get there, Don Camillo, we'll get there,' replied Christ who now seemed to everyone more beautiful than ever.

And they did get there. Old parish priests, even those with a tender heart, have strong bones and for this reason the Church of Christ, which weighs mainly on their shoulders, resists all storms.

*Deo gratias.*

## The Young People of Today are Complicated

THERE CAME TO the presbytery a 'gravedigger from the competent ministry'[53] to see the famous crucifix that the newspapers had talked about so much and to study it, and when he had seen and studied it, he said that he would send someone to collect it for the necessary restoration.

'The crucifix does not move from here,' answered Don Camillo sternly. 'There is nothing to restore.'

The gravedigger of the competent ministry was accompanied by the Bishop's secretary, and the young priest, who regarded Don Camillo as 'smoke in his eyes', jumped into the fray:

'Reverend Father, let us not talk nonsense. Christ's right hand is broken at the wrist and the arm of the cross is broken in line with it, which some scoundrel has mended badly by screwing a piece of iron behind it. Did you not notice?'

'Certainly,' replied Don Camillo, 'as I am the scoundrel who carried out the repair.'

The ministerial gravedigger was one of those diligent officials capable of blocking the crucial construction of a bridge for twenty years if – in digging the footings for the

---

[53] An interfering antiquarian from the Ministry of Education.

supports – a fragment of an earthenware pot from 1925 was discovered, while barely opening his mouth if someone were to demolish the Arch of Titus to install a petrol station in its place.[54]

The man shook his head and gave a pitying chuckle: 'Let's not waste time, Father. Whoever comes to collect the crucifix will give you an official receipt.'

Don Camillo, with admirable frankness, explained to the gravedigger what use he would have made of that sheet of paper and reminded him that the door out of the church was the same one he had used to enter it. But the gravedigger had a degree, which allowed him to cover an important seat with his backside, and swelled his chest like a turkey.

'*Reverendo*,' he cried, 'I represent the Ministry of Education!'

'No ministry of public education was here on the morning of October 15, 1944,' replied Don Camillo. 'But those *I* represent were.'

'Reverend, spare us your jokes!' the Bishop's secretary exclaimed.

'It's no joke; I have at least 300 eyewitnesses to what actually happened. If you want me to I'll bang the hammer bells for a moment and they'll all be here.'

As much as the young priest was from the mountains and as much as the ministerial gravedigger was from Rome, they both knew that there are people in this patch of fertile earth scattered along the south bank of the Great River who are quick to anger.

'Don't bother to ring the bells,' said the gravedigger. 'You tell us all about it instead.'

'The "joke" occurred during the war,' explained Don Camillo. 'The Germans invaded the village and hid

---

[54] A triumphant arch on the Via Sacra, Rome, commemorating a victory by Titus and Vespasian in the Jewish-Roman War (66–73 AD).

Panzers and vehicles under cover of the roadside avenues of trees and under the arcades and in the courtyards of houses. Then came others with a secret radio transmitter, who reported all the movements of the Germans to the Allies. So, the liberators were immediately informed and their planes swooped over the country one Sunday morning. It was hell: but people didn't move from the church, where Mass was being celebrated. I didn't move either; but there was no courage involved as far as I was concerned because I'd been a military chaplain and was familiar with bombs.

'At the moment of the Elevation,[55] a bomb exploded on the roof of the sexton's house. A piece of shrapnel shot through the window in the choir, behind the High Altar, but Jesus protected us. He took the force of it on the right arm of the cross. Of course you can laugh: the Crucified Christ above the altar is only painted wood, but those men and women here that day were not made of wood, they were flesh and blood. And their faith was stronger than their fear, for no one moved. The splinter of shrapnel severed the end of the arm of the cross and, at the same time, the hand of Christ. And the hand, nailed to the piece of wood, fell in front of the altar rail and everyone saw that poor shrunken hand on the ground. *Agnus Dei qui tollis peccata mundis . . .*

'Now, understand me, a joke like that, told at the Vatican Council, would have gutted the holy Fathers with laughter: but here, people rather like this sort of joke and so everyone – the oldsters who saw it firsthand and remember, and the young who learned about it from the old – the image of that poor wounded hand will never leave them.

---

[55] The ritual raising of the Host by the celebrant at the climax of the Mass.

'I'm like those people too. I am an old priest and I believe that Christ does not have to resort to cosmetic surgery to hide the signs of his wounds. The "piece of iron" – as the Secretary rightly called it – and the splinter of shrapnel that severed the cross and the wrist of Christ: I pierced them with a drill and screwed them together to keep the cross in place. War must serve some purpose. Anyway, I understand your position: you can't afford to listen to our jokes because you represent the State . . .'

'Not always,' said the ministerial gravedigger. 'Sometimes it happens that I represent myself. For me everything is fine as it is. The crucifix is a truly exceptional work of art but I don't think there is any need for me to recommend that it be restored.'

'I am pleased to concur,' answered Don Camillo bowing.

*

Men have managed to find ways to harness nuclear energy, but no one has yet discovered a way to harness crazed brains like Cat's. Stratagems were her meat and drink, and there was every reason to suspect that she was adopting a new one. One minute she locked herself away in the sexton's house reading or scribbling, then every now and then she jumped on that damned motorcycle and disappeared. Where was she going? Nobody knew and Don Camillo only had a bicycle and could hardly track the pestiferous mini-brain. So he decided to ask for help and, the first time Peppone passed in front of the presbytery, he called him inside.

'Comrade Mayor,' he said, 'I would like to talk to your son, Michele: would you let him know?'

'No,' replied Peppone. 'The only thing I'd do to that wretch is hit him on the head.'

'I am amazed, Mr Mayor. The whole area has been quiet for some time. There is no news of more beatings or those other witty acts of hooliganism, the unmistakable style of your son. We don't even see him around anymore, so much so that one wonders whether your baby boy is sick.'

'Well, he is!' Peppone shouted. 'Sick in the head. Now that he's been called up, he refuses to do military service. He wants to go into hiding, can you credit it? He's decided to become a fugitive!'

'You should be proud of him, Comrade!' exclaimed Don Camillo. 'Evidently the good Michele listened to your ardent anti-war speeches. I remember that in your last one you said that if prisons are the training schools for thieves, barracks are training schools for murderers.'

'I was talking about America, about Vietnam!' protested Peppone. 'Michele heard about conscientious objectors not in my speeches but in your church!'

'I am not responsible for what Don Chichi may have said,' returned Don Camillo. 'I am me, Don Chichi is Don Chichi.'

'Two bloody priests speaking from the same pulpit in the name of the same God . . . Sounds to me like the Church playing both ends against the middle.'

Peppone, who was quickly aroused, said things about priests that would make a bald man sprout curly hair. Don Camillo answered in kind, but when he was about to lose complete control, he suddenly found an inner calm.

'Comrade,' he said quietly, 'in this world where no-one gives a damn about anyone else, in this world dominated by selfishness and indifference, you and I continue to fight a war that has in fact been over for a long time. Do we not seem like a couple of ghosts out of their time? Do you not realise that, before long, having fought so long, each for his flag, we will be kicked out of office – me by my people and you by yours – and we will find ourselves miserable and broken and having to sleep under a bridge?'

'So what?' Peppone replied. 'We will continue to fight under the bridge.'

Don Camillo thought about this and conceded that in a dirty, lousy world, in which it is not possible to have a true friend, finding one true enemy was indeed a great consolation:

'All right, Comrade,' he said, 'but send me Venom.'

*

When Venom arrived he wore a dark expression and hair over his eyes.

'If you're hot, do take off your wig,' Don Camillo suggested.

'The wig is at home, in the chest of drawers,' replied Venom. 'This hair is mine. Even Samson's hair grew back.'

'Indeed, and like Samson you have regained your strength and are contemplating picking a fight with anything and everything, starting with the army.'

'I don't want to destroy anything,' the long-haired man muttered. 'I don't want to be a soldier, that's all. Enough with wars: we young people want peace. If you want war, you old folks can have it.'

'I don't want to make wars either,' explained Don Camillo. 'I just want to know what the hell Cat is up to. Every now and then she disappears: I'm afraid she's back in touch with those city thugs. Do you know what she's up to?'

Venom shook his shaggy head: 'Actually, I thought about it too and one time I followed her. But she saw me, stopped and told me to mind my own business. Then I sent her to hell. In the end, I have no right to be on her case.'

'I, on the other hand, have not only the right but also the duty,' Don Camillo declared. 'Get a rental car and be ready. I will pay you for your trouble.'

'You just need to pay for the car. The satisfaction of annoying that brat is the most beautiful way of paying me. When it's time, give me a whistle.'

Don Camillo did not even need to whistle. When, two days later, Cat jumped on her motorbike and shot off, Venom, arrived with the car in front of the presbytery a minute later. Don Camillo jumped up and together they set off in pursuit. Venom was driving as if he had a lap to catch up at the Indianapolis speedway track and soon Cat was in sight.

She was making her way quietly, arousing no suspicion, and they followed her with ease. About ten kilometres from the city, she left the provincial road and turned onto a secondary road that was soon swallowed up by the countryside. Venom turned off too and, after a while, Cat slipped through a gate, the beginning of a very long avenue flanked by tall poplars. Don Camillo and Venom found the gate closed and had to stop. To the left of the gate was a little hut: Venom pounded on the horn and the caretaker appeared.

'Are you members?' the man inquired.

'Members of what?' Don Camillo asked.

'If you don't know, it's pointless me telling you,' grumbled the man, who must have had a particular dislike for priests and longhairs. He retreated into his hut. The property was enclosed by a high wire mesh that skirted the road.

'Let's go around until we find a way to get in or at least to see what it is,' said Venom, restarting the car.

The impression they had was of a huge rectangle of land and, after turning the first corner, they found the situation as before: ditch, wire mesh, thick hedge.

Venom stopped the car: 'Father,' he said 'if you want, I'll take the pliers, cut the net and go inside to see. This business doesn't smell right.'

'No,' answered Don Camillo. 'Let's go once round first.'

At that moment they heard the roar of an engine. An aircraft was approaching, travelling no more than fifty metres high and coming from the far side of the fence to pass over their heads. They got out of the car to look: the plane rose up and returned to repeat its carousel until it had risen around 2,000 metres. Suddenly, something fell from the craft and a large white flower opened in the blue autumn sky.

Venom shook his big head and mumbled: 'I don't understand how there can be crazies that actually enjoy parachuting!'

Now that they were there, they might as well enjoy the show: the little man hooked to the big white umbrella played the ropes wonderfully and it seemed that everything was working well, but suddenly from God knows where, a gust of wind took the parachute and blew it off course in the direction of the river.

'That wretch is going to fall who knows where!' exclaimed Don Camillo. 'Let's go!'

They got back into the car and set off in pursuit of the castaway in the sky, while Venom muttered: 'Typical priest! As soon as they see the possibility of grabbing a dead person to send – recommended – to the Eternal Father, they forget everything else.'

Slowly the parachute lost altitude and Venom, proceeding like a demented man through lane upon lane, kept closely in pursuit of it.

'Look out, high voltage!' Don Camillo suddenly shouted, seeing the parachute approach a series of national grid power line pylons. But, if there is a God for the mad, for paratroopers, it seems, the complete Trinity is at work, for the flying bundle swept over the wires.

'It's going to end up in the Po!' Venom screamed shortly afterwards.

Instead the skydiver managed to bring the parachute down in a meadow at the foot of the embankment and the great white umbrella collapsed on the still green grass.

Venom careered down from the embankment along a suicidally steep road, then crossed a farmyard threshing floor at full speed, causing havoc in a herd of chickens and finally managed to slip onto a cart track before splashing onto the wet meadow grass and catching up with the paratrooper. The little fellow had already unhooked himself from the ropes and was taking off his helmet, when Cat's red hair was caught glistening in the sun. Don Camillo took the last few steps jumping like a kangaroo.

'Is it possible that you can only do crazy things?' Don Camillo shouted.

Cat lit a cigarette and replied ironically: 'Of course, this is not a sport for priests or rural bully boys.'

'What on earth made you do it?' Don Camillo panted.

'If my father did it, why wouldn't I do it?'

'Your father did it because there was a war on and war requires men to do the craziest things!' Don Camillo said.

'My father did it because he had guts. And when he proved he had guts, he could claim respect as a soldier.'

Soon, officers from the training school arrived, worried at what they might find, but Cat reassured them:

'Everything is fine. The only unfortunate incident was the arrival of my Very Reverend Uncle Priest, accompanied by his sexton. You know how it is: misfortunes never travel alone.'

'I wouldn't agree,' said Don Camillo. 'The only real disaster is that your parachute opened at all.'

Venom was devoured by his ire and only found the ability to speak when he dumped Don Camillo in front of the presbytery.

'I'll let that brat see what a sexton I am!' Veleno said, and there was so much hatred in his voice that Don Camillo was seriously worried. But from that day on, Venom disappeared as if by magic.

Only a long time later did Don Camillo learn from Peppone what had become of him. Indeed, it was Don Camillo who asked Peppone about it and Peppone replied:

'Your God alone knows what happened to him! First he didn't want to go into the military and talked about going into hiding. Then he signed on a month early and did crazy things until he managed to get enlisted in the paras! Do you understand? The paras! Those crazies who jump out of planes with a parachute. Do you understand anything about these young people?'

'I don't,' replied Don Camillo. 'Young people today are a complicated lot.'

'Crazy lot!' exclaimed Peppone. 'And he doesn't realise – that idiot! – that we've lost sleep thinking about the danger of his parachute jumping.'

'There are worse dangers than that,' muttered Don Camillo.

## San Michele Had Four Wings

THE DINING ROOM looked the same, but Don Camillo felt uneasy. Habit is such a business that it can trick you into seeing something even when it is no longer there. Alternatively, the subconscious may notice something out of the ordinary that you don't see at first and nag you into a second look. A slight discrepancy, perhaps in light and shade or how full or oddly empty the scene feels, can give the subconscious a clue that what stands before your eyes is somehow *different*.

For the fourth time, Don Camillo looked around and at last realised what it was: the small, very old painting of San Giovannino was missing. Desolina said that she knew nothing about its disappearance and, after searching in vain, Don Camillo concluded that the picture must have been stolen and said:

'I'm going to report the theft to the *carabinieri*!'

'I wouldn't do that,' said Cat, walking into the dining room wearing her leather jacket, glistening from a long motorbike ride in the fog.

'And why not?'

'Because the painting is here,' she replied, taking it out of the bag she had with her and hanging it up in its usual place.

'I took it to a city dude: he's willing to drop five hundred big ones for it. Half a million!'[56]

'I'm not interested,' Don Camillo replied curtly. 'My old Bishop gave it to me twenty years ago and I care about it deeply. Why would I want to sell it?'

'To avoid gossip,' Cat explained coolly and a little suggestively. 'Just think, the Very Reverend Parish Priest has his niece entrusted to him for a little unconscious bias training, and the sweet child gets a bun in the oven! Since I can't go back to my mother in this state (or she'll go mad), I thought I'd go far away from here, get a job and drop the sprog on my own. But, to do this, I'll need money. Unless you want me to go to the city and work in a brothel.'

'What I want is for God to strike you down!' Don Camillo roared in horror. 'I had no idea you were such an out-and-out delinquent!'

'There's nothing delinquent about having a child.'

'You, monster, didn't you think about what this will do to your mother?' Don Camillo shouted.

'No, at the moment of conception I was actually thinking about what Venom was doing to me.'

'Venom! But you can't stand the sight of him!'

'Nor did I have to: it was two in the morning.'

Such shamelessness demanded God's vengeance. Don Camillo clenched his fists:

'Don't run away . . . this time I will break your bones!'

'Would you dare to beat a woman in this state?' she reproached him. 'Oh, but then you have never been a mother so you cannot understand . . .'

Don Camillo was a man of quick decisions: floored by the girl's impudence he ran out of the house and from

---

[56] Approximately $800 or £300, a sizeable sum in 1966.

the garden threw open the shutters of the dining room window, which was protected also by a large metal grille:

'Stay at arm's length from me so that I cannot stretch out, grab you and strangle you. Answer me: *was* it that rascal who got you into trouble?'

By this time Cat had sat down in front of the fire in the dining room fireplace and having lit a cigarette was quietly smoking.

'I'm not in trouble, Reverend Uncle. *You* are in trouble. In any case, there are no delinquents or victims in all this. If I hadn't wanted to, then of course Venom . . .'

'Venom!' roared Don Camillo, clinging to the grille. 'That thug will have to bear the weight of his responsibility. We need a shotgun wedding, *now*!'

The girl sneered:

'So, Very Reverend Uncle, are we throwbacks to a time when in order to save a family's honour it marries off its fourteen-year-olds? Girls who then continue to give birth to children like rabbits and camp out in the piazza or under the town arcades because, so they say, society must feed them and find them a place to live? Is this Catholic moral sense? How can a marriage between two foolish youngsters be regarded as conferring a sacrament upon them? What would it do for the institution of family? It is much more immoral to marry two irresponsible youngsters than to put 200 single mothers into circulation! Precisely out of the respect I have for family and for marriage, I will never marry an idiot like Venom! Shotgun wedding? To close a small hole, you would open an abyss, Uncle. Let's be honest: to drive a lousy little Fiat Cinquecento legally you have to take a serious test to get a licence. To get married and start a family, which is a thousand times more important and potentially dangerous for society, it is enough simply to say "Yes" in front of an old fossil of a country priest!'

Clinging to the metal grille, Don Camillo was suffering terribly, dripping with sweat and anger in equal measure.

'I'll have you locked up in a home for lost girls,' he gasped.

'Yesterday I came of age, Reverend, so no one can tell me what to do.'

Not being able to bite into and break off one or more of the bars in the iron window grille, Don Camillo screamed instead:

'Take the painting, sell it and go to Hell!'

Cat threw the butt of her cigarette on the embers of the fire, got up, took the painting, put it back in her bag and headed for the door.

'Okay, Uncle,' she said. 'If it's a boy, I'll name him Camillo.'

*

Peppone's wife had become obsessed: she wanted a fur. Not a diva-style fur coat, you understand, but a little thing worth no more than a million lire. But Peppone was dead set against it.

'Imagine! They accuse me of being bourgeois as it is, and now you want me to buy you a fur stole!'

'This is not China and there are no Red Guards,' replied his wife.

'Here we live in a village and there are a thousand scoundrels who will say that I exploited the people for their money and got rich on the back of them.'

'Nonsense: the shop is yours and you paid for it with your money and mine too!'

'Maria! Don't you understand that if I go to the piazza protest that the people are suffering and then I buy you a fur, I'll be out in the cold?'

'Then stop shouting that the people are suffering. The only suffering people do these days is when they have an accident driving their cars. Besides, if someone really is in a bad way he'll be in a bad way whether I wear a fur or an ordinary overcoat.'

At that moment there was a knock on the door and Peppone took a breather. Peppone's wife went to answer it and returned with Cat.

'Mr Mayor,' the girl began, 'I would like some information.'

'Then go to the town hall and see the Town Clerk,' replied Peppone.

'No good,' Cat went on. 'The father of my child is not the son of the Town Clerk, he's the son of the Mayor.'

Peppone looked at her and his mouth dropped open.

'*Signorina*, are you crazy?'

'No. According to the obstetrician, I am expecting a baby.'

'Well, go and expect it wherever you like, but not here!' Peppone's wife screamed fiercely.

'Very well,' Cat replied calmly. 'Since my uncle has chased me out of the presbytery and as the child's father – I'm talking about Venom – is away in the army, I'm going to wait for our baby sitting on the stairs of the town hall.'

'We have no evidence of our son having an affair with you!' Peppone said in a manner precluding debate.

'To me there is,' Cat giggled. 'And in a few months it will be evident to everyone.'

Peppone's wife was on the warpath. 'These are things my son has to deal with,' she shouted. 'We have nothing to do with it. Get out!'

'One moment, Maria,' Peppone intervened. 'This young girl is deranged and it takes nothing to create a scandal!'

'My Reverend Uncle came to the same conclusion and dropped half a million to get me out of the way.'

'You slut!' Peppone's wife exploded. 'I see now, you want to take advantage of my husband's delicate position to blackmail us! If you think you're going to force Michele into marriage . . .'

'Marriage?' came back the grinning Cat. 'Do you think a beautiful, smart girl like me would make a move like that with a stupid thug like your son?'

Peppone made a grab for his wife who had hurled herself towards Cat to tear her to pieces, and said:

'Signorina, if it's not about marriage, would you like to tell us what you are after?'

'I want to go far away. Find a couple of rooms, have my baby in peace and raise him on my own. I don't have the slightest intention of starting one of those screwed up families by marrying a man like your son. I have my dignity and my moral principles.'

'Listen to her!' howled Peppone's wife. 'How dare you talk about dignity and morals after what you did!'

Cat sat down and lit a cigarette.

'Sure, Ma'am,' she replied, smiling at her. 'I did with your son exactly what you did with your husband, unless your first child's four month term is a unique medical phenomenon. The only difference is that I don't humble myself by sobbing and lamenting that if I don't get married I'll throw myself under a train!'

'I have never threatened to throw myself under a train!' Maria protested.

'That's right,' Peppone confirmed. 'She threatened to throw herself into the Po. So, young lady, what does that mean you want from us?'

'I don't want anything more than an honest job.'

'Work? I have no work to give you!'

'Mr Mayor, the Reverend Uncle's money has been used to buy a magnificent second-hand station wagon and to rent and furnish two small rooms at La Rocchetta. I'll go around selling stock from your shop and you'll pay me a commission on every piece sold.'

'And why don't you go directly to the manufacturers?' Peppone muttered.

'I've tried, but everywhere they want too much of a kickback from me that I don't feel like signing up. Of course, I won't officially sell your stuff. It will appear that I'm in competition with you.'

The girl's perfidy was boundless: while standing outside in the corridor she had heard what Peppone and his wife had been saying and was now scheming to take advantage of it.

'Don't be surprised, Lord Mayor. I know people. People enjoy the misfortune of others more than their own luck. The farmer enjoys it when his harvest is good, but he is even more satisfied when his neighbour's harvest is bad. In church it is the same: many people behave all holy not for the pleasure of going to Heaven, but for the pleasure of knowing that others will go to Hell. Ditto in politics: property-less proletarians struggle not in order to improve their condition but to worsen the condition of the landowners.

'Why, *Signor* Mayor, since we cannot count on the goodness and intelligence of our neighbours, do we not exploit their wickedness and stupidity? Why, instead of sending your wife out dressed like a rural housewife, don't you buy her a big fur and a big diamond to match? A lot of people hate you and they will buy from me if only to spite you. We'll both benefit!'

'I would give it a go,' advised Peppone's wife. 'This girl is damned – she knows more than the Devil.'

*

This statement was unfair, because Cat knew at least twice as much as the Devil. Cat, more beautiful, perfidious and dazzling than ever, got her enterprise underway speedily and flooded the land with washing machines, dishwashers, refrigerators, televisions, transistors and such-like merchandise.[57]

Unaware of the colossal activity going on in the back room, the people of the village very much enjoyed seeing Peppone's clientele at the shop gradually disappear and, when Signora Maria came out in her fur coat and glitter, they grinned anticipating the joy of the moment in which the poor woman would have to sell the fur and diamonds to pay off the company's debts.

After four months, Cat had set up a terrific business and everything was going beautifully, when suddenly Venom turned up on a short leave. Let us, therefore, return in a theatrical way 'as you like it' to the *Paese del Melodramma*: Peppone was speaking from the grandstand in the piazza about Vietnam and the barbarity of the American military machine. In full flight, he was able to say *'strumentalizzazione'* with precise 'z's, which seemed to have been engraved by Bodoni[58] himself, but, suddenly, something appeared before his eyes that left him speechless.

There, in the front row, was Venom in full para uniform. He seemed to be at least two and a half metres tall and Peppone decided that all he lacked to be the Archangel San Michele were two wings on his shoulders and a sword in his hand. He didn't give a damn about Vietnam and America anymore and cut his speech short . . . 'Which we conclude with the fateful cry of "Long live freedom, long live peace!"'

[57] In Italy, between 1958 and 1965, the percentage of families owning a television set rose from 12% to 49%, washing machines from 3% to 23%, and refrigerators from 13% to 55%.

[58] Giambattista Bodoni, a famous 18th-century typesetter and compositor.

Peppone's wife, seeing Venom before her, lacked none of her husband's reservations and decided that he did actually have two magnificent wings and a sword in his hand. She could also see a golden halo on her son's head. And, of course, she melted into tears and said the one thing she shouldn't have said:

'And now, Michele, what shall we do about poor Cat, who's been so good and industrious in your absence . . .'

Venom replied that he knew nothing about what she'd been up to and his mother explained that the girl was expecting a baby and that he could not leave his progeny scattered around the world. Venom got on his bike and set off towards La Rocchetta. He met 'the poor girl' in the Stradaccia where a light mist caught the scene and gave everything something of a fairytale flavour.

Cat was driving her station wagon loaded with appliances and Venom had swerved, coming to a halt in front of it, blocking her path. Cat turned pale and clung desperately to the wheel. Coming upon San Michele himself, with double wings, double golden halo and a large flaming sword in his hand, in a lonely country road was enough to make anyone catch their breath.

'Are you . . . on leave?' she stammered.

'Yes . . . They tell me you are expecting my child.'

'I've heard that too,' Cat admitted. 'Anyway, I'm not expecting anyone's child.'

'Just as well,' said San Michele, twirling his flaming sword. 'But what on earth made you say something like that to my parents and your uncle, when there was never anything at all between you and me.'

Cat observed that the wings of San Michele numbered but two and that his sword did not flare at all.

'I also have the right to a place in the sun, right?' she made bold. 'I had to find somewhere to live! How else could I have persuaded my uncle to stump up the readies and your father to give me a job? Or do you think you alone have the right to a life?'

'No,' muttered Venom. 'I meant . . . why me?'

'Why you!'

Cat pressed forward now with *her* flaming sword, (looking a lot like Joan of Arc).

'What *are* you? Are you not a rebel like me, ranged against this foolish filthy world? We may belong to different gangs, but aren't we on the same wavelength? Answer, great Venom, great Rebel: do you go along with the lousy world that the old fools have saddled us with? Tell me, do these filthy old hypocrites deserve our respect? Or has your shearing at the hands of the paras also stripped you of your anarchist spirit?'

'No!'

'So why not use these foolish old self-deluders to build a world that *we* would like? If cowards and hypocrites are terrified of scandal, why not terrorise them with a scandal. I needed you as my pretext: I used you because I thought you were one of us. And aren't you? Don't you want to go along with it? Or do you want to go home and explain that it's not true, that you have nothing to do with it, that you are a good boy while I am a slut? . . . Well, if so, you go!'

'No,' replied Venom. 'I haven't changed and I know what solidarity means. Anyway, we might as well . . .'

'*What?*'

'As you've said you're expecting my child, we might as well do it. The protest would be more . . . concrete.'

'I'm not into extremism,' Cat explained. 'Besides, you're not my type.'

'And what would your type be?' Venom protested. 'That lousy Ringo? I'm going to smash his face in.'

'No don't do that: he arranged for his aunt to buy a fridge from me and I sold a dishwasher to his sister, a washing machine to his sister-in-law . . . Also, I never said that Ringo is my type.'

Venom shook his head: 'I don't see why I'm not your type.'

'Are you bailing out yet?'

'I'm one of the first on the course. They say I'm good.'

'Like I'm good, huh?'

'You are not good, you're crazy . . . I'm also doing well with judo and I'm learning karate.'

'That's a step in the right direction,' Cat acknowledged.

'Speaking of the child,' Venom persisted, 'when they see that nothing's . . . happening, how are you going to handle that?'

'I already have my round, my clientele. But for now I need you to play along.'

'Sure. Venom knows what he is and would never betray others of his kind.'

'Are you staying long?'

'I leave tomorrow morning. If you want, I'll give you my address. You might need it.'

'Taking you up on that would be very difficult. But give it to me anyway. I'll give you my card. Well, you may need a fridge in the barracks.'

Having the Cat company card, San Michele tore a white feather from one of his wings, wrote his address on it and passed it to Cat. Then he left without saying goodbye. Young people today are like this: tough . . . Tough as leather.

Seeing him speed away into the mist, Cat saw that his wings were after all not two, but four.

'I knew I wasn't wrong,' she muttered to herself as she shifted into first gear, forgetting to squeeze the clutch.

*The Sheep's Roar is Fashionable*

DON CAMILLO WAS roasting chestnuts on the fire in the dining room, when a voice startled him:

'Good morning, Very Reverend Uncle!'

'We agreed that you would never come back here,' replied Don Camillo without turning around.

'I know,' Cat concurred, 'but when I realised you needed me, I got over the repulsion that this dump finds in me and here I am.'

'*I* need *you*?' Don Camillo shouted.

'Not me personally, rather a good 200-litre fridge freezer.'

Don Camillo withdrew the pan from the fire, jumped to his feet and cried out in front of the hateful girl:

'You and your refrigerators can go to hell!'

'Maybe we should!' Cat giggled perversely. 'I'd do some great deals over there.'

She pulled an illustrated catalogue out of her bag and dropped it on the table:

'This is the fridge for you. Twelve instalments; you won't even know you're paying for it.'

'What do I need a refrigerator for?' roared Don Camillo.

'First of all because the deal's a good one. I'll give you a hefty discount. Second: buying it from me is one in the eye for Peppone. Third: you can give me the fridge as a wedding present when I get married.'

Don Camillo gasped. 'Ah, so you are getting married!' he exclaimed.

'Of course I'll get married . . . sometime. Do I look like the type who can't catch a husband, what with all the jerks there are out there?'

Disappointment rekindled Don Camillo's anger.

'Then there is no hope of avoiding a scandal!' he cried.

'Ah, but wouldn't it be a scandal to you if a girl gave birth to a child after only two or three months of matrimony? Is that not the morality they taught you in the seminary?'

'Are we to start all over again?' Don Camillo exploded, pounding his fist on the table.

'No, so long as you're happy with twelve instalments of 8,000 lire a month.'

The girl's shamelessness knew no bounds and so proved Don Camillo's temper too:

'You brazen hussy, you stole my *San Giovannino* and now you also want to take 8,000 lire a month from me?'

'What sacrifices would an uncle who wasn't a priest make for his orphaned and pregnant niece?' she groaned without conscience.

Cat was always beautiful, cynical, mocking: but now a shadow of sadness veiled her eyes: she also seemed to have gained weight recently.

'All it takes is your signature here, in this little contract,' she explained. 'I'll leave it for you: think about it.'

'Okay, I'll think about it,' muttered Don Camillo.

'Well,' said Cat. 'Now let's go to the shop.'

'What shop?'

'Yours. I want to make my confession.'

'You mean to confess to me!' Don Camillo screamed in horror. '*Me?*'

'Sure,' Cat calmly confirmed, peeling a chestnut. 'If Magdalene was listened to by Christ, why shouldn't a poor country parish priest listen to me? Are you more important than Christ?'

'No!' Don Camillo roared. 'But I'm your mother's brother and I don't know what to do with a niece like you.'

'Relationships have nothing to do with it. I am here as a sinner and I want to confess to the parish priest.'

'Go to another to empty your cesspool!'

'But why, Very Reverend Uncle? You already know all that I have to say, so it would be easier . . .'

'No! I could not compose myself properly with you. I could not strip myself of my righteous resentment. I could not judge you with due impartiality.'

'I don't care about your judgment, Father. You are not the Eternal Father. You listen, report to the Eternal Father and he, then, will decide. I understand: the business with the painting of San Giovannino is still grating with you. Surely a priest has a sacred contempt for money . . . Huh, for the money of others, it seems: but woe to you when it's his!'

'I don't care about the picture. I would have given you everything I own as long as you left me alone. It is your immoral behaviour that makes me angry.'

'Being frankly honest is not immoral,' replied Cat. 'I am honest in that I do everything out in the open!'

'When I speak of immorality I am referring to the part of your conduct undertaken not in the light of day but in the dark, which, before long, will put an unhappy fatherless creature into circulation. Also, I despise your wickedness. I understand your treacherous game: to take revenge on the man who got you in this trouble, you try to ruin his parents by stealing their customers.'

The girl laughed: 'I don't steal anything: I know how to sell better than they do and I sell more than they do. Those two are waiting for the blackbirds to fall into their net, I am going to catch the blackbirds in their nests. It's the same with you lot. You parish priests are sitting here comfortably in your armchairs like employees of the tax office, waiting for the sheep to arrive. The trouble is that at the tax office the sheep have to turn up to be shorn, otherwise their belongings will be seized or they will end up in jail. But no law obliges the sheep to come to *you*.

'Reverend Uncle; if you want to win clients, you have to do what I do: go and find them. New priests like Don Chichi understand this and go into taverns, places of entertainment, factories – to work like workers. So they learn to drink, to play cocincina,[59] to swear, to dance the shake,[60] and to hate the rich employers. Then, maybe, they get married and avoid becoming bureaucrats as you old pastors have become.'

'If you've come here to make sacrilegious speeches,' roared Don Camillo, 'you can leave!'

'I came here to confess. And, if you refuse to confess me, I will go and protest to the Bishop's secretary.'

'Okay,' Don Camillo surrendered, as he strode towards the church.

\*

Cat knelt in the confessional. 'Father, bless me for I have sinned,' this paragon of perfidy began. 'Before telling you my other sins, I will start with what weighs heavily on my heart because I have committed it with malice.'

---

[59] A traditional Italian card game.

[60] A fashionable dance involving a free-form jerkiness of limbs and head and developed from such numbers as *Hippy Hippy Shake*, recorded by the American Chan Romero in 1959, by the Beatles in 1963, and a few months later by the Swinging Blue Jeans.

'Speak, child: I am listening.'

'I took advantage of the naivety of an old country parish priest and made him believe I was expecting a child in order to persuade him to give me the money I needed to set up a small business. Also, this morning, I bandaged a tightly folded sheet around my waist to trick him into buying a refrigerator. Then I told him everything, irreverently taking advantage of the seal of confession, so preventing him from punishing me.'

'Daughter,' Don Camillo replied with tremendous effort, 'the exact same thing happened to me once. Twenty years ago a guy, who one night had ambushed and beaten me, came to confess.[61] I respected the confidentiality of the confessional then, but I gave his backside a boot even so.'

*'Errare humanum est, diabolicum perseverare,'* admonished Cat.[62] 'God would not forgive you a second time.'

'Daughter, I hope with the help of the Lord to be able to strip myself of all my animosity. Are you saying, then, that there were no sinful relations between you and that young man?'

'Neither with him nor with anyone else,' Cat said. 'And I'm ashamed to confess it, but there it is.'

'Do you mean, then, that, despite appearances, you have sound moral principles?'

'No! I don't care about morals. I would say my type has never appeared on my radar, that's all.'

'Daughter, you walk the path of sin. Sin is not only in acts, but also in words, thoughts and omissions. It is a pity to cause scandal as you did. It is not enough that a girl does not materially commit sin. She is forbidden from behaving *as* a sinner. In your particular case you

---

[61] 'A Sin Confessed' in *The Little World of Don Camillo* (Pilot, 2013).

[62] 'To err is human, to persist at it diabolical' is Cat's re-working of the Latin proverb.

have committed a grave sin, which is not that of having deceived your old uncle priest, but that of having blamed an innocent young man for a grave error. What will that boy say when he learns that you have falsely accused him?'

'He already knows,' said Cat. 'He and I talked about it.'

'And what did he say to you?'

'What could he say, poor fool? For him, it's okay.'

'Daughter, does it seem to you right what harm you plan against that poor boy?'

'I don't intend to do him any harm,' Cat protested.

'You want to marry him, child, that is clear. Do you sincerely believe that his faults are such that they deserve such severe punishment?'

'I don't want to marry him to punish him, but because I like him,' said Cat.

'And if you don't want to punish him, why are you hurting his father so much by ruining his business?'

'I work *for* Peppone,' Cat confessed. 'I compete with him, but he supplies me with all the goods I sell.'

Mentally Don Camillo pleaded to Christ for help.

'Lord, help me: this is the first time I have ever confessed the Devil himself. What should I do?'

'Don Camillo,' came the distant voice of Christ, 'you must discover whether the girl is repentant or not. Everything depends upon it.'

'Daughter,' Don Camillo asked Cat, 'are you sorry for what you did?'

'Not even in your dreams,' said the pernicious creature. 'I never regret anything when things turn out well!'

'Lord, did you hear that? *No repentance!*'

'Exactly what I was hoping to hear from her,' replied Christ.

'*Ego te absolvo,*' wailed Don Camillo.

'For penance you will go to the small chapel of San Martino and recite, in front of the sacred image of the Madonna, three *Our Fathers*, *Hail Marys* and *Glorias.* Hurry up, child! Have pity on a poor old country parish priest who is persecuted by the spasmodic desire to cover your face with slaps . . .'

Don Camillo's voice reflected the harsh struggle that raged within and Cat understood this and darted away like a doe. A few moments later, on hearing the girl's station wagon pull away at high revs, Don Camillo left the confessional and went to vent the sadness of his soul with Christ above the High Altar:

'Lord, if these young people make fun of the most sacred things and they are the up-and-coming generation, who will ever swell the congregations of your Church?'

'Don Camillo,' replied Christ calmly. 'Do not let yourself be influenced by the cinema and newspapers. It is not the case that God needs men: it is men who need God. Light continues to exist when the world is blind. It is written, "They have eyes but do not see."[63] The light is not extinguished if the eyes do not see it.'

'Lord, why is the girl acting like this? Why, when to get what she wants could so easily be done? Whatever it is she wants she has to extort it, steal it, rob it.'

'Because, like many young people, she is dominated by the fear of being judged virtuous. It is the new hypocrisy: at one time the dishonest would try desperately to be considered virtuous. Today, it is desperately unfashionable among young people to be seen to be pure.'

Don Camillo spread his arms wide: 'Lord, what is this mad wind of change? Does it mean that the circle is about

---

[63] *Ezekiel,* 12:2.

to close and the world is racing towards rapid self-destruction?'

'Don Camillo, why such pessimism? If you are right, would not that make my sacrifice pointless? Would not my mission among mankind have failed because man's wickedness has proven stronger than the goodness of God?'

'No, Lord, all that I meant was that today people only believe in what they can see and touch. But there are fundamental things that cannot be seen or touched: love, goodness, pity, honesty, modesty, hope. And faith. Things that life cannot be lived without. This is the self-destruction I was talking about. Man, it seems to me, is destroying all his spiritual patrimony. The only true wealth that he, in thousands of centuries, has accumulated. One day, not far off, he will find himself exactly like the prehistoric brute that lived in caves. The caves will be tall skyscrapers filled with marvellous machines, but the spirit of man will be that of the caveman.

'Lord, people fear terrifying weapons of mass destruction, but I'm beginning to think that only these will restore man's true wealth. Because they will destroy everything and, freed from the slavery of earthly goods, man will seek God again. And he will find him and rebuild his spiritual heritage, which today he is laying waste.

'Lord, what should I do?'

*Il Cristo* smiled.

'What the farmer does when the river overwhelms its banks and invades the fields: the seed must be saved. When the river returns to its bed, the earth will re-emerge and the sun will dry it out. If the farmer has saved the seed, he will be able to sow it on the land made even more fertile by the silt of the river, and the seed *will bear fruit*, and the swollen and turgid ears of corn will give men bread, life and hope.

'The seed must be saved: faith. Don Camillo, we must help the faithful to keep their faith intact. A spiritual desert is spreading more and more every day; every day new souls perish because their faith abandons them.

'Every day more men of many words and no faith are destroying our spiritual heritage and the faith of others – men of all races, of all backgrounds, of all cultures.'

'Lord,' asked Don Camillo, 'are you suggesting perhaps that the Devil has become so cunning that he can even sometimes disguise himself as a priest?'

'Don Camillo!' Christ reproached him, smiling. 'I only just survived the Vatican Council, do you want to embroil me in yet more trouble?'

'Forgive me,' apologised Don Camillo. 'My head is an empty vessel. *What should I do?*'

'You might sign that contract for the fridge.'

'Lord, do you too deal with household appliances now?'

'Not I, Don Camillo, but that poor girl does.'

Don Camillo returned to the dining room, more confused than ever: he couldn't believe that Christ had called Cat 'that poor girl'. Anyway, he signed the contract but perhaps from the smoke from the fireplace, perhaps from the demonic sulphur fumes left in Cat's wake, he struggled because his eyes filled with tears.

*Remembering a November Long Ago*

WHEN ONE FINE day Don Chichi unaccountably disappeared, Don Camillo alerted the Curia to the fact and the reply came that they knew all about it and he should not worry.

Don Camillo didn't. If anything, only the *presence* of the little priest could ever worry him, never his absence. So he thought no more about it, but four months later, on a visit to the city, he met a priest from a parish in the mountains, a former seminary friend, and learned that immediately after his disappearance Don Chichi had been assigned to the small parish of Rughino, the one selected earlier as a punishment for Don Camillo.

'He is a very dynamic young man,' the mountain priest told him. 'You know that Rughino is a depopulated franchise because the good men and women of the village are all now working abroad, leaving only old people to look after their children and their houses. It is only three kilometres from Lagarello, my village, but, until a few weeks ago, to get from Rughino to Lagarello you had to travel a lot more kilometres, because there was no direct road and only a tiny bridge – it's a story as old as the cuckoo up there. Well, these old men, assisted by the old women of the village and the older boys, worked like hell and now, finally, they have a direct route in. All thanks to your Don Chichi who launched the initiative, researched and organised the work, even taking up shovel and pickaxe and working on it himself.'

'I am pleased to hear it,' said Don Camillo. 'It must be very satisfying to Don Chichi.'

'Yes . . . and no,' replied the priest laughing. 'In fact, now that there is a road, the people of Rughino, rather than having to put up with his socialist sermonising every Sunday, prefer to make the round trip of six kilometres to attend Mass with me. But I do believe that if other villages play their cards right, Don Chichi will go on to fix the entire network of mountain roads.'

This was undoubtedly a good idea, but the men in charge at the Curia did not see it as the way forward and, so, some time later, Don Camillo was summoned to an audience with the Bishop himself.

'Our Don Francesco,' explained the Bishop, 'is now completely recovered. He had a spiritual crisis and we sent him to Rughino for treatment, where this fine young man did great things, managing to convince his parishioners to build a road they had aspired to for centuries. We, together with the civil authorities, inaugurated it and the Signor Prefect was enthusiastic in his praise of Don Francesco's work on it.'

'I am delighted!' exclaimed Don Camillo. 'It is a triumph indeed.'

'A stupendous *double* victory,' the Bishop pointed out. 'Thanks to the connection between Rughino and Lagarello, we have been able to eliminate a useless parish like that of Rughino. As a result, once Don Francesco has accomplished his mission, he will again be available and can return to help you, Don Camillo.'

'Truly,' Don Camillo respectfully averred, 'we have no problems with roads . . .'

'Don Camillo,' the Bishop interrupted him, 'your long experience combined with Don Francesco's youthful enthusiasm will give fresh impetus to your parish. Indeed, with regard to this, we wish to advise you to find a more . . . convenient accommodation for that young niece of yours who, if you will allow me to say so, does not seem the kind of girl ideally suited to hanging about in a presbytery.'

'That young girl,' explained Don Camillo, who was beginning to break out in a sweat, 'has always been a guest of the sexton's family. Moreover, for several months now, she has settled in another part of the municipality.'

'So we have been told,' said the Bishop. 'We just wanted to advise you to keep her as far away from the presbytery as possible. For obvious reasons. Do you understand me?'

'No, Excellency . . .' replied Don Camillo.

'Don Camillo,' the young Bishop was getting impatient, 'apart from everything else, the girl's particular political position makes her presence in a presbytery highly inappropriate!'

'I understand *that*, Excellency,' said Don Camillo with some difficulty, 'but it is not the girl's fault that her father was murdered by the communists.'

'No: but our job is not to keep hatred alive, but to drive it out. The presence of that girl is an obstacle to the relaxation of old enmities, and living testimony to a past that must now be forgotten. When all's said and done, she is hardly the sort of girl that would fit well in the ranks of the "Daughters of Mary"!'

'That is certainly not really her thing,' Don Camillo granted, 'but she is a modern girl – exuberant, but honest.'

'Honesty!' the Bishop exclaimed shaking his head, 'even fire is honest, but it is better not to put it close to petrol.'

*

Don Chichi resurfaced a few days later and surprised Don Camillo, who was busy with some design work: he was in fact working on a sign to be displayed on the church door and he had already drawn the following, in capital letters:

MASS IN MEMORY OF THE SOULS . . .

The paint brush was difficult to guide with his massive hands, and Don Chichi offered to help:

'May I, Father?'

'Thank you,' replied Don Camillo, continuing his work, 'but I learned from His Excellency the Bishop that you are recovering from a serious illness and I would not like you to get tired.'

'Don't worry about me!' Don Chichi exclaimed laughing and relieving Don Camillo's hand of the brush he set to work. 'My illness is a far distant thing!'

But in fact it was very close and it entered the room at that very moment.

'Good morning, Very Reverend Uncle!'

Hearing Cat's voice, Don Chichi went pale and leapt to his feet.

'Oh, Don Francesco!' exclaimed Cat in a diabolically angelic voice. 'You're finally back! If you only knew how much we need you here!'

'This'll be worth seeing!' Don Camillo growled grimly. 'Anyway, nobody needs *you* here! Be off with you!'

'I brought your refrigerator,' Cat said in a tearful voice.

'I don't need any refrigerators!' Don Camillo shouted. 'I'll pay for it as agreed, but you take it home and keep it for that gormless one that will marry you.'

'Marry me!' Cat protested, blushing adorably. 'I'm not thinking of getting married at all. In fact, I have decided to become a nun.'

'You *are* crazy!' Don Camillo shouted.

'Does one have to be crazy,' the girl asked, 'to feel the need to pray for the salvation of a humanity that has lost the fear of God?'

Cat's shamelessness made Don Camillo lose his temper: 'I don't care!' he shouted. 'Go away and give me no more trouble. The Bishop does not want you to hang about the presbytery.'

'And why on earth not?'

'Why? He doesn't like you!'

'His Excellency doesn't know me,' Cat said with an angelic smile, 'but the good Lord does and *he* likes me. Reverend Uncle, why do you want to extinguish the holy flame of faith and banish me?'

Don Chichi, who, meanwhile, had returned to work with Don Camillo's paint brush, said: 'Reverend, so far you have written: "Mass in memory of the souls . . ." How should it go on?'

'Mass in memory of the souls of the Hungarian dead,' mumbled Don Camillo. 'In three days, it will be the tenth anniversary of the Soviet repression of the Hungarian uprisings.'[64]

Don Chichi put down his brush and shook his head.

'Don Camillo,' he said in a voice that trembled with indignation, aroused by the parish priest's barbaric treatment of the small and fragile Cat, 'you have lost touch with the world. All the press, newspapers and magazines, while remembering those tragic days in Budapest, now

---

[64] The Hungarian Uprising of 1956 began as a student demonstration. It was the first major threat to Soviet control after Russian forces drove Nazi Germany from the territory at the end of World War II.

rightly place emphasis not on Soviet repression but on the rebirth of Hungary.'

'Let's raise a glass of beer to born again Hungary!' shouted Don Camillo. 'None of those poor people crushed under the tracks of the Soviet Panzers have been born again. Nor have those poor boys who were kept in prison until the age of eighteen so that they could be handed over to the executioner and hanged "legally"!'[65]

'Don Camillo,' said Don Chichi in a firm voice. 'All this belongs to the past. Let *God* think of the dead. We must think of the living, because dialogue can only be entered into with the living. Why rekindle past hatred? Why poison the souls of young people who don't even know what happened ten years ago in Budapest? The Church is about love, not hate. The Church says: "Love your enemy."'

Don Camillo's ears had turned red, he was at boiling point.

'It is almost 2,000 years since Jesus was crucified,' he said, 'and still today the Church represents him nailed to the cross. Not to make his enemies hate, but to remember his self-sacrifice for the *love* of his people!'

Cat intervened: 'Reverend Uncle: you must concede that the New Liturgy tends increasingly to exclude representations of 'the martyred Christ' in churches, and that sacred art increasingly disavows the crude realism of the crucifixion. Don Francesco's understanding of this is important, Jesus suffered as a man and as a man he died for the *love* of mankind. Of all mankind, especially those

---

[65] 'Let's raise a glass of beer . . .' is an ironic reference to the infamous execution of thirteen Hungarian generals after Austria persuaded Russia to invade Hungary during its War of Independence (1848–9). The Austrians celebrated the execution of the thirteen patriots – martyrs for defending the cause of freedom and independence for their people – by clinking their beer glasses, before subjecting the country to brutal martial law with Russia's help.

who crucified him and whom he forgave when he was dying on the cross. By continuing to represent the martyrdom of Christ in a ferociously realistic way, like you might find in a wax museum, will only fan the flames of hatred for those who crucified him. Reverend Uncle, does it mean nothing to you that the Council Fathers have solemnly exonerated the poor Jews, who, for nineteen centuries have been accused of deicide? So, returning to our discourse, why remember the dead of Hungary and not those of the St Bartholomew's Day Massacre[66] or those of the French Revolution?'

'Because their executioners are dead,' Don Camillo shouted. 'They are not keeping alive a regime that threatens the freedom of the whole world *today*! Because Cardinal Mindszenty,[67] who represents the oppressed Church, the Church of silence, is still a prisoner of these same executioners.'

Don Chichi smiled: 'The Church of silence does not exist, because God is everywhere and speaks to all those who want to listen to him.'

'So, then,' asked Don Camillo who was by this time dripping with sweat, 'what use is the Church? Why did the Son of God need to come down to earth as a man and suffer and die as a man . . .? Anyway, you just write what I told you. I'll take care of the rest!'

Don Chichi, seeing the parish priest pouring sweat and anger from every pore, chuckled his amusement:

'Don Camillo, I see that there is another sign already painted. I think you want to announce a solemn Mass for November 4th?'

---

[66] The massacre of Huguenots by a Catholic mob in 1572.
[67] The post-war Leader of the Catholic Church in Hungary and personification of uncompromising opposition to fascism and communism in his country.

'Sure! You don't want me to neglect Victory Day!'[68]

'Victory!' Don Chichi said with bitter disgust. 'An ill-omened date to be celebrated. There are no winners in wars. In wars most everyone loses; only evil wins. It's not a victory to remember.'

'I want to remember the dead of that war,' explained Don Camillo.

'The same old story. The dead as usual!' Don Chichi chimed sarcastically. 'It makes the Church look like an undertaker who spends his time in the cemetery of history unearthing limed bones and displaying them in the shop window. Father, what is this cadaverous religion of yours with its dismal slogans? "We were born to suffer", "Remember that you must die" ... No! Remember you must *live*! This is the meaning of Jesus's revelation; this is the meaning of the Resurrection.'

Cat looked admiringly at Don Chichi with ecstasy in her eyes.

'Don Francesco,' she said, apparently much moved, 'this is a very profound observation. This is the reason why young people distance themselves from the Church – because it speaks only of death, teaches only how to die and not how to live. Because it denies man his rights and charges him only with *duties*. Because it does not admit happiness on earth, but promises heaven only in Heaven, while those who live according to God's law and understand the meaning of social solidarity[69] can in fact find happiness on earth too, improving life for others. It is an

---

[68] November 4 is National Unity and Armed Forces Day, commemorating victory in World War I, an event recognised as completing the process of the unification of Italy. But, as Don Camillo knows only too well, November 4 was also the day in 1956 when 200,000 Russian troops attacked the anti-Soviet protesters in Budapest.

[69] 'Social solidarity' means the rising sense of the interdependence of people within society, which encourages people to feel that they can enhance the lives of others.

inhuman Church that forces its priests to withdraw from life and ignore its essential problems. Its priests are black crows for whom the happy, innocent chirping of multi-coloured birds singing praises to the Lord with their throats wide open, is a mortal sin.'

'Cat,' screamed Don Camillo, 'don't talk nonsense!'

'What I say is true, Reverend Uncle. What about that sweet "Sister Sorriso" who sings the praises of the Lord with her guitar, moving the hearts of millions of people who listen to her, hasn't she been forced to abandon the nun's habit and leave the Order? Didn't the black crows chase her away?[70] Don Francesco, would you ever have done such a thing? You, a young, intelligent, cultured, modern priest, would you have prevented that nightingale from happily singing the praises of the Lord?'

'Never!' Don Chichi exclaimed. So moved was he that he was amazed to see that although she was wearing a soft, thick wool overcoat, Cat had sprouted two white wings from her shoulder blades.

'Don Francesco,' continued Cat's caressing voice, 'leave the dead to the old parish priest: it is all that remains of a long and useless life. Give him the signs. Some old fossils will come to the Mass on November 4th: but there'll be none there for the Hungarian dead. And, then, this old parish priest will understand that now is not the time for death but for life! If it's any comfort to

---

[70] 'Sister Sorriso', dubbed 'the Singing Nun', was baptised Jeanne Deckers. She entered the Dominican convent at Fichermont in Belgium in 1959. Highly appreciated by her sisters for her musical skills, a record company became interested and, in 1962, she released her first album, *Dominique*, which became a huge hit around the world. In 1966 she left the convent, but her second album was not a success and although remaining a Christian and dedicating herself to good works, she committed suicide at 52 with a French friend, Annie Pescher, with whom she'd been living in a small apartment near Brussels.

you, Don Francesco, I am fully, enthusiastically, devotedly in complete agreement with you . . .'

'Indeed it is!' exclaimed Don Chichi, getting back to work.

Cat turned to Don Camillo, who was still staring at his hopelessly shameless niece:

'Rev, where do I put the fridge?'

'I don't care,' roared Don Camillo.

'I'll have it put in your room. Instead of getting into bed every night, you should shut yourself in it, it'll preserve you much better. The traditionalist Church always needs well-preserved corpses.'

Don Chichi sniggered his amusement. Don Camillo went to supervise the unloading of the refrigerator. Then, when Cat was about to get back into her station wagon, he grabbed her by the shoulder.

'Mischief-maker,' he said softly. 'What have you got up your sleeve now for Don Chichi?'

'To sell him a fridge,' Cat replied simply.

'Stay away from here! Don't get me in trouble with the Bishop!'

'Oh, don't worry, Rev. I'll sell the Bishop a fridge too,' the wretch giggled.

'Don't say such things even as a joke!'

'Why shouldn't I? I sold one to the Bishop's secretary to give to his sister. Why can't I sell one to the Bishop too?'

As Cat flew off in her Giardiniera station wagon, Don Camillo turned his eyes to heaven:

'Jesus,' he said, 'what do you make of all this?'

'I cannot say,' came the distant voice of Christ. 'I do not deal with refrigerators.'

*

The evening before the Mass for Hungary's dead, Don Camillo received a letter in which the Bishop's secretary, on behalf of his Excellency, expressed his disapproval of the politically inappropriate initiative. He also received a box containing, a large, well-framed colour photo of Cardinal Mindszenty, accompanied by a note: 'Compliments of the Cat Appliances Company'.

Don Camillo threw the letter in the fireplace and went to hang the portrait under the sign that now dominated the main doorway of the church. Don Chichi watched him do it. Then, when Don Camillo came back down the ladder, he shook his head and said, looking at the portrait of the Hungarian cardinal:

'Why this desire for martyrdom? Couldn't he too have found a way of living with authority in his country?'

'We must pity him,' replied Don Camillo. 'He was led astray by that other guy who got himself nailed to the cross. Typical extremists.'

*

It was a strange Mass because, except for the few old ladies who always jump on the bandwagon when a sacred office is celebrated, none of the clericals were present, which goes to show how Catholics in those days disapproved of any initiative deemed to run counter to dialogue and detente.

Nevertheless, all the socialists were present, intending to demonstrate that, although Marxist to the core, they thought very differently from the communists. And Peppone and his gang came, intending to demonstrate that, although communist, they were of a completely different kind of communist to the Soviet and Chinese extremists.

Don Camillo said a few words:

'Brothers, there is much dialogue between those on opposite shores. These souls that today we remember stand on the shore of death and speak to us who stand on the shore of life. Let us listen to what they ask of us and in our hearts we will find the right response. Amen.'

The Great River was swollen with muddy water and all those who, coming out of Mass, went to the bank to see if the level increased or decreased, remembered Don Camillo's simple words. Someone even saw on the water, towards the opposite bank, red flashes as of blood.

*The Little Boy Who Saw Angels*

A THIN, TATTERED BOY was walking barefoot in the mud along the Stradaccia and on his slender shoulders he carried a sack, which seemed very heavy. The silence, the bare black trees emerging like ghosts through the icy fog and then plunging back into it, made the scene seem part of another century, perhaps that of Cosette, the orphaned child in *Les Misérables.*

Don Chichi caught up with the boy, and brought his car to a halt.

'Where are you going?' he asked, opening wide the car door.

'To Filotti's farm,' replied the boy, putting down his sack by the roadside ditch.

'That's a long way to go and it's cold.'

'No matter,' the boy replied with a shy smile. 'I like walking in the fog because I can talk to the angels.'

Don Chichi loaded the boy and his sack into his car.

'It's a bit heavy,' the boy explained. 'They are potatoes: the little ones that the farmers set aside for the pigs. I earned them with a few jobs and they even gave me a pumpkin. Pumpkin, cooked under the ashes, is sweet and my younger brothers really like it.'

'Are there many of you?'

'Four sisters and four brothers. But Cetti, my older sister, is sixteen already: she works in the city.'

'What does your father do?'

'We live alone with our mother: we have no father.'

'So how do you manage to get by?'

'No idea, Reverend. The Lord knows, and he's the only one who needs to know. You should turn right now: we live in that yellow house over there.'

It was more a miserable outbuilding than a house. The one large room, divided in two by a rickety wall of crates for the grape harvest, served as an encampment for eight children and a woman whose poor clothes barely made her shapely thirty-year-old body respectable. For beds there were pallets, for furniture old packing cases. The only luxury was a very battered stove, which looked like it had been picked up in a scrap yard.

Don Chichi was moved to indignation by the injustice of the scene and said that it was not right that anyone should live in such a hovel.

'Father,' replied the woman 'we are not complaining. It would be enough if the owner repaired the leaky roof and made a window in that wall, because it always seems like night in here.'

Filotti's house was not far away and Don Chichi left, determined to take it up with him. He found the old farmer in the stable and didn't hold back for a second:

'Don't you think it is your duty to do something for those people?'

Filotti spread his arms wide: 'What can I do, Reverend? I went to the Mayor, I went to the *carabinieri* and they told me to sort it out myself. The roof needs replacing, but I'll have to wait for the Spring to do it.'

'Replace the roof?' Don Chichi screamed in horror. 'You have an obligation to repair it *now*, to make some windows, install sanitary facilities, make that shack habitable!'

Filotti looked at him in amazement.

'That filthy girl with her tribe came here one night from God knows where. I found them camped in my woodshed the next morning. When I tried to get them out, the woman began to scream that they were poor flood victims and when the children began sobbing as if I was gutting them, I let them stay.'

'And now you don't feel it is your duty to help those poor people even after the fury of the Great River has stripped them of everything? Haven't you seen the horrendous desolation of the flooded areas on television?'

'Yes,' the old man roared, 'but the floods occurred between October and November, while those wretches arrived here in June.'

'Misery is misery in all months of the year!' Don Chichi insisted. 'Here is a poor widow with nine children and society has specific obligations towards these poor things.'

'I am not society,' shouted Filotti. 'I am only a very small part of society and it is not right that all society's obligations weigh exclusively on me. They've taken over my shed, ransacked my garden, robbed my chicken coop, burned my wood, milked my cows, stolen my linen and you tell me I should have mended their roof and made their house comfortable? I work hard to make a living and keep the farm going for me, my wife and daughter!'

'That poor widow is young and robust,' observed Don Chichi, 'why don't you give her a way to earn something?'

Filotti let out a scream: 'Reverend, this summer I employed her and her older children for the tomato harvest. I paid them the going rate and those no-goods denounced me as an exploiter of widows and orphans: they had a labour inspector swoop in here and, between fines and the rest, they cost me a cow!

'And it was lucky that was all I lost. Had I not reported her arbitrary occupation of the woodshed to the *carabinieri* and filled in a lot of stamped paper, the inspectorate would have eaten me alive, saying that the woman "was a qualified salary worker residing on the farm without a contract, booklets, insurance, stamps . . ." and other rubbish!'

'It is right that the State should protect workers' rights!' Don Chichi said.

'And we, the employers . . . Are we, as the cry of old goes, "to live like vagabonds scratching our bellies"?'

'Christ said: woe to he who denies the worker just wages.'

'I know!' screamed the old farmer, 'but he was talking about *mercede* [fair remuneration], not "Mercedes". Workers today are no longer satisfied with the Millecento (1100) or the Seicento (600), they believe they are entitled to the Mercedes!'

Don Chichi was getting angry. 'Shame!' he exclaimed. 'Don't joke about the misery of the working class!'

Then he left because Filotti had a pitchfork in his hands and seemed willing to introduce it by way of a concluding argument in his impassioned speech.

\*

Don Chichi felt inspired with a holy mission and after describing the terrible misery of the widow and her orphans to Don Camillo, he said:

'Reverend Father, we have conflicting ideas about many things, but on this we must surely agree: we must help those less fortunate than ourselves in any way we can.'

'Don Francesco,' replied Don Camillo, 'I do have something I'd like to say about this business, but I will keep it to myself. That woman has nine children: we can accept the youngest of them in our parish nursery, clothing and feeding them for free.'

'That at least is something, Don Camillo, but I cannot stop thinking about that little boy walking barefoot in the mud, talking to the angels. He must be a sensitive and intelligent child; let's have him live here with us: he can serve us as altar boy, distribute the newsletters and circulars to the parishioners and keep the church in order. We will clothe him, feed him and pay him what we can. Father, he told me a wonderful thing when I asked him how they managed to live: "I don't know, only the Lord knows, but for us it is enough that he knows." That poor boy's misery and hunger and hardship have not poisoned his heart, as so often happens. His misery has, indeed, given him faith in the Lord and enabled him to commune with angels. If we help him we will nourish a vocation in him, which will probably make him into a worthy priest. A true priest of the Church of the Poor, because he was born into and lived in poverty. Don Camillo, remember Matthew, where Jesus identifies with the poor: "I was hungry and you gave me meat . . . I was naked and you clothed me . . . Inasmuch as you have done this unto one of the least of my brethren, you have done it also unto me . . ." Don Camillo, remember Matthew and also Mark, Luke and John about what Christ said: "Whoever welcomes a boy like this in my name welcomes me . . ."'

Don Camillo did remember Matthew, Mark, Luke and John, but the rest of it he consigned to oblivion.

*

Marcellino proved to be all that Don Chichi had predicted: a perfect altar boy, a heavenly voice in the choir. He wandered around the presbytery all day, always ready to jump on his bicycle to run an errand. He was kind of face and appealed to people. On Sundays, when he took the collection, his smile made even the stingiest dig in their pockets. At other times he spent long hours in church talking to angels or reading the books that Don Chichi lent him.

Then, one Sunday morning after Mass, Marcellino approached Don Camillo in the sacristy and, handing him the small collection box full of coins, said in a sweet, hushed voice:

'Father, we should talk about the percentage.'

'What percentage?'

'Mine,' answered Marcellino with a smile. 'I collect the money and am entitled to a percentage. I should be entitled to fifty percent but I would settle for forty-five.'

Don Camillo look at him puzzled.

'Marcellino,' he asked the boy, 'did the angels tell you this?'

'No, Father,' the boy replied. 'When I'm with the angels we talk about other things.'

'Well that changes things,' said Don Camillo, booting him out with a kick in the pants. 'Don't bother to be seen here again.'

Marcellino vanished without a word, but the afternoon saw the arrival of his mother. She was in full combat gear and proceeded in the classic wedge formation, with the smallest child in her arms, two little girls of five and four years clinging to her hips and Marcellino's four brothers behind her. Her invasion of the presbytery began with a dramatic gesture indicating these unhappy creatures and the following words:

'Reverend, you would ruin me by sacking Marcellino right now, for my Cetti has lost her place in the city too!'

Don Camillo stepped in, demanding precision:

'She has not lost *her* place: for the umpteenth time she has been fired and now she has to *change* jobs!'

The sacred claims for workers' rights were all the rage at the time. The principle was: 'The employer is always wrong.' So there were people, like the good Concettina, known as Cetti, who got hired and, after a while, behaved in such a way as to get fired. Then, immediately she would run to her Trades Union denouncing her ex-boss for a variety of rights violations. Immediately, efficient officials would then rain down on the ex-boss, confiscate his books, search his bed, and inevitably find violations which were punished with tremendous fines and adequate compensation for the defrauded worker. It was a very ingenious system for not working and making money anyway and, more importantly, doing down the hated employer.

La Cetti had played the game fourteen times already, always successfully. Then, of course, her reputation had spread and no one wanted to see her at their door anymore.

'She is not to blame, poor thing, if she has always had dishonest employers,' her mother protested. 'You cannot put Marcellino on the street: I am a poor widow with nine dependent children!'

'No one but you has brought them into the world!' replied Don Camillo.

'Reverend!' the woman screamed indignantly, 'I'm not one of those sluts who go on the Pill.'

'I know,' Don Camillo replied calmly. 'You are a slut who has given birth to nine children without taking a husband and now you expect society to support them for you. Be gone!'

The woman left screaming, accompanied by the screams and sobs of seven of her children. Don Chichi, who had been present at the scene, protested heartily:

'Don Camillo, this is a case of a poor mother defending her dependents.'

'She is not a poor mother and she does not defend her children, she lets herself be defended by them. Too many people give birth to herds of children just to hide behind their hunger and their suffering. It's the worst exploitation.'

'But is it the fault of the children?'

'I do not blame the children,' Don Camillo affirmed. 'I simply say that one should not encourage or even applaud – as is too often the case today – their wretched parents. But we must prevent them from transforming their children into so many enemies of society.'

\*

Two days later a union official turned up at the presbytery. He accused Don Camillo of having employed a thirteen-year-old boy and making him work during the holidays.

'Serving the Mass is not a job,' explained Don Camillo. 'It is voluntary participation in a religious rite.'

'Any business that produces something involves work,' the official said.

'The Mass does not produce anything concrete or tangible, it is a spiritual manifestation.'

The official laughed.

'Neither does a theatre produce anything tangible: it provides entertainment and workers in the theatre have specific rights enshrined in the law. In the context of Trades Unions, the Mass can be considered a spectacle. The boy played an important part in it and should have been regularly paid. He is entitled to extra pay for holiday work, compensation for dismissal and a redundancy payment. He also had to have employment certification, health insurance because he worked in a public place, and national insurance contributions should have been paid for him.'

The Union official was, of course, a tough guy, accustomed to seeing employers tremble with terror: he was surprised, therefore, when Don Camillo said to him, pointing to the door: 'I understand your case: I will pray for you.'

'You are wrong, Reverend, if you think you can get away with this!' the official shouted.

'*Errare humanum est*,' answered Don Camillo, slamming the door in his face.

*

Naturally, in the newssheet posted on the People's Palace there appeared a fierce attack on Don Camillo, who preached love for his neighbour and then kicked out a poor boy and denied him just pay.

Peppone was not satisfied with the attack, but hired Marcellino as a boy in his home appliance shop: and did so observing all the rules established by the unions. And he found a way to let the whole region know about it.

Marcellino responded in such an exemplary way that one day Don Chichi pointed this out to Don Camillo:

'Father, I was right. Marcellino is a good boy and you failed to understand him.'

'Maybe so,' Don Camillo admitted, 'who knows, maybe he continues to see angels even among the refrigerators and washing machines?'

In truth, Marcellino no longer saw angels but, as he possessed great sensitivity, he saw, cunningly hidden inside a washing machine, a certain register marked "confidential" and took it home to study it. Then he let Peppone know that, if he wasn't paid 150,000 lire, he would take that register to the district attorney for direct taxes, who made a hobby of investigating confidential and secret accounting registers.

Peppone certainly couldn't be seen to be accused of defrauding the working class and he himself brought the money to Marcellino's mother and personally retrieved the register.

He found the poor woman in bed, about to give society her tenth orphan.

*Another Tale of the Old River*

A T 11 P.M. ONE FGRIDAY, Cat received a phone call. It was Tota, one of the Scorpioni girls:

'Cat, what the hell did you do to Ringo?'

'He kept bothering me and I told him to go to hell,' explained Cat laughing.

'Ringo is wild and vows revenge. He knows who all Venom's boys are and where they live: he's coming with the gang to fish them out one by one and he'll cut them into small pieces. ETD is tomorrow morning; I'll call you as soon as they leave.'

Cat knew what a beast Ringo became when he forgot he was a human: without losing a second she ran to warn the leaders of Venom's gang. The three rural longhairs shrugged in dismay and then stammered that they didn't know what to do.

'Raise the alarm with all the boys immediately. Meet me at the Macchione at seven tomorrow morning.'

Before returning home, Cat went to Peppone's and knocked on his door. Peppone was getting ready to go to bed and he said plainly that, at that hour, he didn't want to hear about refrigerators.

'In fact, I'm not talking about that,' explained Cat. 'Give me Venom's black leather jacket and help me load the motorbike on the Giardinetta. Tomorrow morning the Scorpioni are coming down here to cause mayhem.'

Peppone's ears immediately pricked up:

'Those hooligans again? I'll warn the *carabinieri* and have them all rounded up!'

'Don't bother,' Cat replied. 'It's our business. Help me sort out the stuff and go to bed and dream about Stalin. Maybe he'll give you some good numbers to play in the Lotto.'

At seven o'clock the following morning, the gang of rural longhairs were all gathered in the deserted hollow of the Macchione. Without Venom, they felt like kids. The morning was cold and the bad boys had lit a big brush fire to warm themselves: but fear is a kind of cold that's hard to get out of your bones. They discussed the situation and, after an hour, the decision was made: to jump in the saddle and cut out for the mountains. But just at that moment they heard the powerful and well-known roar of a motorcycle approaching and jumped to their feet. Cat was swallowed up by Venom's leather jacket and looked even tinier on top of the big motorcycle: but everyone thrilled to her arrival.

'They've left,' said Cat. 'Thirty, as we are. In order not to attract attention they'll be travelling by different roads. Then come together halfway along the Stradaccia. We'll wait for them stationed behind the embankment and, as they arrive, we'll comb them. Let's motor!'

Cat, already a thrilling sight when seen from the front, reversed with a reckless spin-out across the road, and when the longhairs saw on her shoulders the white skull and the word 'Venom', all without exception started to paw their engines and jumped in the saddle ready to split the world.

The tip-off was accurate and the first Scorpioni to arrive at the Stradaccia were quickly overwhelmed. Then, when the rest came, the battle got tough. Cat directed strategy from the top of the embankment, which she already knew was reinforced by steel mesh Gabion baskets of stone on the floodplain side. Seeing that her gang was losing its bite, she summoned four rural longhairs up onto the embankment and handed each a pair of wire cutters:

'Quick, cut the mesh baskets: it's time to throw the artillery on the field.'

This brought matters to a new and worrying level, because the four rural longhairs obeyed Cat as the Old Guard once obeyed Napoleon.

'Guys,' Cat screamed, as she saw stones in the hands of her gunners as big as melons, 'aim at that ball-like extremity between their shoulders, the one you see covered with long, lice-infested hair!'

'Cat,' Ringo screamed from below, 'if I get hold of you, I'll throw you!'

A large stone creased his pumpkin; three fingers further and the Scorpion leader would have wound up dead. The young man paled:

'Ah, you shoot to kill!' he shouted. 'It means we're going to get serious too. Guys, *iron out*!'

The Scorpios drew the knives out of their sheaths. The Rurals jumped back and, after a moment, each was holding a piece of motorcycle chain. In another minute, there'd have been an obituary to compose: the two gangs were ranged against each other and all the longhairs were silent, motionless, ready for a massacre, waiting for the order from Ringo and Cat respectively to attack.

But the order did not come: in the silence a thunderous voice exploded:

'Throw all that junk in your hands to the ground!'

Peppone and his henchmen had appeared on the embankment, their shotguns levelled.

'Good thinking,' laughed Ringo. 'To prevent a brawl, you're going to kill us? Don't make me laugh.'

'Who wants to kill you?' replied Peppone. 'Our cartridges are loaded with grains of salt. Lead gives better results, but I assure you that a shot of salt has a certain . . . effect. So drop all that junk or we'll get on with it!'

At that moment Don Camillo also appeared on the bank.

'Reverend, get out of the way,' Peppone shouted. 'You are not involved!'

'I have good reason to be here. When any of these cretins die they will need Extreme Unction.'

'Arms down!' Peppone repeated. But he was worried: he knew that he would never find the courage to shoot.

Cat noticed: 'Instead of talking, shoot!' she yelled, snatching the shotgun from Peppone's hand and pointing it at Ringo.

The blood drained from the young man's face and he dropped his knife.

'Take the gun off her!' he screamed. 'She'll shoot for sure. I know that well enough. If she didn't have it in her, I wouldn't have chosen her to be my girl!'

Cat laughed wickedly:

'You lousy worm! I was never your girl and I never will be. I'll be whose girl *I* want to be!'

It was Ringo's turn to laugh: 'You brat: when a Scorpio chooses a girl for himself, she must be his or no one else's. That bastard with the death's head on his back dared to set his sights on my girl and he, along with all his band of yokels, will have to pay.'

'I venture to say that it was *she* who set her eyes on *him*,' Don Camillo corrected Ringo. 'However, that has nothing to do with your punitive expedition.'

'It absolutely does have to do with it!' Ringo screamed. 'Whoever offends a Scorpio offends all Scorpioni. That is our law. In any case, why hasn't that coward shown his face?'

'He's got other things to do. And I'm enough to sort out a lousy guy like you!' yelled Cat and pulled the trigger.

Don Camillo knew it would end like this, so he was ready. Swiftly, his hand came down on the barrel of the gun and the saline discharge spattered the ground between the two gangs with a sizzle. All the longhairs had by this time thrown down their weapons and Smilzo went down from the Embankment to pick up the various knives and chains.

'And so,' said Don Camillo to Ringo, 'you see yourselves as protestors, even when you break each other's bones. Is that what you mean by being a rebel?'

'Sure,' Ringo replied. 'It's as good a way as any to disrespect your rotten system and replace it with ours.'

'And what would this new system be?' inquired Peppone. 'The rule of the strongest. The law of nature. The weak must be eliminated?'

'I understand perfectly,' said Don Camillo derisively, 'I read yesterday that an eighteen-year-old Russian boy killed his aged parents because they annoyed him.'

'That's not our way,' Ringo corrected him. 'For us the old are already dead. They are corpses on shore leave. Even *your* law forbids killing the dead. Desecrating a corpse.'

'And when does "old age" begin exactly?' asked Peppone, who was building up steam.

'The putrefaction begins after forty,' Ringo explained.

'You are the ones who'll be rotting,' shouted Don Camillo. 'You and other lice like you. You're cowards who waste your lives on chatter and song. Who shirk all responsibility and live by begging or stealing your rotten parents' loose change.'

Ringo took a step forward: 'Reverend, I have no respect for your greasy black petticoat or your old age. If

I don't front up and slap you down, it's only because I pity you.'

'Pity is an honourable sentiment which, unfortunately, does not stick in my craw,' replied Don Camillo, now trundling quickly down the bank.

Ringo was practised at boxing, judo and karate, but the first two flutters caught him on the ear and made him forget everything, even his home address. Grabbing him with both hands by his long mane, Don Camillo loaded the youngster on his right shoulder ready to launch him into the stratosphere, but Cat's voice stopped him.

'No, Uncle! Don't skin him! Venom has to skin him!'

'Young people do have certain rights,' Don Camillo conceded, letting go of the youngster's lice-ridden head and climbing back up the embankment. 'If you weren't scoundrels,' Don Camillo resumed in a thunderous voice, 'if you really wanted to raise a fierce protest against this putrid world of ours, instead of playing at war, you would, for example, make yourselves available to help those poor people that have lost everything in the flood.'

'The flood victims? They're the walking dead,!' Ringo yelled, getting to his feet.

'They will die for sure if some rebel doesn't help them!' Don Camillo replied.

It was the second day of the famous flood that had ruined a third of the country and the flood victims, perched on the roofs of submerged houses, were still waiting for someone to rescue them.[71]

'Behold a real protest!' continued Don Camillo. 'Protest against the wordsmiths who solve everything with their chatter and with television broadcasts that

---

[71] In the great flood of 1966, Florence may have received the brunt of attention from the world's media, but out in the countryside, the floodwater stranded people in their homes and on their roofs, leaving them reliant on volunteers in dinghies or improvised boats for vital resources.

transform cataclysms into variety shows to amuse the couch potatoes in their selfishness. To take a hand in the outcome, to help these poor people, to spite the politicians and bureaucrats. Here is a real man's protest!'

'And what should be done, in your opinion?' Ringo chuckled. 'Go swimming into the flooded areas. All the roads are flooded and cut off?'

'Not all of them,' answered Don Camillo. 'Ill-fortune has favoured one way in. A good mayor, if one could be found, would collect together food, blankets, etc, he would load everything on a couple of boats and ship them to where the river and the sea have flooded the countryside and villages.'

'We have a good mayor!' Peppone screamed.

'Yes, Comrade,' Don Camillo agreed, 'But, to make a move, he needs permission from the Kremlin or from Mao.'

'Permission is not the problem,' replied Peppone. 'The issue is that people are no longer willing to give. Too often have people seen where their help ends up.'

'Not this time, Mr Mayor' said Don Camillo. 'If we personally guarantee that we will distribute the stuff, they will be generous.'

'Us? In what sense?'

'You and me. Whoever doesn't trust the Priest will trust the Comrade and vice versa.'

Peppone turned to the longhairs:

'All cowards get back on their motorcycles and go home to listen to the protest songs on their turntables. The rest of you come with me.'

'I'm for it,' Cat replied. Then she looked at the rural longhairs and added, 'Me and team Venom.'

'I don't give a damn about the flood victims: but, if it means we will spite someone, I'm there too!' said Ringo.

'Us too,' cried the deputy chief of the Scorpioni. 'And it'll be fun to see how the old fogey in charge manages to turn the relief organisation into disorganised chaos.'

The battle had been very balanced and, when they martialled their forces, twenty long-haired men from each gang proved fit for purpose. Among the broken head, arms and ribs brigade, 10 Rurals and 10 Scorpioni had to be released from duty.

*

Peppone picked up a truck and, with Don Camillo at his side, he went around the whole town. The word went out: 'No money, just stuff!' An intelligent motto because a farmer would rather give you a sack of flour than 500 lire.[72] In any case, everyone offered something because they remembered the flood that had hit the country fifteen years earlier, and they knew well enough that, despite all the promises then, they had had to put everything back on its feet on their own.[73]

While the collection continued, Bigio, Brusco and Smilzo, aided by the longhairs, set up the fleet. They commandeered two motor barges, huge heavy cargo boats of a type that are used to transport sand and gravel. Plus two barges connected into a pontoon and used to ferry vehicles from one bank to the other, pulled by a tugboat. On the dock they had a truck and a four-wheel drive tractor with trailer. The collected stuff, all neatly packaged in waterproof plastic bags, was divided between the four barges. It was a lightning-fast operation: on the barge commanded by Peppone, Ringo's twenty Scorpioni took their places; on the other, commanded by Don

---

[72] Less than $1.

[73] Earlier, during the dramatic flooding of 1951 in the Polesine lands, Guareschi had put Don Camillo on guard to the village: see 'The Right Bell', *Don Camillo and Peppone* (Pilot, 2016).

Camillo, the twenty rural longhairs led by Cat. Don Chichi would have liked ever so much to participate in the expedition, but Don Camillo reminded him that he should not leave the parish unmanned.

'And then,' he added wisely, 'I am already on the expedition and you can have too many priests.'

The fleet left shortly after midnight, in the rain: the crews, full of dents from the earlier action and dog tired, sheltered under large waterproof tarpaulins and fell immediately to sleep. Don Camillo's boat spearheaded the formation, followed by Peppone's barge and the towed pontoon. A small fast boat with outboard and equipped with headlights acted as reconnaissance and went on ahead.

Towards ten o'clock the rain stopped and the weather brightened up; it was logical that Don Camillo should take advantage of it: besides everything else it was a Sunday. At the stern of the boat were a large block of crates full of canned goods: on it, Don Camillo set up his old field altar and set about celebrating Mass.

Even on Peppone's boat the whole crew woke up and emerged from beneath the tarpaulin.

'Typical priest!' muttered Peppone, taking off his hat. 'Any opportunity to put on a show!'

Ringo was about to laugh, but the engines of the barges and the tugboat were still and, in that solitude, in that silence, the priest's words swelled over the boundless expanse of muddy water and Ringo gave up the idea.

Now you'll appreciate, a longhair without a guitar is like a soldier going to war without a gun. So the Scorpioni had their guitars and at the Elevation they broke into a chorus of Old Man River and at the Communion they gave it some of their plaintive 'beat' whining.

'Lord,' said Don Camillo 'why don't you shut them up? Why don't you stop them from disturbing this sacred rite with their profane songs?'

'Don Camillo,' replied the distant voice of Christ, 'everyone sings the praises of the Lord as he can.'

'Yes, Lord, but listen: now they are even whistling!'

'On certain occasions the praises of the Lord may also be whistled,' Christ explained.

'Lord, where is it all going to end? Who could ever have imagined that a poor old country priest would be celebrating a Catholic rock Mass?'

'I, Don Camillo,' replied Christ.[74]

With the end of Mass the clear weather also ended: the engines resumed their roaring and everyone ducked back under the tarpaulins to shelter from the rain.

*

They arrived at the flooded lands of the Delta in the early afternoon and when they saw the first semi-submerged farm houses, the trouble began.

It was a time for coordination. The coordinators sent from the capital arrived one after the other to coordinate the rescue operations, to establish the various sectors of competence. Whereupon the super-coordinators would come to coordinate the coordinators. Meanwhile the people perched on the roofs of the houses and waited.

And a speedboat with officers and guards aboard blocked the fleet:

'Who are you? What are you doing here? Who are you with? What are you carrying? Why are you messing with things, unsolicited?'

---

[74] Elsewhere, later in the Sixties, the rock Mass would become a common feature, its chief architect jazz saxophonist and ecology activist Paul Winter, whose 1981 work, *Missa Gaia/Earth Mass*, defined the genre.

'They'll end up fining us because we don't have the appropriate bill of lading!' Cat screamed in anger.

'Shut up,' returned Don Camillo. 'Don't you understand that state inefficiency cannot tolerate private efficiency?'

The longhairs were getting agitated: Ringo proposed to board the motorboat and throw the officers and guards into the water. The idea was a good one, although there was no need to put it into action: all in good time the coordinators left, judging that they'd delayed the rescue work sufficiently and the fleet was able to move off once more.

The longhairs loaded people camped out on the roofs of half-submerged houses. They ferried the poor people to high ground, provided them with provisions – each person received food, blankets and clothing – and then, with the truck and the tractor, they conveyed them to villages unaffected by the rising waters.

The last operation of the day involved a farmhouse called Cascina Rossa, a small house where the water had reached almost to the ceiling of the first floor. An old couple had found shelter in the attic with various select possessions. They didn't want to leave their home or the things they'd managed to gather together around them. Reasoning with them was useless and eventually Peppone cut the nice stuff short and ordered Ringo:

'Take those poor wretches and their junk and throw them on the boat!'

The Scorpios loved violence and carried this out without question, ignoring the protests of the old man and his wife. The boat had just left the farmhouse when the little house crumbled and disappeared into the muddy water.

'There!' exclaimed the old man bitterly. 'Are you satisfied now!'

'You should be!' cried Ringo in fury. 'If we'd waited five minutes before saving you, you'd both have been drowned!'

'Exactly!' the old woman moaned. 'It'd be all over. Instead we are condemned to a life with no house no vegetable garden not even a chicken coop!'

'The State will support you,' Ringo replied.

'The State!' the old man muttered, 'They'll put us in an old people's home, me on one side, she on the other – divided forever, while we could have died together, in our home.'

'What nonsense!' Ringo sneered. 'Dying alone or in company is still dying.'

'Young lad,' replied the old man 'you have your whole life ahead of you, we have ours behind us. At a certain point – and you will come to this – the problem is no longer that of living well but of dying well.'

The two barges were by this time alongside and Don Camillo had heard what the old man had said:

'My dear fellow: I understand what you're saying, but those boys cannot. They don't care how old people die. He's for the oldies to kick the bucket as soon as possible.'

'Then why didn't they let us die?' asked the old woman.

'If you really want to die, no one's going to stop you jumping into the water!' Ringo screamed.

'Only he who gave us life can take it away,' replied the old woman. 'You don't understand, boy, but the Reverend does.'

'Engines!' Don Camillo shouted. 'Mission over, back to base!'

'Shouldn't we dump them first?' asked Peppone in a low voice.

'We're responsible for their sad situation. I'll take them to my old chapel house. It is run down but there is one habitable room and there's a nice piece of land: we can clean it up, plant a vegetable garden and make a chicken coop for it.'

The old woman's eyes lit up. 'A chicken coop!' she exclaimed, but was immediately saddened: 'My poor hens, all drowned . . .'

'Spanish galleon to port!' Cat yelled.

A large, solidly not to say finely constructed chicken coup was sailing slowly, steaming even, over the muddy water. And, on this floating dunghill around twenty hens were scratching sadly among the chicken manure.

'Malayan tiger cubs, boarding!' Cat yelled.

They pulled over to the foul hen house and caught the chickens.

'Now you have the chickens too!' Ringo shouted to the oldsters. 'What more do you want?'

'Thank the Lord,' replied the old woman, spreading her arms wide.

'Go to the shop next door,' growled the young man. 'We have no truck with Jesus Christ!'

Don Camillo heard nothing above the powerful roar of the engines. Jesus heard, but let it go. After all, he too had been a long-hair and had annoyed so many people with his rebellion that he ended up nailed to a cross.

And this is another of the stories that the Great River will tell to anyone who likes to listen to fairy tales and finds himself in one of the poplar groves on its hallowed shores.

*Don Chichi Proceeds Like a Panzer*

DON CHICHI, DON Camillo's young coadjutor, had clear ideas.

'The Church,' he explained to Don Camillo one day, 'in its centuries-old inertia, has transformed priests into so many indifferent bureaucrats who wait in their office for someone to come and get married, have a child baptised, have a relative buried and so on.

'The ancient metaphor of the flock and the shepherd is outdated. Progress has changed customs and mentality: the good old days are gone when it was enough for the shepherd to ring his bell to make the whole flock run to the fold! Priests still want to ring their bells, as they did when once upon a time the sound of church bells was the only voice to rise – powerful and commanding – through the great silence. But today the great silence has been blitzed by the roar of engines, the shouts of people and music pulsating through loudspeakers. The voice of church bells is just one of a hundred thousand noises that deafen us. It is no longer a solemn summons, it is part of what has become . . . a nuisance.

'Caught up in the anxiety of mass production and the new demands of progress, the flock is more and more deaf each day to the call of the Church. And the good shepherd who, *temporibus illis*, abandons his flock to track down lost sheep, now finds himself with his fold empty, because *all* sheep are lost. Do you see what I mean?'

'I do,' said Don Camillo. 'You would advise giving up herding and going into more productive activities.'

'Far from it!' protested Don Chichi. 'What I'm saying is that if the sheep no longer respond to the shepherd's call, the shepherd must go out and hunt down his sheep, one by one. If our sheep no longer come to the fold for their spiritual food, let's bring it to them.'

'Oh, I see,' said Don Camillo approvingly. 'In short, follow the example of edible food shops and set up home delivery.'

'No, Father!' Don Chichi yelled. 'Return to the original strategy, to Christ and to his Apostles, who brought the consoling word of God to the suffering people! Go house to house, knock on doors, take an interest in all the problems of the faithful, actively intervening where possible. Transform the priest-bureaucrat into a friend. This I would like to do.'

The strategy could not be faulted: moreover, it had the great advantage of freeing Don Camillo from the little priest's presence, so Don Chichi obtained the unconditional approval of the parish priest and was soon feverishly busy. There were, of course, a number of people who told him in no uncertain terms that they knew where the church was and if they needed the priest they would send for him. But there were also those who welcomed him amicably and opened their souls to him. One of these was Zelinda Brugnazzi, wife of the tenant of La Palazzina.

'Father,' the good woman confided to Don Chichi one day, apparently in great distress, 'you knows how it is. Young people today no longer want to be farmers and, unless you're to condemn your children to working in a factory, one way or another you have to do something for them. Anyway, we made tremendous sacrifices and bought the boys a car. For a poor peasant, buying a car is a big commitment, but we got one and now we have to save every penny to keep up with the instalments. Then came the calamity, old Tolini died. He was a good man, but his son is another matter altogether!'

All the while moaning and groaning, Zelinda then spelt out her tale of woe. A few years earlier, the Brugnazzi had risen from being sharecroppers to becoming tenants and had taken on livestock, machines, tools and stock from old Tolini, the owner of the farm they tended, making a commitment to pay for it all bit-by-bit. They'd already paid part of what they owed but, just as they'd taken on the commitment of the car, Tolini had died and his son and heir was demanding the balance *on the nail*.

'Reverend,' Zelinda whined, 'we have to pay two million within a few days! Where do *we* get two million?'

The Tolini farm took its name from the house that the old man had built a few years before the war about fifty metres from the tenant house. It was a large, beautiful, solid dwelling with a large garden around it, a real country squire's house, equipped with all the comforts but with a certain showiness that was rather annoying. Looking at it and thinking of the lucky people who lived there, one couldn't even say, 'May God smite you with a bolt of lightning!' because Tolini had installed a lightning rod on top of it.

These are details that wouldn't occur to most people, but about which poor peasants feel deeply.

'Isn't it enough for his son to have inherited everything?' Zelinda persisted. 'Why does he want to ruin poor people, who sweat blood for his farm from morning till night?'

Don Chichi, seized by red-hot fury, reassured the poor woman with a gesture and decided to sort things out at La Palazzina.

Tolini's widow, a very thin and battered old woman of around sixty-five, greeted Don Chichi with a certain detachment. Discovering that he wanted to talk to her son, she led him to the first floor of the house: 'A sudden chill took him,' she explained, 'and the doctor ordered him to stay in bed.'

The interior of the house, with garish but solid and expensive furniture, was as eye-catching and pretentious as the exterior. The heir, in his mid-thirties, thin and already grizzled, had a face marked by deep wrinkles, which Don Chichi, without hesitation, figured was an unequivocal sign that he led a hedonistic lifestyle.

They talked about this and that, and then Don Chichi came to the point.

'I would like to draw your attention to the poor Brugnazzi,' he said.

'The Brugnazzi?' the heir asked in surprise. 'What do they want?'

' . . . And to the debt owed to your late father. They are unable to pay.'

The heir was anything but uplifted at this news but managed to summon the strength to laugh:

'Reverend, you *are* joking! They can and must pay! And immediately! In fifteen years, of the two and a half million owed, they have paid only half a million, and that piecemeal. Bear in mind that the money is now worth half of what it was fifteen years ago.'

'On the other hand, the property is worth twice as much as it was fifteen years ago,' replied Don Chichi. 'Every cloud has a silver lining. Divine Providence has given you this magnificent house and the magnificent farm that the poor Brugnazzi have been working on for twenty years . . .'

'Divine Providence has given us nothing!' the heir interrupted angrily. 'This farm was bought by my father and mother from their honest toil and their sacrifices, under the illusion that it would afford them a slice of bread in their old age. What Divine Providence did give me was a dicky heart that forced me to liquidate the small transport company that I, again from my efforts alone, created from nothing in the city. And now Divine Providence forces me to live here, with my poor old mother. We've had no handouts from Providence: we are people who have always worked hard!'

'Working is the most fundamental of duties,' Don Chichi replied firmly. 'Remember St Paul and the second letter to the Thessalonians: "Whoever does not work will not eat."'

'But I can't work anymore,' the heir protested panting. 'I am an invalid. If my old mother could not take care of the garden and the chicken coop, what with tax reducing the rent we receive by more than a third, the fair rent initiative and other robberies, we would starve!'

Don Chichi was a modern priest who did not question for a moment his point of view.

'It's sad,' he said, 'the sight of a poor man lamenting his situation. But when it is a rich man who bewails it, the spectacle is not so much sad as disgusting. How can someone who has inherited capital worth God knows how many millions claim to be on the edge of starvation?'

'Ninety-seven, to be exact,' said the heir. 'When my father died, the tax authority established the value of our assets at ninety-seven million and, therefore, I had to pay thirty-five million by way of inheritance tax.'

'Taxes must be paid not only by the rich but by the poor,' declared Don Chichi aggressively. 'Don't whine: sell the farm, pay the right tax and you will have more than sixty million left! Sixty million is not to be sniffed at!'

'Of course,' said the heir wearily, 'sixty million is something, but that assumes that I'll get sixty million for the farm when I sell it. And the fact is that the new law obliges me to sell the farm to the tenant, who, poor man, cannot pay the two million he has owed us for the past fifteen years, but is ready to buy the farm at the price set by the Special Commission, on the nail. Which is only thirty million. So, my inheritance will actually leave me five million in debt.'

Don Chichi would have none of it: 'Signor Tolini, don't treat me like a fool! Don't tell me fairy tales!'

'You are ignorant of the Law of Pre-emption.'[75]

'I know it and I know it is a very just law!' Don Chichi yelled. 'He who, with his own sweat, has worked a piece of land for so many years, has the sacrosanct right to first refusal before anyone else, because he has earned it! He does not receive it as a gift like you did. What did you do to have a right to this land?'

The heir was struggling to breathe:

'This farm represents the labours of my father and mother,' he protested weakly.

'God created the earth as nourishment for all men. The earth belongs to all humanity, like air, light, water! Nobody can possess common property! Even if he buys it legally, he steals it!'

'Even the Brugnazzi?' objected the heir. 'What gives them the right to have it?'

'Because they work it! Because they produce bread for everyone. Ultimately, the Brugnazzi just want to sacrifice twenty years of hard and honest work, to buy the right to continue to work hard and honestly for the community.'

'And my dad didn't work hard and honestly for the community?'

---

[75] According to Italian law, the holder of the right of pre-emption has right of first refusal on equal terms over other interested parties.

'Your father is out of it now, peace to his soul, he has nothing to do with it. He already has his piece of land at the cemetery.'

'But my mother is alive,' exclaimed the heir, animated. 'And these scoundrels, the Brugnazzi, will throw us out and come and live here! How are we going to survive without a house or any means?'

'Society will take care of you,' said Don Chichi. 'Democratic society uses the money of its citizens wisely and cares for the old and the elderly. Certainly you will experience poverty. But poverty redeems you from the sin of wealth, which marks your past. This is how social justice is brought about: and you must help, not hinder the new course, extending the hand of fellowship to those poor peasants by renouncing your father's legacy. Only then will you be able to say to God without being ashamed: "Forgive us our debts as we also have forgiven our debtors!"'[76]

Tolini jumped up in bed and, grabbing the bottle of water from the bedside table, shouted:

'Damn crow, I'll break this on your head!'

Don Chichi shot off like a bolt of lightning as the old woman entered and, approaching her son, implored him: 'Calm down! You know how bad it is for you. Lie back down and don't worry: the Brugnazzi will pay and will never come in here. Nobody will be able to steal this house from us because it is ours and ours it will remain.'

*

Don Chichi ran to vent his indignation with Don Camillo and, panting, related his dramatic adventure, concluding: 'Don Camillo, the ruthless selfishness of the rich is the number one enemy of society. The first goal of the born

---

[76] *Matthew*, 6:12.

again Church must be to fight the rich. Wealth is a crea-
tion of Satan and by fighting wealth you fight Satan. This
is why Jesus wanted to be born poor: this is why we must
be the soldiers of Christ the Worker!'

'To be precise,' said Don Camillo calmly, 'Christ was
not a worker but a craftsman.'

'Worker or craftsman, it doesn't matter,' shouted Don
Chichi.

'It does matter,' explained Don Camillo. 'We must
actively insert ourselves in the new social course by being
perfectly in compliance, from the start, with the unions.'

'Father,' Don Chichi said indignantly, 'you simply
want to make a joke of what's happening. Don't forget
that repellent fellow threatened to throw a bottle at my
head and I only escaped because I could.'

'Tolini behaved very badly,' Don Camillo acknowledged. 'He shouldn't have threatened you, he should
have thrown the bottle at your head right away. Then
you wouldn't have been able to escape.'

*

Tolini died a few days later and his old mother went to
the presbytery to sort out the funeral.

'Don Camillo,' began the old woman, then pointed to
Don Chichi: 'and you the cursed one who dealt him the
final blow. Either you, Don Camillo, make sure I won't
even see your deputy, or my son will be buried with a civil
funeral.'

'Madam!' jumped in Don Chichi, 'be careful what you
say: remember that you too will have to go before the
court of God!'

'I know,' the old woman replied grimly, 'but I'm not
afraid because you'll never be part of the jury.'

On the day of the funeral, Don Camillo sent Don
Chichi to town and everything worked fine. It was a cold

and foggy December afternoon: old Tolini, having buried her son, slowly made her way home. When she arrived, she shut the front door and the windows on the ground floor and sealed them with adhesive tape. When evening came, she rolled the two large cylinders of liquid gas, which had been delivered that morning, into the kitchen, opened the taps and, after having closed and sealed the stairway door with tape, sailed up to the first floor. In the dark she lay down in the big bed and waited. The kitchen was under the bedroom and the old woman could hear the hiss of the gas coming out of the cylinders.

When she didn't hear it anymore, she said:

'They won't have our home, my son!' and she pressed the little button that sparked the electric bell in the kitchen.

Liquid gas cylinders represent one of the greatest social achievements of the century because they put an explosive more powerful than dynamite within the reach of all citizens. The explosion was terrifying and shattered everything: the furniture, the house and the old woman. In addition, the explosion set light to the woodshed, which passed the flames to the fir trees in the garden, so that only debris and ashes were left. When all's said, Divine Providence is clearly pro-bourgeois, for otherwise why would the barrage of bricks, having broken down the Brugnazzi garage door, also have taken out the sparkling 'Giulia' of poor peasant stock.

Don Chichi became very agitated:

'Why did she have two large cylinders of liquid gas delivered that morning? Why, after the debris was examined did it emerge that the cylinder valves were not broken but had been opened wide? It is no accident, as you say, Father: and being a suicide, the old woman has no right to be buried in sacred ground.'

Don Camillo looked him in the eyes:

'Of course. On the other hand, if, taken by sudden madness because you oppose a religious funeral, I kick you to death, her remains would have the right to rest in blessed land.'

Don Chichi knew that Don Camillo would never kill him. But he also knew that he possessed two elephant legs clad with heavy shoes, Size 45, and did not insist.

'*Fate vobis*!' he said. 'The parish priest will see Zelinda Brugnazzi to the Eternal Father. I am going for a nice bike ride along the river.'

'It is better that you do,' muttered Don Camillo.

'But,' exclaimed Don Chichi when he had reached the door, 'let me tell you that the bourgeoisie cannot lose!'

'That may be because the enemies of the bourgeoisie do not know how to win,' replied Don Camillo calmly. 'Anyway, if you happen to be in the area, tell your Brugnazzi friends that the two million debt will have to be paid by tomorrow because old Tolini turned the bills over to me, giving the money to the kindergarten.'

On the road to the embankment Don Chichi came across Cat's Giardinetta and the girl saw him and pulled up. The little priest was deeply depressed and the diabolical girl took cowardly advantage of him by managing to sell him, in instalments, a washing machine and a floor polisher to give to his sister and cousin at Christmas. Then, spreading her white wings, she flew gently into the grey sky and disappeared beyond the speed of light.

At least that's how it seemed to Don Chichi and the fact that he bought a washing machine and a polisher from an angel was some sort of consolation.

## Two Robbers Become Three

THESE WERE PROSPEROUS TIMES.[77] It is not known how the thing worked, but it had to be well thought out because people laboured less and less and earned more and more. A sense of well-being brought with it a lot of stuff quite new to us: like night, cabaret, striptease, festivals, Whiskey a Go Go,[78] sexy cinema, beat music, beat fashion, even beat Mass.[79]

The women no longer nursed their babies and instead raised them with tinned feed. They didn't even cook anymore, either because they didn't have the time, or because the modern, beautiful kitchen interiors would have been wasted on it. So they bought everything ready

[77] In the twenty years from 1950 to 1970 per capita income in Italy grew more rapidly than in any other European country.

[78] The famous nightclub in West Holywood, California, founded in 1964 and the springboard for many successful bands.

[79] Guareschi's repeated use of the colloquial English 'beat' in his otherwise Italian manuscript reminds us that the word alluded in those far-off days to the Beat Generation, which came to maturity in the late 1950s as the immediate forerunner of the hippies of the mid '60s. There's a sort of irony in Don Camillo's vilification of them. In exuberant celebration of their rejection of bourgeois conventions, the novelist Jack Kerouac coined the phrase 'Beat Generation' for this race of 'crazy, illuminated hipsters . . . ragged, beatific, beautiful in an ugly graceful new way . . . down and out but full of intense conviction', but later revealed that 'beat' had in fact been chosen as a shortened form of 'beatitude', a hidden reference to the fact that he was a Catholic.

made: canned food, frozen food, hot food from rotis-series, even delicatessens and 'frying tonight' shops.

Comfortable, ready-made living meant that every family had to have special zones in the house for a televi-sion, an enormous quantity of household appliances, and the essential car in order to escape from home for the weekend and to spend summer holidays by the sea, in the mountains, or on a cruise.

All wonderful things, but they cost a lot of money: therefore those who worked to live were forced to go on never-ending strikes to get more pay; while whoever did not have a job made do in various other ways. For example, a man might put a women's stocking on his head and go robbing jewellers, banks and post offices. At Christmas, as comfortable living required considerable extra expenses, these robberies intensified.

So it happened that, late one afternoon, just as the postmaster of Don Camillo's village was about to close up shop, he was confronted by two guys standing in front of them with their faces covered up to their eyes with black handkerchiefs.

The larger of the two, settling in front of the counter, forced the postman – gun in hand – to pretend he was writing something, while in a matter of seconds the other emptied the safe. Then they departed, got back on their motorcycles, which they'd left out front and disappeared. It took the postmaster a long time to regain the use of his tongue. However, he had not lost the use of his eyes and ears, so he was able to divine that they were two long-hairs whose names were Ringo and Luky.

In the excitement of the hold-up they had in fact called each other by name. Ringo was the one with the black mop, while Luky was the carrot-head. The postmaster was also able to take note of the number plates of the motorcycles.

It took nothing for the city police to establish that the motorbikes belonged to Ringo, leader of the Scorpioni, and red Luky, his lieutenant. As if that were not enough, Ringo and Luky had disappeared from circulation.

The police knew all about the Scorpioni and found it very interesting that Ringo's girlfriend lived in the very town where the hit had taken place. So, immediately they dropped their line in the water to wind her in. The girl, sensing imminent conflagration for her rebellious life-style, had taken refuge with Don Camillo, and that is where the policemen found her.

'You are Ringo's girlfriend,' their chief asserted confidently.

'Doubly wrong,' Cat replied calmly. 'I am an adult citizen with a clean record and deserve to be addressed respectfully as an independent woman. Also, my relation-ship with Ringo and his gang has been over for some time. These days I sell household appliances, hold a regular licence from the Chamber of Commerce and I can account for my every move. I can't understand why you're looking for these two guys – the Scorpioni were never into theft.'

The police chief was no fool and was not impressed:

'Strange coincidence,' he replied with no little sarcasm, 'that the two robbers were called Ringo and Luky, had black and red hair respectively, like Ringo and Luky, and rode motorcycles registered to Ringo and Luky.'

'Stranger still that they did not give the postmaster an autographed photo and even stranger that, after having worked so hard to make themselves identifiable, they did not actually hand themselves in,' replied Cat giggling.

'So,' screamed the boss man, 'where are Ringo and Luky? And why did they disappear?'

'Ask the police who know everything, not an appliance dealer,' Cat said.

'That's enough!' the chief decided, very annoyed. 'Come with us: we will continue the interrogation in my office.'

Don Camillo intervened; 'Captain, I'm the girl's uncle,' he said. 'If you want to slap her about, you are free to do it here.'

'Reverend!' protested the chief. 'We don't beat up anyone and don't have the slightest intention of slapping your niece around!'

'Shame!' sighed Don Camillo, sincerely sorry. 'An opportunity like this will never occur again.'

Cat was taken away at nine in the morning and returned in the cab at nine in the evening.

'How did it go?' Don Camillo inquired.

'Very Reverend Uncle,' Cat replied, 'I confess that, at one point, I *was* afraid.'

'Why on earth so? Isn't it true that you had nothing to do with it?'

'I was afraid precisely because it is true. How can an innocent person defend herself? The truth always sounds so idiotic, dull and unconvincing. If you don't tell lies, you have little chance of getting away with it.'

'So you told lies?' Don Camillo shouted.

'Of course: otherwise how could I prove that I was telling the truth?'

'You are a scoundrel! You'll see, they'll do it again.'

'Hope they do!' Cat replied. 'I've sold them a fridge, two washing machines, a dishwasher and a floor polisher on instalments and I do rather worry about those poor boys, Ringo and Luky.'

'You have the shamelessness to pity two robbers?'

Cat shook her head:

'Very Reverend Uncle: you're in the wrong job. You should have been a policeman. You have the right cut and besides anything else, a bad priest is more destructive than a bad cop.'

*

Things swung into action at two o'clock that same night. Someone rapped on the window of Don Camillo's bedroom with a knocker-upper's pole. After looking to see what was up, the priest took his shotgun and went down to open the front door of the presbytery.

Trudging behind two battered bicycles were Ringo and Luky, soaked and in very bad shape.

Don Camillo kept his shotgun trained on them:

'What are you doing here?'

'*Pulsate et aperietur vobis*,' said Ringo, managing a smile.[80] 'We are cold, hungry and our bones are broken from fatigue. We have been living in the bush for four days and nights, like dogs.'

'Like wolves, more like it!' Don Camillo replied harshly. 'Anyway, my duty is to call the *carabinieri*.'

'Go ahead,' Ringo said bitterly. 'We wouldn't even have the strength to get back on the bikes. At least give us something to eat.'

'The Marshal will feed you,' answered Don Camillo, making for the telephone.

'No need to trouble yourself, Very Reverend Uncle,' said a voice behind him. 'I cut the line.'

Cat, already dressed, entered the dining room and placed herself between Don Camillo's shotgun and the two boys.

'I'll feed them,' she said. 'I have my Giardinetta in the garage. Get it out, you two and wait for me.'

'Cat,' shouted Don Camillo, 'get out of the way and don't get involved with those two thugs.'

---

[80] *Matthew* 7: 7–8: 'Knock, and it shall be opened unto you.'

'I'm not a deadbeat priest, tired and bitter,' replied the girl. 'Before I condemn people, I want to listen to them.'

'Forget it, Cat,' Ringo said. 'He's right. You don't have to meddle. Give us a piece of bread and cover our backs until we make ourselves scarce.'

The two young men felt sorry for her and Don Camillo felt ridiculous with his gun. In any case, that damned Cat had walked over and covered the mouths of the shotgun with her hand.

Don Camillo drew back and set the weapon down in a corner.

'Light the fire and feed them,' he said. 'Not even I condemn people until I have listened to them, although I don't imagine what you two wretches can have to say.'

'We can say that we had nothing to do with this dirty business,' replied Ringo, as a bundle of kindling began to flame and crackle in the great fireplace. 'Some damned villains set us up. They stole our motorbikes and made the hit in order to lay the blame on us.'

'That's what I told the police,' Cat agreed, bringing bread, salami and wine to the table.

'Rubbish!' Don Camillo shouted. 'If that were the case, you'd have reported the theft to the police and you'd be off the hook.'

The heat and the wine had revived the two bikers.

'Are you kidding, Father?' sneered Ringo. 'The chief and deputy chief of the Scorpioni not only get ripped off of their motorbikes like rookies, but then go whining to the police like two bourgeois plebs? We have our dignity. Also, we don't trust your rotten justice system. The only justice we believe in is the one we abide by ourselves. This is a matter that exclusively concerns us Scorpios and the two fools that dropped us in it.'

'Three,' Cat corrected. 'There must have been three: two with motorbikes who made the hit, and a third who was waiting for them in a car. They got rid of their motor-cycles and drove off safely in a car. Only a policeman or a priest would be incapable of picking up on something so elementary.'

Don Camillo had great respect for the forces of law and order, but he was more than a little bothered by being compared to a policeman. He looked with concern at the two bad boys. He had watched them laughing as they risked their skin to save the flood victims. With their long, dishevelled hair, straggly beards, and dirty, battered clothes, they certainly looked like brigands. But usually – he felt bound to admit – real brigands don't look like brigands.

'Who can corroborate your story?' he muttered.

'We can,' the two replied as one.

'That's not enough for me,' said Don Camillo. 'I need an oath, which you cannot give me because you have no time for God.'

'That's not true,' Ringo countered. 'God has his agenda, we have ours. Peaceful coexistence.'

'For heaven's sake,' exclaimed Don Camillo, 'do you believe in the existence of God or do you not?'

Ringo laughed: 'If we were to deny the existence of God we would deny our existence and the existence of the whole universe. We are rebels, but our revolt is against men, not against God.'

Don Camillo was a typical product of *la paese del melo-dramma*[81] and never passed up an opportunity for a bit of theatre:

'Follow me!' he said to the two lads as he made his way out.

---

[81] The land of Guareschi's imagination, where hilarious and unearthly things do happen.

The church, lit only by a few votive candles, was deeply redolent of mystery and icy cold with it. They stopped in front of the old High Altar:

'Cross yourselves!' Don Camillo intimated to the two young men.

They crossed themselves.

'Do you swear by the Crucified Christ that you are nothing whatever to do with that robbery?'

'We swear it,' the two said in a firm and confident voice.

They returned to the fire.

'Was their word good enough for you?' Cat asked. 'Or do you think a person can swear falsehood before a high altar?'

'For sure, it's possible,' replied Don Camillo grimly. 'But then the person that does so opens an account with God. It's one thing to deceive a poor country priest, quite another to try it on with God.'

'We are not trying to deceive anyone,' said Ringo. 'We're more interested in what we do now.'

'For the time being you will stay here. Of course, not looking like you do now. We will get you some decent clothes and cut your hair.'

'Anything you want, but not that!' Ringo exclaimed.

'But don't you understand that if someone sees you with those lice-ridden locks we're all in trouble?'

'We understand that,' Ringo replied. 'Thank you for the hospitality, but rather than cut our hair, we'd prefer to give ourselves up.'

Don Camillo found a compromise solution: they would remain behind closed doors on the penultimate landing of the bell tower.

'And Don Chichi?' Cat put in, obviously worried. 'That one pokes his nose in all over the place; he'll find them out.'

'He will not discover them because I will tell him all about them myself,' Don Camillo calmly stated.

'And he won't betray us?' said Ringo understandably concerned.

'No,' explained Don Camillo. 'It will be enough to make him believe that you are the two real robbers and that you did it driven to it by social injustice. He will support you to the hilt. The important thing is not to make him suspect that you are innocent.'

'Not sure you're the best person to be in charge of that, Reverend Uncle,' said Cat laughing. 'I'll explain it to Don Chichi. I know the little peccadilloes of progressive priests! And I'll take care of the rest of the business too. When the police raised the alarm, they set up roadblocks but did not see any motorcycles. The two bikes must therefore be here in the area. We have to find them.'

Cat mobilised Venom's gang and her orders to them were precise:

'Act in twos and threes and look for two motorcycles. If you find them, don't touch them: stay with them and send one person to report their position to me.'

The Great River had exhausted its gift of raw power and its waters, previously released to lap the base of the main embankment, had withdrawn. At the foot of the slope, which from the embankment road led to a barn in the floodplain area, two motorcycles now emerged from the mud. Advised by Cat, the *carabinieri* went to recover them. They were the two motorbikes used for the robbery and inside the saddlebags were found a black wig and a red wig, two pistols and two black bandannas.

It was Don Camillo himself who brought the news to the bell tower. Ringo laughed:

'Father, if we had listened to you about cutting our hair, what trouble would we be in now, finding ourselves bald?'

The next day, a stolen car was found in a small street near the city and, inside, were documents that the robbers had stolen in their haste, together with the money from the safe of the post office. The car, returning from the scene of the crime, had had to refuel at Castelletto and the gas station attendant there remembered very well the faces of the three occupants. They were three well-known professional thugs from the city: subsequently, the police caught them and made them sing. The story was told in detail by the newspapers.

'Now,' said Don Camillo to the two boys who had come down from the bell tower, 'now you can easily go to the police and clarify things.'

Ringo shook his head: 'The police can take care of their own dirty business. Now it is simply a matter of settling accounts with the three thugs who have made us look foolish. We know them, but they don't know who Ringo and Luky are. They are about to discover that.'

'How will you go fishing for them in jail?' Don Camillo asked.

'It's about being patient for a few months,' Ringo explained. 'Next amnesty, when they come out, we'll catch them and fix them.'

Don Chichi, who was present, intervened:

'Boys, don't do this! Remember that those three poor young people are victims of social injustice and their gesture is a justifiable revolt against the selfishness of the rich!'

'What's this, the Eleventh Commandment?' laughed Ringo. 'Don't worry, Reverend, we'll take your words into account and assure you that we'll use softwood sticks to break their bones.'

'That's a kind thought,' Don Camillo conceded. 'It would be another nice thought if, before you left, you spent a minute in the church thanking God for helping you.'

'No need,' Ringo replied. 'We'll see to that once we get back to base. God is also in the city, you know.'

That was very comforting news and Don Camillo was delighted.

## All Psalms End with the Gloria

PEPPONE WAS SO furious that if you'd touched him with the tip of your finger he'd have given off a shower of sparks.

Up to now, Peppone and his gang had ruled over the Municipality completely uncontested and this was because the communists and socialists together had been able to call on more than double the support enjoyed by the Christian Democrats.

It was then that the comrades from the hamlet known as La Rocca had formed an autonomous Communist Section in support of Maoist ideology, headed by the young and vigorous pharmacist Bognoni, who was also one of the leading communist members on the Municipal Council with Peppone.

Then, after the catastrophic flood that devastated a third of the nation, came the reunification of the Socialists nationally in a new coalition party with the Christian Democrats and suddenly, Peppone and his comrades were left isolated and with voting rights no more than equal to that of the new clerical-socialist block.

Thus did the pharmacist come to hold the balance of power on the Council, because her vote could now tip the scales in favour of one side or the other. And since, in those days, the sins of the children were visited on the innocent fathers, rather than the other way round, the young Bognoni (who, in her time had been lubricated with cod liver oil by Venom) enjoyed blocking any and all of Peppone's initiatives.

Peppone resisted for a while, but then resolved to consign socialists, clericals and pharmacists to hell and let them get on and deal with his affairs, if that is what they wanted.

The world does not collapse if a mayor resigns, but Peppone was not any sort of mayor, he was unique. He had put himself at the helm of the deranged municipal boat in the storm of the immediate post-war period and, despite having raised the Red Flag on the flagpole, he had managed to keep the *Navicella*[82] on the right course. Therefore, when it was election time, even those who saw communism as smoke in the eyes gave Peppone their vote without hesitation.

When it became known that Peppone wanted to resign, people became worried. Two foreign industrialists who had decided to set up a plywood factory and a plastics factory in the area and had already begun to dig the foundations in the land granted to them by the municipality, suspended the work and returned home. Then the owner of a workshop that produced agricultural equipment immediately set about relocating to another more propitious municipality.

It was then that Don Camillo hooked up with Peppone and tried to convince him to go back on his decisions to resign.

'Comrade, your position as Mayor was not given to you by your party but by the vast majority of citizens.'

---

[82] Guareschi uses 'Navicella' for 'little ship', making a not altogether ironic reference to the famous mosaic by Giotto di Bondone, which shows the apostle Peter's fishing boat, tossed by a storm until Christ appears, walking on the water. *Matthew*, 14: 22–32.

'The majority proposes and polity disposes,' replied Peppone. 'I cannot remain in office on the whim of that woman!'

Peppone, once he'd made up his mind, proceeded like a Panzer and it is well known how difficult it is to reason with a Panzer. Don Camillo went to the pharmacy to try to persuade the Maoist 'Red Guard' to give up their revolution and re-enter the fold. The pharmacist sneered at him:

'The fact that it is a priest who asks me is the best proof that Peppone has betrayed the Leninist ideal and the working people. You should hire him as a sacristan.'

When they are involved in politics, women can be even more difficult to reason with than a Panzer and Don Camillo, without wasting time discussing the subject, fell back on Belicchi, one of the socialists, who until a short time ago had made common cause with Peppone.

Belicchi listened to him and then responded with evident distaste:

'It is shameful that you, a priest, should support the communists.'

'I am trying to improve the administration to everyone's advantage,' replied Don Camillo.

'The administration doesn't matter,' Belicchi insisted. 'What matters above all is *the Party.*'

'Too bad that foul water doesn't understand politics, otherwise it'd manage to leave the region without a sewer. What about the two factories? And the workshop? They'd have provided jobs for 250 workers.'

Belicchi laughed: 'Better 250 workers without work than supporting three filthy capitalists. We will come to power and, with planning, we will make everything right.'

'*Il Socialisti*! Such is always their refrain,' thought Don Camillo and spread his arms wide: 'May I at least ask you for some information?'

'Sure.'

'What would you say if, one of these evenings, at dusk, someone rained a volley of blows on your back with a stick?'

Belicchi burst out laughing:

'Reverend, Peppone no longer scares anyone. The communists are too bourgeois these days.'

'But I'm not,' countered Don Camillo.

'And you would beat me up on Peppone's behalf?'

'No, on my own account, Comrade Belicchi. In the days when I was a little left-wing priest like Don Chichi, you marched with the fascists in a black shirt and, one evening, you beat *me* up. I might return the compliment. And on my own, without needing three thugs to assist me, as you did.'

Belicchi made a gesture of impatience: 'Reverend, this is childish stuff! Those days are long gone; who even remembers them anymore?'

'I do,' answered Don Camillo. 'Those who dish it out easily forget, but those who take it, don't.'

'But I was a mere boy and I redeemed myself by fighting in the Resistance!'

'I'll take that into account: I won't beat up the ex-partisan in you, only the ex-fascist.'

Don Camillo had seized Belicchi by his jacket lapels and Belicchi paled:

'You can't do this! Everyone knows that, even as a fascist, I was playing a double game!'

'My back doesn't know it,' explained Don Camillo, starting to bang Belicchi against the wall.

'And what, in your opinion, should I do?' the little man stammered.

'Remove yourself from the Socialist party and join the Communist one.'

'Are you really asking me to do such a thing? You, a priest?'

'For me, you Marxists are so much flesh from Hell,' replied Don Camillo. 'I don't care whether you fry in a frying pan or in a bedpan.'

Don Camillo had some very persuasive arguments and Belicchi did decide to take himself from the frying pan into the bedpan, with the result that Peppone had an absolute majority and the pharmacist's vote against him became no more than a pathetic tribute to Mao.

Naturally, Don Camillo needed to be seen to have operated in the strictest secrecy and Peppone, taking advantage of a rally for peace in Vietnam, showed his gratitude to Don Camillo with a hot denunciation of failed clerical conspiracies to undermine the democratic municipal administration. It was a really good speech that left Don Camillo speechless. He listened to it with Cat and at the end exclaimed:

'I can't understand how that bumpkin managed to put together a speech like that!'

'He just read it. He gave me the broad ideological outline and I wrote it,' Cat explained with her diabolical smile.

'Ah! And how did you manage to find all those quotes from St Paul, St Augustine, St Thomas, *Rerum Novarum* and Pope John?'

'Even Don Chichi is good for something,' said Cat.

'And you, thankless child,' protested Don Camillo, 'have you turned against your uncle?'

'No, Reverend Uncle, I simply helped the grandfather of my future children.'

Don Camillo looked at her with a pained expression:

'And do you really think that boy is stupid enough to marry you?'

'What's he got to do with it? I'm the one marrying him!'

'And, tell me: does he know that you have decided to marry him?'

'Sure. I wrote to him and he replied that he is delighted.'

'Ridiculous! I can't believe that such an idiotic man can exist. Unless you would allow me to read his reply.'

'That is technically not possible,' explained Cat calmly. 'There was a postal strike and so as not to waste time I took him my letter in person and he replied verbally.'

Don Camillo jumped: 'You really did that! Is your mother okay about it?'

'My mother?' giggled the girl. 'Do you mean that boring little woman who tittle-tattles around the house and keeps reminding me of all the things I shouldn't do?'

'Stop messing around! Does your mother know or does she not know that you are getting married?'

'She'll find out about it: there are enough gossips in this woebegone world.'

Don Camillo felt like grabbing Cat and banging her against the wall.

'So this is what we've come to!' he yelled. 'A girl gets married without even telling her mother!'

'Did she warn *me* when she got married?' the shameless girl laughed and then added: 'Take care, Very Reverend Uncle, or I'll get married in a miniskirt. Like it or not.'

'Like it or not, you will only enter here decently dressed and with a clean face!' replied Don Camillo.

'Imagine if I, in front of the boys, showed up dressed like a "Daughter of Mary"!'

'Don't you worry about what they'd think: those thugs with their lousy mops won't be there. All joking aside, marriage is a serious matter.'

Cat went wild: 'I intend to get married dressed as *I* like and with the guests *I* like! Either that, or I'll get married in the town hall!'

'Young lady,' said Don Camillo showing her his hoof, 'you will see that I wear shoes sized 45. Well, if you don't get out of here in five seconds, you will feel one of them!'

The girl took off like a rocket.

That seemed to be that regarding Cat's wedding, but a week later the subject returned to the surface and it was Don Chichi who raised it:

'Father, your niece is an impulsive girl but is not without common sense. She has had second thoughts: she wants a marriage blessed by God, but naturally not devoid of her unquestionable personality.'

'So?'

'He will come as a paratrooper, and she will come a paratrooper: they will pronounce the fateful "I do" while jumping out of an aeroplane. There has already been such a wedding. It seems beautiful to me! Think of the solemn promises made far from the ugliness of the earth, in the clear blue sky. Closer to God!'

'I see,' muttered Don Camillo. 'And the priest marries them looking up at them from below with binoculars, I suppose?'

'But no! The priest throws himself out of the plane together with the couple. From tomorrow I'm starting to take skydiving lessons.'

'Ah,' exclaimed Don Camillo. 'Cat managed to convince you.'

'It only took a little while, Don Camillo,' explained the little priest. 'Think of it, a band of the groom's companions-in-arms will participate in the rite and will also launch themselves from the plane. I envisage a wonderful blossoming of garments exceeding white as snow proud against the clear blue sky. Yes, even a progressive has poetry about him. In the meadow, above which the wedding launch will take place, I will set up a field altar and we will celebrate Mass in paratrooper overalls. Believe me, Father: this is another way that the renewed Church can be seen to be updating itself and adapting itself to progress.'

Don Camillo gravely nodded his approval: 'It is a marriage that will surely define an epoch,' he said.

Don Camillo saw Cat again after a month. 'As you will have heard, she said cheerfully, 'we have the best of both worlds, we will have a Christian marriage but also an unusual one. Don Chichi is a treasure: he has already begun to jump. He does very well and will be ready for the big day. This is how priests should be: modern, dynamic. To make the ritual more artistic, the launch will take place from 2,500 metres. For 2,000 metres we will fly together with the parachute closed and have ample time to say, "I do." At 500 metres Don Chichi will open his parachute and detach himself from us. At 400 metres Venom will open his; at 300 I will open.'

'It would be more artistic if you didn't open yours at all,' muttered Don Camillo. 'That idiot who is going to be your husband, is he okay with this?'

'Of course.'

'Will the witnesses also jump?'

'Of course. Venom is fine because his witnesses will be his Lieutenant and a fellow Private. Mine will be Luky, the Scorpioni's deputy chief, and Venom's deputy chief, Krik. Both are taking a parachuting course.'

*

Venom finished his military service, came home and immediately showed up with Cat in the presbytery. Venom looked a little embarrassed: 'Father,' he stammered, 'your niece and I . . . are going to get married.'

'I know,' replied Don Camillo 'I regret not being able to marry you. The fact is that, at my age, I don't feel like jumping from 2,500 metres.'

Venom cast a questioning glance at Cat, then said: 'What is this jumping from 2,500 metres?'

'We'll talk about it,' Cat replied quickly.

'Anyway, Reverend, can you organise something quick or will it turn out something like *The Betrothed*?'[83]

'If the health authority doesn't intervene to commit you to an asylum, in eight days you will be able to commit the greatest stupidity of your life.'

*

Venom rose to the surface again three days later:

'Could you marry us, here in church, on Saturday morning?' he asked.

'Of course,' answered Don Camillo. 'Are the bride's witnesses still Luky and Krik?'

'For the time being,' Venom replied grimly, 'But there are still five days left.'

Venom was very nervous and had a deep scratch on his right cheek and Don Camillo did not press him further.

That Saturday morning, when Don Camillo entered the church, which was full of people, he was in a cold sweat and his heart stopped when he saw Cat walking towards the altar on the arm of her father's brother. Thank God, she was not wearing a miniskirt, but a gown so long that it appeared never to end. The only oddity

---

[83] An allusion to the delays that afflicted the wedding of Renzo and Lucia in *The Betrothed* by Alessandro Manzoni.

was a black bruise under her left eye. Balancing this, Venom had deep scratches on his left cheek.

But Don Camillo caught his breath when he appeared in front of Cat's witnesses. Dressed properly in dark grey and with very short hair, Luky and the Krik had done something incredible.

'It's our wedding present to Cat,' Luky explained softly, touching his hair.

Don Camillo felt a shiver down his back thinking about what that gift must have cost the two bad boys. But most worrying was the approaching moment when Cat was to say, 'I do.'

'Lord,' Don Camillo thought to himself, 'keep a hand on her head or the wretch will respond, "I don't," just to spite me.'

'There is no need,' replied the distant voice of the Christ.

In fact, Cat did as she was supposed to do without hesitation and at that very moment, Don Chichi, deeply embittered (but not beaten), launched himself from 2,500 metres. It was a perfect launch, but at low altitude a rascally breeze so blew the paratrooper off-course that he got caught on the top of a tall poplar and the ropes of the parachute became so entangled that the fire brigade had to come with their ladders to bring him back to ground.

Nevertheless, he spent a long time up there in the tree and had the consolation of seeing Cat and Venom's car pass by on the provincial road, followed by a wild herd of eighty various longhairs on motorcycles, before reaching the highway.

And all this because, even when a priest is stuck on top of a poplar, all the psalms end in the *Gloria Patri*.[84]

---

[84] Gloria Patri, et Filio, et Spiritui Sancto, Sicut erat in principio, et nunc, et semper, et in saecula saeculorum. Amen.